The Lottery Winners

A J WILLS

Cherry Tree
Publishing

Cherry Tree Publishing

The Lottery Winners

Copyright © A J Wills 2023

Chapter 1

The atmosphere turned ugly the moment the boys piled on board, charging the air with a threatening undercurrent that crackles like electricity. They're all drunk, or high, most likely. Behaving like feral animals. Treating the bus as if they own it and none of the rest of us exists.

As they swarmed noisily up the stairs like angry wasps, I willed them to leave us all alone. But they won't. Not unless someone says something, and we all know kids like that don't take kindly to being told what to do, which is why we're all pretending to ignore them. That we can't hear the foul, aggressive language that makes my insides curl. I'm no prude, but there's a time and a place, and it's not here. And it's not now.

The girl they've picked on can't be much older than sixteen or seventeen. A child, really. I noticed her as I took my seat, glancing around to locate the source of an overwhelming stench of vinegar flooding the top deck of the night bus.

She's a pretty girl, yet to fully grow into her looks, wearing her strawberry-blonde hair in tight braids and sporting a bright yellow puffer jacket over a tiny white crop top that shows off an enviable, taut, youthful stomach. She has a cluster of silver rings in her ears and a wrapper of chips on her lap, which she pops into her mouth as she stares, glassy-eyed, out of the window. Probably on her way home from visiting a friend. Or a boyfriend. A trip to the cinema, maybe.

At first, I was just grateful it wasn't me who'd become the focus of the boys' attention. I'd avoided eye contact with them as they poured onto the top deck with their noise and rowdy horseplay, pretending to find something more interesting on my phone and silently praying they wouldn't give me any trouble.

But now they've closed in on that girl, crawling all over her, I feel bad. I ought to do something. It doesn't look as if anyone else is going to intervene. Not the elderly couple at the front staring at the road ahead, plastic shopping bags at their feet and fingers interlaced as if they're still in the first flush of love. Nor the broad-shouldered, thick-necked guy with 'SECURITY' emblazoned across the back of his jacket, who's more interested in the creased paperback in his enormous, tattooed hand. And as for the overweight, spotty teenager four rows in front of me, he's totally oblivious, his head bobbing rhythmically in time to the thumping beats pulsing from his headphones.

Like a concrete yoke, the collective weight of their indifference is pressing heavily on my shoulders, and leaving me with an impossible choice.

Whatever I do, I have a feeling I'm going to regret it either way.

Why can't they just mind their own business and sit quietly? It's late. I'm tired. And my blistered feet are so swollen, they're throbbing in my shoes. I don't want to deal with this. I'd prefer just to close my eyes, rest my head against the window and let the rhythmic motion of the bus rock me to sleep.

I've been rushed off my feet all evening. It didn't help that we had to cater for a big office party. Someone's leaving do. Fifteen of them crammed in around three tables we'd pushed together. Most of them had drunk too much and, although they all behaved themselves, by the end of service I was frazzled and just wanted to get home to my bed.

It's not as if I had a burning career ambition to become a waitress. It's just a job that pays the bills. Or at least it used to. I've not had a pay rise in three years and with the tips being shared between the waiting and kitchen staff, I'm not bringing in much extra these days. Callum and I are supposed to be saving up for a house of our own so we can start a family, but at the moment, unless we have a massive change in fortune, it's a dream beyond our reach.

The boys all have the same look. Hardened faces. Tracksuits, hoodies and trainers. Fingernails chewed down to the skin. Beer fumes and cigarette smoke radiating from their scrawny bodies. Lads from the estate. Outcasts. Prison fodder. They're the type not to be messed with or told what to do.

It's not that I'm a shrinking violet. You get used to looking after yourself when you have to constantly

3

slap down the advances of drunken businessmen who still, unbelievably, think it's acceptable to paw at your body just because you're waiting on their table. But this is different. There's an edge of danger to the boys' behaviour. If I say something, they're liable to turn on me. I can save the girl from their attention, but at what cost?

It starts innocently enough, but you can always sense when trouble's brewing.

'Give us a chip, love,' one of them demands.

Paper rustles. Hands dive in. The pack swoops in like wolves around a wounded deer.

'Hey,' the girl whines. 'Give those back.' A voice so childlike it tears at my heart.

I glance behind. They've snatched the wrapper out of her lap and are handing it around. Jeering and showing off, lobbing chips across the seats. Grounding them into the floor, leaving a starchy mess.

'What's your name?' a tall, skinny lad asks, sliding onto the seat next to her, pressing up against her rudely. The hunter sizing up his catch. 'What's wrong? Cat got your tongue?'

The others huddle closer, mobbing her. Their excitement bubbling into a frenzy.

'Where d'ya live?' another kid barks. 'You from around here?'

And then they're all yelling at her. Trying to get her to engage.

You got a boyfriend?
Come on, I'm only asking your name.
What school you at?

I like your earrings.

'My mate says he fancies you,' one boy slurs. My stomach tightens. 'Do you fancy him or what?'

Surely that guy up front with the security jacket is used to dealing with situations like this. He's a big guy. I wouldn't have thought he'd have been intimidated. Why's he not saying anything?

'Give us a kiss then,' one of them demands.

'Get off me!' the girl shrieks.

'Come on, I'm only asking for a little kiss.'

The rest of them bay like animals.

I twist my head, chancing another glance behind. They're all over her. Hands clawing, touching her arms. Her hair. Her face.

'What you looking at?' the skinny lad at her side hisses at me as he catches me staring.

I snap my head back around and fix my gaze on my phone, my throat dry.

'Oi, I'm talking to you. I asked you a question.'

Now what do I do? Keep my head down and hope they lose interest? Or do the right thing?

If it was me they were picking on, I'd want someone to stand up and take my side.

'You've had your fun,' I say, swivelling my body around in my seat, trying to exude a confidence I don't feel. 'Now leave her alone.'

Another boy, shorter and stockier than the lad at the girl's side, jumps up with his shoulders back, chin jutting out. He has the dark growth of a prepubescent moustache and pitted, acne-ravaged skin. 'Mind your own business, bitch,' he snarls.

His naked aggression shocks me, but I can't back down now. It would look like weakness.

I take a breath, my hands trembling. 'I said, leave her alone.'

'Yeah? And what are you going to do about it?' His face tightens into a scowl. He struts towards me, knees kicking sideways. 'You should mind your own business, innit.'

I slide out of my seat, my heart thumping. He's a good two inches shorter than me. Another one of life's diminutive men with a point to prove.

His mates momentarily fall silent, observing with amusement.

I glance at his hands.

What if he has a knife?

I hadn't thought about that.

His hands are empty, but that's not to say he doesn't have a weapon concealed somewhere under his clothes.

He takes a step closer. 'I said, what ya gonna do about it?' he repeats, slowly. Menacingly.

I raise my phone and point it at him, jabbing the screen so his face comes into focus. Making sure he's captured clearly.

His eyes narrow, momentarily confused. 'You filming me?'

I continue to point the camera directly at him for a few seconds before panning away towards his four grinning mates.

'These five delightful gentlemen on the 157 bus,' I say, loudly and clearly so the microphone picks up my voice, 'seem to think it's acceptable to sexually

6

harass a young, vulnerable woman travelling alone, late at night.'

'You ain't got my permission to film me,' the boy screams, waving his arms aggressively. He lurches forwards, snatching for my phone, but I swipe it from his grasp, holding it behind my head. 'You'd better delete that footage or I'm gonna cut you up,' he snarls, shifting nervously from one foot to the other, like a toddler desperate for the toilet.

'I'm not filming you,' I tell him. 'I'm livestreaming. And I already have a big audience. I'm sure it's only a matter of time before someone recognises you. Your mother will be so proud.'

It's something I saw on a TV drama a while back. I remember thinking then how clever it was, putting the footage out for the world to see instantly. He doesn't need to know there are only two participants in my impromptu live recording. I've made my point.

The boy glances at his mates, like he's looking for answers, but their stupid grins have dropped and they're all staring at me, clueless.

'We ain't done nothing,' the boy protests.

'You were harassing that girl.'

'We weren't 'arassing nobody.'

'Tell it to the police. I'm sure someone will share the link with them any moment and they'll be able to see for themselves.'

The boy's jaw falls slack, his fury morphing into panic.

One of his gormless mates, a boy with a decorative crucifix tattoo on his neck, stands, almost losing his balance as the bus slows to a stop. He slaps the boy on the shoulder.

'Come on, Gaz. Let's go.'

The boy facing me down deflates, lowering his eyes to the ground in defeat. I pin him with my hardest stare and step to one side to let them pass, my heart rattling in my chest.

One by one they troop off, hurrying along the gangway and down the stairs, with their tails between their legs.

Below, the doors hiss open and through the window I watch them slope off, hands in pockets. The boy who'd squared up to me turns and flicks his middle finger in my direction. Charming. My jelly legs buckle and I have to grab a rail on the ceiling to stop myself falling.

The bus finally moves off, and I let out a long breath of relief.

The guy in the security jacket shoots me a tight-lipped smile and mouths, 'You okay?'

I nod.

He returns to his book. Fat lot of use he was when I needed him.

The girl's huddled up against the window, her eyes red and her knees jacked up to her chest.

'Are you alright?' I ask.

She nods. 'I'm fine.'

There are chips everywhere, strewn all across the floor, the empty wrapper left screwed up on one of the seats.

I contemplate sitting with her in a show of solidarity. It's what I'd have wanted if it had been me.

But she's giving off some serious 'leave me alone' vibes and I don't want to make things any more uncomfortable for her.

'Where are you getting off?' I ask.

'Next stop,' she mumbles.

'Me too. Is there going to be someone there to pick you up?'

'I only live around the corner.' Her gaze is fixed on the row of shops blurring past.

The teenager with the headphones continues to nod his head in time to his music. The elderly couple at the front are still staring ahead, motionless, pretending they're invisible.

The bus lurches forwards as the driver accelerates and snatches a gear.

I retake my seat, perching on its edge, my body still filled with adrenaline and my pulse galloping like a herd of wild mustangs. I allow a smile to creep across my lips as a fizz of euphoria foams in my stomach. It's a minor victory, but I did the right thing. That's what's important.

As the bus slows and pulls in again, I jump up and stagger towards the stairs, following the young girl with the braided hair. The doors swish open and a light flashes on. The girl hurries off into the darkness with her head down and her hands planted in her coat pockets.

Callum's waiting for me, half-hidden in the shadows of a dark alley, leaning against a wall.

I step onto the pavement, watching the girl disappear, her legs moving comically quickly, not quite running, not quite walking. I hope she makes it home safely. Maybe I should have offered to walk with her.

'Hey.' Callum puts a possessive arm around my shoulders and kisses me on the lips, his breath sour with alcohol. He usually picks me up from work, but Tuesday is five-a-side football night. 'How was work?' he asks.

'Tiring.'

'Who's that?' he says, noticing I'm distracted by the young girl hurrying away.

'Just some girl who was getting hassled by some kids on the bus.'

'Is she alright?'

'I think so. How was football?'

'Great. I scored twice,' he grins.

As we head for home, hand in hand, I notice he's limping slightly. He still thinks he's a teenager, the way he throws his body around the pitch like a man ten years younger. One day, he's going to do himself a serious injury and that will be the end of his playing days. But there's no telling him.

'Well done,' I say, with as much enthusiasm as I can muster.

'Busy night?'

'Frantic. There was an office leaving party in, but they left a big tip, so...,'

'Yeah?' Callum grins. 'That's great.'

Whatever I take in tips, we've been putting away towards a deposit on a house. We've been rent-ing our current place for the past five years, and although it's lovely, it's not ours. But the deposit we'd need for even a small mortgage on a modest two-up two-down property around here feels like climbing a never-ending mountain. It's not as if our parents are in a position to help, either. And while we continue to save, house prices continue to soar.

Jefferson and Delilah are waiting by the front door for us. When they hear the key in the lock, their tails thump the floor, claws scratch at the lino, and they bark with frantic excitement. Their joy at our return never fails to put a smile on my face.

Callum barely opens the door before they barrel out, almost knocking us off our feet. Jefferson jumps up on me, resting his paws on my chest to offer me slobbery kisses until he calms down.

Usually, after a long shift, I like to head straight for bed. But I'm still buzzing, my mind in overdrive, as if I've shotgunned three strong espressos. The encounter on the bus has shaken me more than I realised. I need to decompress for a bit, otherwise I'll only lie there tossing and turning.

Maybe a cup of chamomile tea will help take off the edge. I'd have a glass of wine, but we finished the last bottle at the weekend and pay day's not until the end of the week.

Callum heads for the lounge and switches on the TV.

As the kettle in the kitchen gurgles and hisses into life, the familiar strains of his mid-week football highlights programme drift through from the other room. A reminder it's lottery night.

We play every week, kidding ourselves we have a chance to win. Although money's tight, we'd never forgive ourselves if our numbers came up and we'd not bought a ticket.

We always choose the same numbers out of a sense of duty and superstition. A mix that vaguely reflects key dates in our lives. Birthdays. Anniversaries. Our ages when we were married. The house number of our first flat. Our respective shoe sizes. I know the chances of winning are slim, but someone has to, don't they? Every week I live in hope, only for my dreams to be dashed. Sometimes, I wonder why we bother.

'Cal, have you checked the lottery results tonight?' I holler as I drop a teabag in a mug.

'I'll do it now,' he shouts back.

I fill the mug almost to the brim and as I stir the bag, watching the colour slowly leach into the water until it turns a brackish brown, I stifle a yawn. Now the adrenaline's slowly filtering out of my system, a wave of exhaustion sweeps through my body.

'So?' I ask, shuffling through to the lounge with my tea. My feet are still puffy, my toes scrunched together from where they've been wedged into a pair of worn court shoes. 'Did we win?'

I used to ask the question with the vague hope that one day Callum would surprise me and tell me we'd won a few thousand pounds. Enough at least to have a splurge in the shops or to treat ourselves to a holiday. A holiday! It's been so long since we've been anywhere hot. But now, it's become a running joke.

I ask if we've won, and Callum answers by asking if I want the truth. Of course, people like us don't win the lottery.

Delilah lifts her head sleepily and whimpers as I scuff past her bed under the stairs. Callum's sitting on the edge of the sofa, bent over, staring at his phone. He has one hand clamped to his forehead.

My stomach lurches. Something's wrong.

'Callum? What is it?' My mind races. Something's happened to his parents. Or his sister. Wild thoughts of disease and disaster flash through my head. Someone's been diagnosed with cancer. Or suffered a miscarriage. Been involved in a car accident. Or maybe someone's lost their job?

He swallows hard, his face ashen. Now he's really frightening me.

'You're not going to believe this,' he croaks.

I shake my head. 'What?' I gasp, fearing the worst.

'Our numbers. We've won.'

He holds up his phone, his hand shaking so violently I can't even read what he's trying to show me.

'What are you talking about?' My stomach somersaults, but my excitement doesn't last long.

Of course, he's winding me up. This is Callum's idea of a joke. We never win anything, especially the lottery. Well, never more than a tenner in all the years we've been playing.

'Ha, ha, very funny,' I grin. Does he think I was born yesterday?

'I'm serious, Jade. Look for yourself.'

Okay, I'll humour him, but I keep smiling to show I've not fallen for it.

I take the phone and stare at the screen and the row of six numbers. Six very familiar numbers.

My head spins and the room seems to spiral away, leaving me dizzy.

'Are you kidding me?' My hand trembles.

Callum stands slowly and scratches the back of his neck.

'Look at the numbers, Jade,' he says. 'They're our numbers. We've only gone and won the bloody jackpot!'

Chapter 2

The harder I stare at the row of numbers, the more rapidly they swim in front of my eyes, looking less and less familiar, until I start to doubt myself.

Are those really our numbers?

Suddenly, I'm not so sure. There must be some kind of mistake.

Callum doesn't seem to think so. He's jumping up and down with his hands on his head, screaming.

'Oh my god. Oh my god,' he's chanting, over and over.

My stomach feels like it's filled with sherbet. I want to believe it's true, but it seems so unlikely. I just can't get my head around it. I collapse onto the sofa, my legs no longer able to support my weight.

Callum falls silent and lets his hands drop, eyes opening wide. 'It's a rollover this week, isn't it?'

'I - I don't know,' I stammer.

'Give me the phone,' he yells, snatching it out of my hands. He prods at the screen while I sink into the cushions like they're marshmallow clouds in a candyfloss daydream.

It all seems so... unreal. This can't really be happening, can it? I can't bring myself to believe it. Not yet. Because if there is some kind of mistake, which there surely must be, I couldn't face the crushing disappointment. I don't want to get my hopes up and have them dashed.

But already my mind is drifting. If we really have won, we could finally buy a house and have a baby. Get a new car. A holiday in the sun for two weeks in the summer.

I try not to get ahead of myself, but it's hard. I've dreamt about what this moment would be like for so long.

Callum's gone worryingly quiet.

'Cal? What is it?'

I knew it was too good to be true. He's spotted something. They're not our numbers at all.

He glances up from his phone and blinks once. Twice. Three times.

And then he swallows, his Adam's apple bobbing up and down.

'The jackpot's over fifty-one million this week,' he says, as if he's not sure he believes it himself.

I hear the words but my brain doesn't register their meaning. He might as well have told me aliens have just landed in the back garden.

'Jade? Did you hear me?'

I shake my head. 'What?'

'Fifty-one million pounds,' he repeats, his grin growing wider by the second.

Fifty-one million?

'Are you sure?'

I can't even begin to imagine that amount of money. I'm pleased if I walk away from the restaurant with fifty quid in tips. But fifty-one million...

A million pounds would be life-changing. It would solve all our problems. We'd never have to worry about money again. We'd never have to save our spare pound coins in a jar by the fireplace. Or look for the yellow-sticker cut-price bargains in the supermarket. Or shop in another discount store ever again. We'd be sorted for life. But fifty-one million? It's an obscene amount of money.

Although, there's no guarantee we've won it all.

'We might have to share it,' I whisper. 'I mean, if there are others who have matched the same numbers.'

'Who cares?' Callum screeches. 'Fifty-one million. Twenty million. Even ten million. We're millionaires, Jade. You can give up your job. I can quit the garage. We can move to Spain if we like. Or get a villa by the sea.'

A villa by the sea? Bloody hell, he's right. We probably could afford that now.

'Never mind Spain. We could buy somewhere in the Caribbean,' I jest.

But it's no joke. If we've won that much money, we *could* afford to buy property anywhere in the world. It's utterly ludicrous.

'We could have a place in Spain *and* the Caribbean,' Callum grins. 'Or buy our very own island, like Richard Branson.'

I've always dreamt of going to somewhere like Barbados or Jamaica. St Lucia, even. But I never

17

thought we'd ever be able to afford it. All those sun-bleached paradise beaches and clear blue waters, drinking cocktails under the midday sun in a little string bikini. It all seemed so far out of reach before, nothing more than a pipe dream. But now...

We probably could afford to buy our own island. A retreat far from the maddening stresses of the world. If only.

'Cal, where's the ticket?' I jump off the sofa and catch his elbow as he jigs up and down.

There's still a niggle at the back of my mind which won't be subdued until I've seen definitive proof we've won. I don't want to get carried away until I know for sure.

'In my wallet,' he says confidently. He rushes out of the room.

I follow him into the hall and watch, chewing my nails, as he hunts through the pockets of his jackets hanging on the hooks on the wall at the bottom of the stairs.

He produces a bulging brown leather wallet and holds it in the air triumphantly. He flips it open and empties its contents onto the stairs.

A ten-pound note. A handful of debit and credit cards. His driving licence. A wodge of receipts and a stack of store loyalty cards.

'I'm sure I put it in here,' he says. I don't like the catch to his voice. The wavering note of uncertainty, bordering on panic.

'Cal?'

He looks up at me, his face hollow. 'It's not... It's not in here,' he says.

We stare at each other in silence, a blooming ache of disappointment and anger swelling in my stomach.

'What do you mean?' I say. 'Please tell me you remembered to buy a ticket this week.'

He gulps. Chews his lip. He looks like a little boy lost.

'Of course I did,' he snaps.

I shouldn't have got my hopes up. He's bought a lottery ticket using the same numbers from the same newsagent every week for the last three years. It would be beyond cruel if the one week our numbers came up, he'd forgotten.

'Well, where is it?' I demand.

He scratches his head, his eyes darting left and right, up and down.

'Hang on,' he says, charging for the stairs. He bounds up them two at a time.

A few seconds later, I hear drawers being banged open and closed.

Oh, well. Our little fantasy was fun while it lasted. A villa in Spain or the Caribbean would have been nice, but I'd have settled for enough money to put down a deposit on a house here in this country. That would have been enough for me. Who needs their own island, anyway?

Callum continues to bang around upstairs.

I won't hold it against him. It's not his fault. I'm sure he didn't mean to forget to buy a ticket. He's going to be feeling awful enough and me going on about it won't change anything.

An hour ago, we had no money. We still have no money. Nothing's changed. Nobody's died. We still have each other. And the dogs. And our health. That's what really matters and we should be grateful for that.

It's what I tell myself, at least, as I slump on the bottom stair, pushing the contents of Callum's wallet to one side. Jefferson, sensing something's wrong, comes up to me and whines.

I stroke his head and scratch his ears. 'It's okay, boy. Nothing for you to worry about.' He rests his chin on my lap and looks up at me with doe eyes.

Behind me, Callum's heavy footsteps plod slowly down the stairs.

'Don't worry about it,' I say. 'It doesn't matter. It was fun to dream, but we still have each other, and the dogs, right?'

I can't bear to face him. The disappointment crushes me like a ten-tonne iron block.

Callum stands behind me, breathing heavily through his nose, as if he's just sprinted around the block.

'Jade,' he whispers.

'Let's go to bed. Watch the football tomorrow.'

Delilah pokes her head around the newel post to check what's going on, her tail curled between her legs.

I stand and turn around with my arms open, intending to pull Callum into a comforting hug. To tell him I don't blame him.

I expect to see a dark cloud of despair hanging over his head, but his smile is even wider than before, his eyes shining with delight.

He pulls his hand out from behind his back and holds up a slip of paper.

A lottery ticket.

The lottery ticket.

'Is that...?' I gasp.

He nods. 'I forgot I took it out of my wallet and put it in my bedside drawer for safekeeping the other day.'

I stare at the ticket. At the faint printed row of numbers. Our numbers.

'And they match?' I ask tentatively.

He nods.

My eyes blur with tears.

'I've double-checked,' he says quietly. 'We've won. There's no mistake.'

'We've won,' I repeat, reading the row of numbers over and over until they start to dance and blur before my eyes.

Callum wraps his arms around me, lifting me up, twirling me around and squeezing me tightly.

'Careful,' I squeal, worried he'll crumple the ticket and somehow invalidate it.

'I can't believe it, can you?' he says, putting me back down on my feet. 'Everything we ever wanted, we can have.' His grin's a mile wide.

'But I already have everything I could ever want,' I giggle, planting a passionate kiss on his lips, more out of relief than lust.

He laughs. 'But now you can have me *and* be a millionaire.'

I pull away from him, my head clouded in bewilderment. 'But this doesn't happen to people like us.'

'I guess it does now.'

'So what happens next?'

Callum shrugs. 'I have no idea. I suppose we need to call someone and get it verified.'

'At eleven-thirty at night?'

Callum laughs. 'I don't think they man the offices twenty-four hours a day. We'll have to call in the morning.'

'And in the meantime? We'll have to find somewhere safe to put the ticket.' I don't want to let it out of my sight.

It's incredible to think that one thin sliver of paper could be worth more than fifty million pounds.

'We should celebrate,' Callum says. 'Do we have any champagne?'

I raise an eyebrow. When have we ever had champagne in the house? 'There's one last bottle of beer in the fridge we could share,' I suggest.

'That'll do.' With a sly grin, he marches off into the kitchen, leaving me standing dizzy with excitement and disbelief.

My whole body's as light as air. I could take off and float away at any moment.

We're millionaires. *Multi*-millionaires.

All our hopes and dreams are going to come true.

I pinch my arm, snagging the skin between my finger and thumb. But I'm not dreaming. This is really happening.

It's a new beginning. The start of a new life. We'll never have to worry about anything ever again.

Chapter 3

'Jade? Are you awake?' Callum whispers in the dark.

'Yes. I can't sleep.'

'Me neither.'

The bed sags as Callum rolls over and flicks on his bedside lamp. He plumps up the pillow behind his head and rests his hands on his bare chest, staring at the ceiling.

I tried to sleep, but it's impossible. My heart's racing almost as fast as my brain. I can't stop thinking about the money we've won and how it's going to change our lives forever.

I keep picturing us in a magnificent house in the country, like something out of one of those glossy magazines, with a dozen bedrooms, a kitchen the size of a small bungalow, a gym in the basement and maybe even a pool in the garden. I keep thinking about the fabulous walk-in wardrobe I'm going to have and all the amazing clothes I'll buy to fill it. It's like every birthday and Christmas I've ever known rolled into one.

And yet, every time my imagination runs away with itself, there's another part of my brain niggling away, prodding me with a stick of doubt. What if the ticket's invalid? What if they reject our claim? What if we've misread the winning numbers? What if? What if? What if?

Callum peels himself out of bed and pads across the bedroom to my dressing table. He flips open the lid of my jewellery box and retrieves the ticket.

'Still here,' he says with a mixture of delight and relief, holding it up for me to see.

I check my phone. It's not even four in the morning. No wonder my eyes are gritty with tiredness and my head is foggy. At least I don't have to go to work today. Or ever again.

It's a strange feeling. I've worked since I was sixteen and had a job picking strawberries at a farm not far from my parents' house. I'll have to call the restaurant later and tell them I'm sick. I guess they'll find out the real reason I won't be in again soon enough. I hate to let them down, but I won't miss the long hours and late nights. Who knows what I'll do to fill my time in future.

'What do we do about telling people?' I ask, as Callum returns the ticket to my jewellery box and comes back to bed. I snuggle up to him, resting my head on his shoulder.

'I don't know,' he says. 'I haven't really thought about it.'

'You'll have to tell your parents. And your sister. But maybe wait until we've had the win confirmed?'

'It would be nice to give them something,' he says, his heart thudding rhythmically against my ear. 'How would you feel if we paid off their mortgages?'

'I think we could probably buy them bigger hous-es, don't you?' I say. If we really have won fifty-one million pounds, there's going to be plenty to help out our friends and family.

'Are you sure?'

'Of course I'm sure. They're our family,' I say.

'What about your mum? What are you going to tell her?'

I take a deep breath and let it out slowly. 'I don't know yet.'

'You can't keep it from her. She's going to find out sooner or later,' Callum says.

'I know. But...'

'Yeah,' he says, 'I know.' He leans over and kisses my head.

It's complicated.

'What time can we ring the lottery people?'

'The offices open at eight o'clock, according to their website. We'll call them as soon as they're open.'

He sits up and grabs his mobile as I roll back onto my side of the bed. My mind drifts back to St Lucia and lying in a hammock strung between two palm trees as the sun sets over the horizon, the only sound the gentle lapping of waves.

'What do you think?' Callum shoves his phone in my face, so close to my nose I can't focus on what he's trying to show me.

'What is it?' I ask, grabbing his wrist and pushing his hand away.

'It's that watch I've had my eye on.' He grins mis-chievously. 'Shall I buy it?'

'How much is it?'

'Three hundred notes.'

'*Three hundred pounds?*' I splutter. 'For a watch?'

'We can afford it. I could afford to have a different one for every day of the week if I wanted.'

'Don't you think we should wait until the money's in the bank?' I grimace.

'Come on, Jade, don't be a killjoy.' He taps the screen a few times. 'There, I've done it. I've ordered one.'

'How've you paid for it?' I sit up, aghast. We don't know we can afford a three hundred-pound watch yet. Not for certain.

'I put it on the credit card.'

'Cal, I really don't think...' But he's not listening. He's continuing to tap away on his phone. 'What are you doing? What else are you buying?'

'Just a pair of trainers. There must be things you want? Go on, treat yourself. We've got the money now. A bag? An expensive necklace? Some shoes?'

I shake my head. Not until I know that money is really ours. It would be awful if we racked up debts we couldn't pay back because our ticket was invalid.

'It'll probably only be a few days until we get the money. We should wait,' I say.

'Hmmm?'

It's too late. I've lost him. He's already spending the money we don't even know for sure is ours. I wish he'd wait, at least until he's spoken to the lottery people in the morning. Is that too much to ask?

'Look, I can book a test drive online. What do you reckon? Should I do it?'

He flashes the phone in front of my face again. All I catch is a picture of a fast-looking red car on a sweeping mountain road.

'There's a Ferrari garage in Sevenoaks,' he says, like a little boy in a sweet shop.

I groan. 'You're not buying a Ferrari, Callum.'

'Why not? We can afford it...'

We don't last much longer in bed. We're both restless, unable to sleep. Our minds too active.

We get up and shower. Take a leisurely breakfast and drink too much tea. Callum can't be dissuaded from ordering more stuff online and I give up trying to talk him out of it. It's hard when he thinks we've won more money than we could dream of.

As the clock slowly ticks closer to eight, we sit at the kitchen table with mugs of tea going cold. Callum's phone and the precious lottery ticket lie between us.

At the stroke of eight, Callum glances at me, and I nod, butterflies dancing in my stomach.

He makes the call on speakerphone. It rings for what seems like an eternity before the call's eventually picked up by a woman who says her name is Nicola.

'We matched all six numbers in last night's lottery,' Callum says. 'We think we've won the jackpot.'

He keeps his eyes fixed on my face as he speaks, leaning over the phone.

'How exciting,' Nicola says breathlessly. 'Congratulations.'

Surely, it can't be as simple as that?

I reach across the table and take Callum's hand,
giving it an encouraging squeeze.

'So I'll just need to take a few details and we can
begin the process of getting your claim verified,'
Nicola says.

'How long will that take?' Callum mumbles.

'Not too long. Now let's start with your name,
address and where you purchased the ticket.'

Callum gives her all the details, spelling out his
name and address while I look up on my phone the
name of the newsagents we always buy our lottery
tickets from. When she asks for our bank account
details, it starts to feel dangerously real, like we
might actually be getting our hands on this money
after all.

'It was a rollover last night, wasn't it?' Callum says.
'Do you know if there are any other claims on the
jackpot?'

I snatch a breath and hold it while Nicola taps on
a keyboard on the other end of the line.

'No, our records show there was only one winning
ticket,' she says.

'One?' Callum says.

'So assuming there's no issue with your claim,
you stand in line to win just over fifty-one million pounds. Fifty-one million, two hundred and
thirty-six thousand, nine hundred and eighty-one
pounds and twenty-seven pence, to be precise.
How exciting for you.'

It doesn't matter how many times I hear the size of the jackpot, it takes my breath away every time. And to think it could all be ours, it's mind-blowing.

'Now obviously, winning that sum of money is going to be totally life changing for you and a massive shock, albeit a nice one. So our advice is always to take a bit of time to get used to the idea. We can help you with that, but I can't stress enough that you need to take a step back and process everything. And, of course, if you have any questions, we're always here to help.' It's almost as if she's reading off a script.

'Right. Sure,' Callum says, but I can tell he's not listening to a word. He's mentally spending the money again.

'One thing we would strongly recommend is that no matter how tempting it might be, don't go rushing off on an immediate spending spree,' Nicola continues.

I raise an "I told you so" eyebrow, but Callum looks away.

'You'll have plenty of time to spend your money, so I suggest you don't do anything hasty,' she adds.

'How long will it take to confirm our winnings?' Callum asks.

'As it's such a large amount of money, we'll send someone out to see you later on today, and assuming all the checks and confirmations come back without any problems, we can begin the transfer process more or less straightaway.'

'Right,' Callum says. He's gone all quiet. After all his dancing and jigging around the lounge last night,

he's almost sombre. I guess it's the shock. I'm feeling numb, too, like we're in a dream we're liable to
wake up from at any moment.

'Can we tell our family yet?' Callum asks.

'I'd hold fire on that until you've had a chance to
speak to your adviser. They'll be able to tell you
how to handle those conversations and also the
inevitable publicity that comes with such a big win.'

Callum's eyebrows shoot up. 'Publicity? We don't
want any publicity.'

I hadn't even thought about that.

'I understand,' Nicola says. 'But that's where your
adviser will be able to help. They'll talk to you about
all the ramifications of your win, but you probably
ought to start thinking about the fact that people
will inevitably find out. They always do. Neighbours. Friends. Work colleagues. It's hard to keep
these big wins secret from everyone, I'm afraid. So
it's best to be prepared.'

'Right,' Callum says, staring at me wide-eyed.

'It's not that I want to put a dampener on your
excitement,' Nicola continues, 'but it's important
to think about how this money is going to change
everything, including your relationships with people.'

I lean forwards. 'Hi, it's Jade. Callum's wife,' I
say. 'I'm not sure what you're trying to say, Nicola.
Surely, people are going to be pleased for us?'

'Of course most people are going to be pleased
for you. But it's inevitable there will also be people
whose reaction is less than positive. Some will be
jealous or resentful. Some people will find your

31

new wealth intimidating. I'm not here to burst your bubble, but you do need to come to terms with life being very different for the both of you from now on. I'm sorry.'

I stare at Callum. I've always thought winning the lottery would be the best thing that ever happened to us, but Nicola's just delivered a steaming dose of reality onto our doorstep. We'll be rich beyond our wildest dreams, but it's going to come at a cost I haven't even considered.

'If people can't be happy for us, then they can jog on,' Callum says. I don't think he appreciates what Nicola's trying to tell us.

'That's the attitude,' she says. 'It's your money. Don't let anyone spoil it for you. Now, unless you have any more immediate questions for me, we'll get an adviser out to you within the next few hours. Sit tight and let it all sink in. Life as you know it will never be the same again.'

Chapter 4

The lottery adviser who turns up at the house a few hours later is a jolly man with a big, oval face and a dazzling smile that shows off an impeccable row of pearly white teeth that look suspiciously like veneers. His short-cropped haircut appears to be an attempt to disguise the beginnings of a receding hairline.

'Marco McCourt,' he says, as Callum and I answer the door together. We've been on tenterhooks all day. 'Call me Marco. Please.' A chubby hand shoots out from the sleeve of a dark suit jacket. 'You must be Callum and Jade?'

He looks genuinely thrilled for us. What a great job to have.

We usher him inside, conscious of the curtain twitchers on the estate, who'll be wondering why we're both at home today, instead of at work, welcoming a suited visitor into the house in the middle of the afternoon. Tongues will be wagging. I can guarantee it.

Marco collapses on the sofa, his legs and feet flying off the floor as he sinks into the soft cushions. His corpulent stomach strains at the buttons of his salmon-pink shirt as he looks around the room, taking it all in, giving me an unwelcome flash of pasty skin and thick, dark hair around his navel.

'Lovely place,' he says with an appreciative nod.

'It's only rented,' I explain. 'We're saving up to buy a place of our own.'

Marco's smile broadens even wider. 'And now you'll have the pick of any properties you want.'

'So we've definitely won?' I ask. I just want someone to say it out loud, to confirm once and for all it's not a joke or a mistake. That we've won fairly and squarely and we'll soon have our hands on the money.

'Well,' Marco says, leaning forwards with his pudgy hands clasped together, 'let's have a look at your ticket, shall we?'

Callum heads to the sideboard and grabs a white envelope where we put the ticket for safekeeping. He slides it out delicately as if it's an ancient map liable to crumble in his hands.

Marco takes it and holds it at arm's length, peering at it over the top of his glasses, his forehead creased, eyebrows arching upwards. Then he flips it over and examines the back of it. He grunts, which could mean anything, and puts it on the coffee table. He pulls out his phone and takes a photo of it.

I can hardly breathe. Every muscle in my body is wound so tightly. Our future entirely depends on Marco's verdict in the next few moments. I've tried so hard not to get my hopes up, but if he tells us the ticket is void, I think I'll cry.

Callum sits in the armchair opposite the sofa, tapping his foot furiously, his face taut and anxious.

I don't know how much he's already spent in anticipation of our win. A three hundred-pound watch and a few pairs of expensive trainers are one thing, but if he's splashed out on an Italian sports car, there's no way we'd be able to pay the money back.

Marco opens his briefcase and jots some notes down on a pad of paper he takes from it, making strange popping noises with his mouth as he writes.

The suspense is killing me.

He glances up briefly, his pen poised. 'Any chance of a coffee?' he asks.

'Sorry, yes, of course. I should have offered.'

'White, no sugar,' he says. 'Thanks. And relax. This is all just a formality.'

My shoulders sag as I breathe out a sigh. Who knew winning so much money could be so stress-ful?

I'm grateful for the opportunity to leave the room. Marco's lovely, but the atmosphere has become strangely oppressive.

When I return from the kitchen with a mug of coffee and a plate of cheap supermarket-brand bourbon biscuits I found in the back of the cup-board, he's going through some details with Cal-lum, checking his passport and driver's licence. He wants to see mine, too, as the winnings will be paid to us jointly into the bank account we share. I'm sure some people would think that's crazy, that we should divide the winnings equally and that I ought to demand my fair share. But I trust Callum. What's mine is his and what's his is mine. It's the way it's always been between us. We've always shared joint financial responsibility for everything, no matter who's earned more. We agreed to that when we wed.

Finally, Callum confirms our bank account details and Marco slides a sheet of paper across the table towards us.

'What's this?' Callum asks.

'The final bit of paperwork.' Marco's still grinning as he hands Callum his pen. 'It's a claim form. I'll just need your signatures here at the bottom.' He points a stubby finger at where we need to sign.

Callum goes first, scribbling with a flourish, before passing the pen to me.

My hand is trembling and my handwriting looks more like a drunken mouse has crawled across the page than my actual signature.

Will they check? If it doesn't match up, will they think I'm an impostor trying to steal the money?

It's funny the crazy thoughts that go through your mind at a time like this.

'Great, well, that all looks in order,' Marco says, sweeping up the form and casting a beady eye over it. 'Congratulations. The money should be in your account within the next twenty-four hours.'

'That's it?' I say. 'We've actually won? You're paying us the full amount?'

Marco falls back into the sofa, his huge frame sinking into the cushions. He laughs. 'That's it.

You're now multi-millionaire lottery winners. It has a nice ring to it, hasn't it?'

I glance at Callum, who's staring at me with big, black eyes.

'Oh my god.'

Callum sucks in his bottom lip and grins at me. 'You want that villa in Spain or St Lucia first?'

My mouth opens and closes, but as tears of relief and happiness prick my eyes, I can't find any words. This is unbelievable. We're rich. Filthy, stinking rich. We have more money than we could ever have earned in a lifetime at the garage and the restaurant. I still can't get my head around it.

Callum jumps up and sweeps me into his arms. 'We've done it. We've won.' He hugs me tightly.

I push him away and shake my head. 'It doesn't feel real. Not yet.'

'It will when you see it in the bank account,' he says, planting a kiss on my lips.

'How many zeros is a million?'

'Six,' Callum says.

'Six,' I repeat. I still won't believe it until I see it with my own eyes.

'You've obviously been giving some thought to how you'd like to spend your winnings,' Marco says, cradling his mug of coffee, 'which is what it's all about. If you can't have fun with the money, what's the point? But it would be remiss of me if I didn't talk to you about coping with such a big win. It's such a large sum, you need to be aware of some challenges you'll face.'

'Challenges?' I ask.

'Well, have you thought about how people might react when they find out about your good news?'

'We don't want any publicity. I already told the woman on the phone,' Callum snaps.

Marco shrugs. 'Of course, and that's entirely your decision. But, whether you like it or not, people are going to find out sooner or later. They're going to talk and gossip. It's human nature, especially if they see expensive new cars parked on the drive and the two of you suddenly wearing designer outfits. People will speculate and you know what rumours are like. Soon the whole town will be convinced you've won a hundred, two hundred million. It's impossible to keep a lid on it. Trust me, the news always gets out one way or another.'

His words buzz over my head like flies on a hot summer's day.

Fifty-one million pounds!

What would that even look like if you had it in bundles of cash piled up on the floor? It would probably fill the room. The house!

Oh my god!

'... and so while it might not be what you thought you wanted, I would suggest you think carefully about holding a press conference,' Marco continues as I tune back into his words.

Callum's on the edge of his seat, with his thumbnails between his teeth, shaking his head.

'We'd organise it all and find a nice venue, plus we'd deal with all the journalists, so you wouldn't have to worry about any of that. You might wonder why we'd recommend it, when winning this much money is a very personal thing, but if you do it, you'll get it over and done with in one hit. The press will get their headlines, and they're generally incredibly positive in their coverage of these stories, and leave you alone. It's good news, after all. And it's also great way of letting everyone know about your good fortune,' Marco continues.

'I'm still not sure,' Callum says.

'Otherwise, there's the danger of a constant drip-drip-drip of speculation on social media, and when that happens, you're likely to get reporters knocking at your door, anyway.'

Social media? Reporters at the door? I shudder. I don't want my mother finding out from one of her neighbours or from people gossiping. She ought to hear it from me, otherwise she'll only come begging and I'll be forced to tell her no. I'm not paying for her booze, or worse, drugs. If she wants to drink herself into an early grave, she can find a way of funding it herself. I'm not going to be the one to facilitate it with handouts because she makes me feel guilty.

'I agree,' I say. 'No publicity. We'd rather try to keep it quiet.'

'Absolutely your decision,' Marco says.

I thought he might be pushier. I'm sure they're desperate for the publicity because every story about a jackpot winner is another reason for someone else to dream it could be them. It's free marketing for them.

'Whatever you do, just make sure you celebrate,' Marco says. 'Mark the occasion. Drink champagne.

Throw a party. Do something and take lots of photos. This is the moment your life changes forever and you want to remember it. Maybe go travelling. Or buy tickets for that concert you always wanted to go to. Treat yourselves, because you deserve it. But,' he says, holding up a finger of warning, 'I would suggest not rushing into any big financial decisions, like buying a house. Take your time to think about it and to make sure you're making the right decision for you.'

'Callum's already been eyeing up a new Ferrari,' I say.

'A Ferrari?' Marco nods appreciatively. 'Nice cars. You ever driven one?'

Callum shakes his head, looking a little sheepish.

'They're powerful machines and not to everyone's taste. I would suggest hiring one for a week first to see how you get on before committing to buying one. They can be tricky to drive.'

'That's a good idea,' I agree. 'And anyway, where would you park it? You can hardly keep it at the house, not unless you want to set all the tongues around here wagging.'

'Exactly, Jade,' Marco agrees. 'That's exactly the sort of thing you need to think carefully about before rushing into any rash purchases.'

Callum slumps into the armchair like a scolded child.

'I'm not saying don't get one. I'm just saying, take your time to think it all through.'

'What's the point of having all this money if I can't spend it?' Callum moans, blowing out his cheeks.

Marco laughs. 'Don't worry, you'll find a way, I'm sure. But you'll also want to think about how to make the money work for you. You don't want it sitting idly in a bank account when it could be earning you more money. I can put you in touch with a financial adviser who can explain your options, if you're interested?'

He opens his briefcase, takes out a couple of leaflets, and hands one to me and another to Callum.

Callum glances at it and stuffs it down the side of the chair. I know what he's like. He just wants to splurge. Who wants to talk about investing and making our "money work"? It sounds so dull, although he's probably right. It would be the sensible thing to do. Even fifty-one million pounds won't last forever.

'And finally, I need to talk to you about what we call the scroungers and the gold-diggers. It's something many people in your enviable position find the most difficult to deal with,' Marco says.

I fold my hands in my lap. Why he's so keen to talk about the negatives? We've just won the bloody lottery. We're rich. We never have to worry about money, or anything else, ever again.

'Some people are going to see you as an easy touch for handouts. I'm not talking about friends and family who you might want to share some of your good fortune with, but strangers who will inevitably come begging.'

'Begging?' Callum sits up straight, his brow creasing.

'You'll get all sorts of sob stories. Parents with sick kids who need money for lifesaving treatment. People posing as charities. Fraudsters who'll try to con you out of your money. Chancers who'll blatantly ask for relatively small amounts because they think you can afford it. You name it, once the news is out, you'll get them all. I'm afraid your postbox is going to be heaving with begging letters and you need to find a way of dealing with that.'

'Seriously?' I ask. 'People do that?'

'You'd be surprised the depths people will be prepared to sink to get their hands on your winnings. So please, be careful and prepare yourselves. You'll have to grow a thick skin and learn how to say no. Otherwise, they'll try to fleece you out of everything you've won.'

I gaze at my hands. It's what Nicola was trying to tell us earlier on the phone. It had never even occurred to me we'd have to contend with beggars and con artists. It seems so degrading.

'I'm sorry,' Marco continues. 'I hate to put a downer on what should be one of the best days of your lives, but you need to understand money is a powerful drug. It can be put to use for so many wonderful and life-affirming causes, but it also has the power to corrupt and cause great misery. It can make desperate people behave in strange and unpredictable ways, even people you thought were close friends or family. From today, you have more money than most people will ever own in their lifetime. So, please, be careful. Keep your eyes open and think with your heads, and not your hearts.

And if you do ever need any advice, no matter how trivial it seems, please just call us.'

Chapter 5

The champagne cork flies out of the bottle with a satisfying pop, bouncing off the ceiling and landing in the sink, narrowly missing the row of glasses I've lined up on the counter.

'Careful,' I warn Callum with a giggle, but it's an instinctive reaction. I couldn't care if he smashed every glass in the house. We can afford to buy as many new ones as we fancy.

As champagne foams out onto the floor, Callum catches it in a tall-stemmed flute and hands the three-quarter full glass to his mother.

We haven't told his parents why we've invited them around this evening, along with Callum's sister, Sally, and her husband, Tim. Given that we hardly ever drink champagne, and it's midweek, they're all looking at us suspiciously.

'You're pregnant, aren't you?' Callum's mother, Miriam, announces. 'I knew it. I said to you the other day, didn't I, Frank? I said I thought she was looking peaky.'

I hold up my hand in protest. 'No, I'm not pregnant, Miriam,' I smirk.

Her face falls and I feel bad letting her down. She's desperate for us to have kids, and we will. In a year or so, now we can afford it and can buy a place big enough for them to run around in.

'Well, what is it then?' Frank frowns as he takes a full flute from Callum. 'Something's going on.'

I negotiate my way to Callum's side. There's barely room to breathe with so many people crammed in our tiny kitchen, but just wait until we find our new home. I'm going to have the biggest kitchen you've ever seen and one of those double-fronted American-style fridges I've always dreamt about. I slip my arm around my husband's waist and place a hand on his chest as he pulls me close.

'We have some news,' he says with a grin that's been fixed on his face since Marco left earlier. He glances at me and I nod.

'Tell them,' I whisper.

'Tell us what?' Sally groans. 'Come on. The suspense is killing me.'

'It's good news. Really good news.'

'Callum,' his father growls. 'Spit it out, son, for god's sake.'

'We've won the lottery!' The words fire out of my mouth with a will of their own. I didn't mean to blurt it out, but I've been bursting to tell someone all day.

The room falls silent. Four pairs of eyes stare at us blankly.

'You've what?' Tim asks, frowning, like we've just announced we've planted a bomb under the Houses of Parliament.

'It's true,' Callum says. 'We found out earlier to-day. We've not told anyone else yet. You're the first to know.'

Callum's grip tightens around my waist. I'm surprised by their reactions. I thought they'd be happier for us.

'How much?' Miriam croaks.

Callum bites his lip, taking his time to answer, as if by saying it out loud it might evaporate into the ether, bringing all our dreams crashing down.

'Just over fifty-one million,' he says.

Miriam's eyes almost pop out of her head. Her jaw falls slack, and she stares at her son in shock.

'Fifty-one million? Bloody hell,' Tim says. 'Congratulations.' He stretches out his arm to shake Callum's hand.

Callum leans over and kisses me. His stubbly chin scratches my skin.

Miriam and Frank continue to stare at us, as Sally rushes to her brother and throws her arms around his neck. 'I don't believe it. That's incredible,' she screams.

'And it's totally tax free,' I find myself saying to Frank. I don't know why, although I was surprised when Marco mentioned it on the way out. It means we get to keep every penny we've won.

'Oh, darling, that's wonderful news.' Miriam's on the verge of tears, which sets me off. My throat swells up with emotion and I start to sob. It's silly, really. I've nothing to cry about.

Callum rubs my back.

'We wanted to tell you all first,' he says. 'Although we're trying to keep it quiet, so please don't say anything to anyone. They've already warned us we're likely to be plagued by people begging for money if it gets out.'

Tim zips his lips shut with his finger and thumb. 'Mum's the word,' he says.

I elbow Callum in the ribs. 'Go on. Tell them.'

Callum clears his throat. 'But obviously, we'd like to share our good fortune,' he says. 'So if it's okay with you, we'd like to pay off whatever's outstanding on your mortgages and buy you each a new house.'

Sally clamps a hand to her mouth. 'You can't do that,' she breathes. 'It's too generous. We couldn't possibly...' She bursts into tears.

'Of course we can, Sally. We want to,' I say.

'That's very generous. Cheers!' Frank raises his glass in a toast and takes a large sip.

'What about work? Will you stay at the garage?' Miriam asks.

Callum tips his glass to his mouth and shakes his head. 'No,' he says, swallowing his champagne. 'I called in sick today, but I'll go in to see them tomorrow and hand in my notice.'

'What about you, Jade? You won't want to be working in a restaurant now you have all this money, will you?'

'God, no! We're both going to quit tomorrow,' I say. 'And it won't be a day too soon.'

I like my colleagues, but my job's hard work, the pay's pitiful, and the hours unsociable. I'm sure they'll be surprised, but it's hardly a career I'm giving up, although it still hasn't really sunk in that I'll probably never have to work again in my lifetime.

'What about your mum?' Frank asks. 'Have you told her the good news yet?'

I glance down at my glass and run a finger around its rim. 'No, not yet,' I say. I know I'm going to have to tell her, but I don't know how. It's not something I'm going to worry about tonight, though. It can wait. Although, not forever.

It turns out it's a myth that decent champagne doesn't give you a hangover. The next morning, my head is banging and my stomach delicate. We went a bit mad and ordered far too much takeaway from an Indian restaurant in town and ended up throwing most of it away. Nobody was really that hungry, but now I regret not eating more. I've never been a big drinker, and drinking on an empty stomach has done me no favours. Sadly, being a multi-millionaire doesn't, it seems, make you immune from the ill-effects of too much alcohol.

Annoyingly, Callum doesn't appear to be suffering at all. He bounds out of bed full of energy and in high spirits, while I bury my head under the pillow and groan.

'I'm going to pop into work and talk to Eddie,' he says, towelling dry his damp hair after showering. 'I want to break the good news to him that I'm quitting face to face.'

I should do the same and have the decency to speak to the restaurant manager in person about my decision to resign, but I can't deal with it today. Not feeling like this. I'm going to spend the morning in bed and maybe, if I'm feeling a little less nauseous later, take a bath. There'll be nobody at the restaurant until this afternoon, anyway. I'll ring then. It'll be easier.

'I'll see you a bit later,' Callum says after he's dressed and grabbed some toast and coffee. 'I don't know when I'll be back. I might look around a few garages. Have a look at a few cars.'

I moan, but I don't have the energy to argue with him. If he wants to waste his money on a flashy sports car, that's his prerogative.

'If you're feeling up to it, why don't you go shopping or look online and buy yourself some stuff,' he says. 'You haven't spent anything yet.'

I slide an arm out from under the duvet and wave him goodbye.

His feet pound down the stairs. The front door opens and slams shut. And I hear his car, a fifteen-year-old BMW that had been his pride and joy, fire up and drive off.

Silence settles over the house, but I'm awake now and, although I'm tired, sleep feels out of reach. Maybe Callum's right. I should treat myself. I can afford some retail therapy. I can buy myself anything I want without a shred of guilt.

But when I do finally rise, drag myself downstairs and curl up on the sofa with a mug of tea and my iPad to browse the online stores, I can't find anything I really want.

It's like when I was little and every year for my birthday, my uncle would send me two crisp ten-pound notes in a card to buy anything I wanted. My mother would dutifully take me to the big toy shop in town, where on any other day of the year I would drool over the latest dolls and games, books and boxes of arts and crafts. But with the twenty pounds clutched in my hand, I was paralysed by indecision, unable to choose anything, until my mother lost patience and finally I picked something simply for the sake of it.

I have that feeling again now. We have more than fifty-one million pounds sitting in our bank account, a vulgar amount by anyone's standards, but I don't know how to spend it.

It's not as if I haven't dreamt about what this moment would be like. Everybody fantasises about winning the lottery and how they'd spend it, don't they? I have a long list in my head, but they're all substantial purchases. Nothing you can buy on a whim online. A big house in the country. Or a clifftop mansion with ocean views. A holiday in the Caribbean. Or the Maldives. A safari in Africa to see lions and elephants.

Eventually, I take the plunge and order a two hundred-pound silver necklace with a diamond-encrusted heart on the end of a delicate chain. It feels like the most extravagant thing I've ever done. It's not the most expensive piece of jewellery in the world, but I still suffer a pang of guilt as I hit the buy button. I suppose I've been used to scrimping and saving for so long that splurging doesn't come easily to me.

From the caravan of delivery vans that turn up over the next few days with piles of boxes and packages, Callum doesn't seem to suffer the same compunction. You can hardly get through the door for parcels. I'm sure he doesn't need half the stuff he's ordered. Watches, trainers, clothes, games consoles, a new TV, two laptops, a fancy camera, a drone and even, bizarrely, a high-end wetsuit. He explained sheepishly that he'd always fancied learning to dive.

And, of course, he went ahead and got himself a Ferrari. A bright red one with soft, cream leather seats and a throaty exhaust. The only consolation is that he took Marco's advice and has hired one rather than buying it outright. For now, at least. He's even rented a lock-up garage on the other side of town where he can keep it overnight. I can imagine the neighbours' faces if he'd turned up at the house with it. It's not exactly a low-key car. They'd have known instantly we'd had a substantial change in our financial fortunes.

Hopefully, he'll lose interest after a few days and send it back. I don't like the idea of him driving around in such a powerful vehicle. He's always loved to drive fast and I worry he's going to wrap himself around a lamppost in it. You hear about these rich kids in their fast cars doing it all the time. And wouldn't that be a tragic irony?

He's out driving again today. I don't know where he goes. When I ask him, he just says, 'Around.' Like it's no big deal. But I'm not his mother or his keeper. As long as he's not up to no good, he can do what he likes. On the other hand, I've hardly been out of the house in days. With no job to worry about, I don't have anywhere to go and I don't fancy shopping on my own.

I've seen a few houses I like the look of, but as yet I haven't plucked up the courage to contact any of the agents. What if they don't take me seriously? I don't want to look stupid. And I can't tell them we've won the lottery. It's supposed to be a secret.

I'm sitting at the kitchen table with my laptop open, looking at new sofas, with nothing better to fill my time, when the letterbox clicks open and clatters closed. It's late for the postman, not that we get much mail these days. Usually just sales brochures, leaflets for the local pizza takeaway, or the odd bill.

My curiosity piqued, I flip the computer closed and head into the hall to investigate. Delilah lifts her head from her bed under the stairs, peering around Callum's unopened boxes of stuff to see what I'm doing. I'll take them both out for a walk later. At least it'll get me out of the house for an hour.

There's a single, solitary white envelope lying on the mat by the door. Nothing particularly unusual about that, but what catches my interest is that our names have been handwritten on the front of it, with no address and no stamp, as if it's been hand delivered.

I unlock the door and pull it open, hoping to catch whoever's pushed it through the letterbox. I peer down the path and into the street. But it's deserted. Nobody hurrying away with their head down, hands planted in their pockets. No one jumping in a car and speeding away. Whoever posted it has gone.

Strange.

Curious, I slink back inside and tear the envelope open. Who even writes letters these days, let alone hand delivers them?

Inside is a single sheet of white paper, covered in cursive, scrawling handwriting in black ballpoint pen that matches the writing on the front of the envelope. It fills both sides of the paper, angling slightly down the page, as if the writer has scribbled it in a hurry.

I don't recognise the handwriting, nor the name scrawled on the back.

It's hard to read, but it looks like Gabriel.

Yes, that's it.

Gabriel Salt.

Whoever the hell he is.

I flip the letter over, confused. Marco warned us to expect begging letters, but I never expected anything like this.

I collapse on the stairs and read the letter slowly, not sure what to make of it, but it's instantly obvious it's going to change everything.

Chapter 6

Dear Callum and Jade,

First, my apologies for reaching out to you like this. I appreciate you don't know me, and that I'm taking a big risk contacting you, but desperation makes people do foolish things.

I am desperate and I have nowhere else to turn.

My beautiful wife, Tilly, was only 32 when she died, and seventeen weeks pregnant with our first child. She was the kind of person who lit up a room simply by walking into it. She was funny and caring and almost impossibly intelligent. I guess that's why she became a doctor.

I know it's a cliché, but she had her whole life ahead of her. Everything to live for. And in an instant of madness, it was all snatched away.

She survived for exactly forty-three minutes after she was knocked off her bike. Even though she was close to the hospital, they couldn't save her or our unborn child. When they phoned me, they were both already dead.

I found out later that she'd suffered serious head injuries and severe internal bleeding. Neither of them stood a chance.

The driver claimed he hadn't seen her. That he'd been momentarily blinded by the sun. But that's all ~~bullshit~~ nonsense. He turned across her path, over a junction, and only stopped because people were waving and screaming at him, while Tilly and her bike were trapped under his van being dragged along the road.

When the police checked his phone, they found he'd been texting his wife in the minutes before he knocked Tilly off her bike.

They should have locked him up and thrown away the key.

But he didn't even lose his licence, can you believe?

The court agreed that if they took it away, he'd suffer "undue hardship" because he wouldn't be able to work. It would be a disproportionate sentence.

Disproportionate sentence??!!

He's never once said sorry or expressed any regret about Tilly's death, and yet all they gave him was a small fine and a slap on the wrist and let him jump back in his van again.

That animal killed my wife and my child and destroyed my life. And his only punishment was a paltry fine.

How is that justice? How can that be right?

I've tried to move on and forget, but I can't. I can never forgive Lee Greenwood for what he did.

He took a daughter. A wife. A mother. A doctor. A friend. And while all our lives have been ruined, he's allowed to continue as if nothing happened.

He's still driving today, in his van, on his phone, a danger to everybody else on the roads.

I thought long and hard about reaching out to you, but after hearing about your good fortune, I felt I had no choice other than to contact you and plead for your help.

I need money to right this wrong. Money I don't have.

I need to take Lee Greenwood off the roads for good and make him pay for what he did.

Please, would you help me? I hate to beg, but what other option do I have?

Imagine if that had been your partner. Your daughter. What would you do?

I don't need much, but more than I have.

And it would mean the world to me if you could help me.

Yours in eternal hope,

Gabriel Salt

Underneath his name, he's scribbled a mobile phone number.

I turn the page back over and start from the beginning, poring over every line, my eyes blurring with tears.

I don't know Gabriel Salt, or his wife, Tilly, but something about his story cuts me in two and wrenches at my heart. It's the most awful tragedy.

56

I'm surprised I didn't hear about it on the news. The manner of Tilly's death is appalling, but the worst part of it all is that the driver was allowed to carry on driving after killing her and her unborn baby. How could the courts let him get away with it? It's a travesty. No wonder he's so upset.

I know Marco warned us about the sob stories, and to be careful not to be taken in by them, but this is different. We have to help him. How could we not? And, anyway, I'd much rather spend my money helping someone like this than frittering it away on stuff we don't really need.

I imagine he needs funds to pay for a lawyer to launch an appeal against the sentence. You can do that, can't you, if you think a sentence is unduly lenient? I'm sure I've read of cases like it. And a decent lawyer can't cost that much. Anyway, the cost doesn't matter. If I can bring this poor widower some justice and some peace, it's a small price to pay.

The only niggle of concern at the back of my mind is how he knew we'd recently come into money. He doesn't mention the lottery, but it must be what he means when he talks about our recent good fortune. What else could it mean? The only people we've told so far about our winnings are Callum's parents, his sister and her husband. I've not even told my mother yet. I can't believe any of them have let it slip, especially when we begged them not to say anything. But that's not important right now. What's important is being able to do something to help this man.

I suppose it could be some kind of elaborate scam. Someone making up a story to tug at our heartstrings and persuade us to hand over a ton of cash. But I'm not stupid. If his story's true, and the case has been through the courts, it should be easy enough to verify. I won't hand over any money until I'm confident he's telling the truth.

I ought to discuss it with Callum first. After all, half the money technically belongs to him. But he never consulted me before splashing out on a sports car, or any of his other extravagant purchases. I don't need his permission or his support. I hope he'll back me on this, but if he doesn't, it's no problem. I'll do it alone.

My mind made up, I trot back into the kitchen and grab my phone from the table, adrenaline racing through my veins. It's exciting to get involved in something so worthwhile. Far better than wasting my money on dresses and shoes I don't really need.

I dial the number at the bottom of the letter and wait for the call to connect.

It clicks and hisses in my ear.

A few seconds pass before it's answered.

'Hello?' A male voice. Quiet. Uncertain. He clearly doesn't recognise my number.

'Is that Gabriel?' I ask, staring out of the window at a bird darting in and out of a hedge in the garden.

'Yes. Who's this?'

'My name's Jade Champion. I've just read your letter.'

Silence on the other end of the line.

'I'd like to help in whatever way I can.'

Chapter 7

Gabriel Salt's house is a typical Victorian terrace, the type you find all across London, in a tree-lined, affluent part of the city. It has a bright red door, and a tarnished brass knocker, but a sad air of neglect in an otherwise respectable area. The front garden is unkempt and shabby, with tangled weeds pushing through the cracks in the path that creeps apologetically up to the front door. Although it's early evening, and it's still light, all the curtains have been pulled closed.

'Are you sure this is the right house?' Callum asks, looking it up and down with a disapproving sneer.

At first, he didn't want to come. He thought it was a scam. Someone trying to defraud us out of our winnings. He accused me of falling for a bleeding heart with a sob story and warned me we'd be bankrupt in a month if I took it on myself to help every charity case that came knocking at our door.

I told him it was an opportunity to do something worthwhile and to possibly make a real difference to someone's life. Eventually, I talked him around. He's still sceptical about Gabriel's story, but he didn't want me coming to a stranger's house alone, and for that I'm grateful. I wouldn't have fancied coming here on my own, either.

I check the back of the envelope Gabriel pushed through the door. I scribbled down the address on the back when I agreed to come and meet him. It's definitely the right house. I step up to the door, rap on the knocker, and step back, my stomach fluttering.

A shadow appears behind the frosted glass panels. A bolt shoots back and the door peels open.

'Jade? Callum?'

'Gabriel?' I ask with a tentative smile.

He's older than I imagined, although it might have something to do with his scruffy beard. It's not a bushy, consciously fashionable hipster beard popular in the bars and cafes around Shoreditch, but more like he's long ago given up shaving or taking care of his appearance at all.

His face is pale and lined, tired eyes partially hidden behind a pair of tortoiseshell glasses. His flannel shirt is unbuttoned, revealing a grey, food-stained T-shirt underneath. I notice he's not wearing any socks.

'I wasn't sure you'd come,' he says, running a hand over his face. 'Please, come in.'

He guides us into a sitting room at the front of the house, sweeping piles of clothes, paperwork and old pizza boxes off the sofa so we can sit. With the curtains pulled shut, the room is gloomy and oppressive, the only light coming from a dull standard lamp with a wonky shade in the corner. I do my best to ignore the unpleasant odour that hangs in the air, like there's a heap of unwashed clothes and sweaty shoes abandoned somewhere nearby.

Gabriel pushes his glasses onto the bridge of his nose as he settles into an armchair, constantly fidgeting, picking, tapping, sniffing and scratching, like he's a man on the edge. From the dark bruised bags under his eyes, I'd guess he's not sleeping much.

'You can't imagine how many versions of that letter I wrote.' He laughs nervously. 'It wasn't an easy thing for me to do.'

I sense Callum shoot me a sideways glance.

'I'm sorry for your loss. We both are,' I say.

In the awkward silence that follows, when none of us knows what to say, I glance around the room, my eyes drawn to some shelves built into the alcove next to a chimney breast. There are a handful of photographs in frames, most of them featuring a beautiful young woman with flowing auburn hair that spills over her shoulders and down her back. A younger, fresher-faced version of Gabriel appears alongside her in some shots.

'Is that Tilly?' I ask.

Gabriel jumps up, grabs one and hands it to me. 'Yes,' he says. 'That one was taken in Italy a few years ago. We'd just been caught in an unexpected shower of rain and we were soaked through, but Tilly just laughed, like it was the funniest thing that had ever happened to us. That picture always makes me smile.'

In it, Tilly's eyes are sparkling, and although her hair is flattened and wet, you can see she's bubbling with joy. A wide smile lights up her face, and laughter lines crease her eyes.

I hate having my picture taken. In every shot, I look like I'm grimacing. Or my eyes are half-shut. Or I'm staring at the camera too intensely, like a rabbit caught in a poacher's lamp. But Tilly looks so natural and at ease. With a rash of freckles across her nose and glistening emerald eyes, she could have been a model.

'She was my soulmate.' Gabriel looks down at his hands. 'My everything. And then she was gone, just like that.' He clicks his fingers in the air.

'I'm so sorry,' I say. 'Your letter was very moving.'

'I'd hoped you'd understand, because I had nowhere else to turn. I've not worked in two years since Tilly's death and it's as much as I can do to put food on the table. I hope you didn't think I was being presumptuous?'

'Don't be silly. Not at all.'

I can feel Callum glowering at me, but maybe when he's heard what Gabriel has to say, he'll feel differently.

'Why don't you tell us a bit about her?' I suggest.

Gabriel looks up and stares at a space above my head.

'She was my life. My light when everything else was dark. And I know she was going to be an incredible mother. She was an amazing woman, always putting other people's needs ahead of her own.' He laughs wryly. 'I guess that's why she became a doctor, because she wanted to help people. It was just who she was.

'She was on her way to the hospital when she was killed. The paramedics who scraped her off the road took her to A&E where she'd been due to begin her shift. They did everything they could to save her life, obviously, but her injuries were so severe, she didn't stand a chance. You can imagine how upset everyone was in the department. They were totally distraught that they couldn't save her. And all because of one arsehole on his phone not paying attention to the road.'

A hard lump forms in my throat and sticks there, refusing to budge. It's utterly heartbreaking. I don't know how Gabriel's coped. If it had been Callum, I'm not sure I could have gone on.

'It's not as if she was an inexperienced cyclist. She went everywhere on her bike. She loved the freedom of it, and I was never worried about her. She knew what she was doing, but I guess you're only ever as safe as the idiots around you.'

He takes a deep breath and lets it out slowly, wrestling with the memories of that day.

'She was in a cycle lane,' he continues. 'Going straight ahead, but the guy in the van turned left straight across her. He claimed he didn't see her. He said he had the sun in his eyes. He didn't even know he'd hit her until he was flagged down by some people who'd seen what had happened. He dragged her almost fifty metres along the road. She never stood a chance. When I picked her bike up later, it was nothing more than a wreck of twisted metal and rubber.'

I feel like I should say something. Offer him some words of comfort. But what can I say? I have no words that will bring him any solace. Instead, I stay silent, gazing at my feet and running my tongue around my teeth, fighting the tears that threaten my eyes. I don't want to cry. This isn't my grief. I didn't even know Tilly.

'I can't imagine what she went through in those last few moments. She must have seen the van turning and been helpless to stop...' Gabriel says.

I pull myself together, reminding myself why we're here. We know what happened to Tilly, how she died, but I'm still no clearer about how Gabriel thinks we can help him.

'And the van driver? He was taken to court?' I ask.

'His name's Lee Greenwood. He's a courier. You know the type. You see their vans pulled up on pavements and on yellow lines all over the place, always in too much of a hurry. That was Greenwood. In too much of a hurry to notice my wife, even when she was trapped under his wheels. Too busy on his phone sending text messages.' There's no mistaking the venom in his voice as a vein throbs in his temple.

'The police charged him with careless driving, but he had a good lawyer.' Gabriel shakes his head in disbelief. 'They claimed it was an accident and that it could have happened to anyone with the sun so low in the sky at that time of the year. But you know, he's supposed to be a professional driver. How could he not have seen her?'

'I don't know.'

'They found him guilty, but his lawyers argued he shouldn't lose his licence because it would deprive him of his livelihood as a delivery driver. Undue hardship, they call it. That if he couldn't work, he'd lose his job and that would be a disproportionate sentence, even though he'd killed my wife and child. So instead, they issued him with a fine. Three hundred and fifty quid. That's it. That's the price Tilly's life was worth to them.'

'You're joking?' Callum says. Now he's taking an interest, like I knew he would. He's so predictable.

'Three hundred and fifty quid,' Gabriel repeats. 'I'd always thought this country had one of the greatest judiciaries in the world, but they don't care about people like you and me,' he says, his face twisting into a bitter grimace.

'Even though he was on his phone, texting, when it happened?' I say.

Gabriel shakes his head. 'They could only prove he was on his phone in the minutes *before* he hit Tilly. Not when he actually knocked her off her bike. So the court discounted it. I mean, it's obvious to anyone that he was distracted and didn't have his eyes on the road. But that's the law for you. And now he's back on the road again and there's nothing I can do about it.'

'It seems extraordinary,' I say. There must be something he's not telling us about the driver. Some extenuating circumstances he doesn't want to admit.

'You couldn't make it up, could you?' he snorts.

65

'So what do you want from us?' I ask. 'You said in your letter you needed help?'

Gabriel chews on his lower lip and rubs a trembling hand across his jaw. 'I heard you'd... recently come into money,' he says. I can see he feels awkward about mentioning it.

'How did you hear?'

He catches himself and looks at me quizzically. 'Through a friend. I'm sorry, I'd rather not say who. I don't want to get them into trouble.'

I shrug. It's a bit late to worry about it now. The secret's out. But maybe it's not such a bad thing if it means helping Gabriel get justice for his wife.

'So, is it legal help you need? Do you need money for an appeal?'

Gabriel frowns. 'Legal help? No. You don't understand.'

'What then?' Callum leans forwards, looking puzzled.

Gabriel wrings his hands. 'You're my only hope because I can hardly go to the bank asking for a loan for what I need,' he says.

'A loan for what?' I ask.

'To deal with Lee Greenwood once and for all. To make sure he's never a danger to anyone else again. I need the money because I want him dead.'

Chapter 8

At first, I'm not sure I've heard him correctly.

'I'm sorry?' I say, frowning.

'I want Lee Greenwood dead,' Gabriel repeats, his face expressionless. 'And I'm begging for your help to do it.'

My jaw falls open as Callum and I exchange a glance. From the look on his face, he's as shocked as I am.

'I - I don't understand,' I stammer. 'What are you talking about?'

Gabriel sighs. 'Look, I know it sounds crazy, and it's a lot to ask, but I'm desperate.'

But I don't hear his words, my mind spinning. 'You want help to kill Lee Greenwood?'

'Yes.' Gabriel wrings his hands, leaning out of his chair. 'I've done some research. There's a man —'

'What?' I gasp.

'He can do it, and make it look like an accident.'

I shake my head violently. This is madness. I can't believe what I'm hearing.

'Like a hit?' Callum says.

'Exactly. He's a professional.'

'A professional?' I scoff.

A look of irritation flashes across Gabriel's face. 'Yes, he knows what he's doing.'

'You can't be serious?' This has to be some kind of joke. I glance around the room, looking for hidden cameras because the whole situation is so ludicrous it can't be genuine. It's a set up. It must be. He's testing us to see how we'll react and at any moment a jolly-faced TV presenter is going to barge into the room with cameras rolling, telling us it was all just a laugh. A social experiment to see how far we'd be willing to go along with such a crazy suggestion.

Hiring a hitman to kill someone? Yeah, right.

I mean, how would you even go about finding someone who kills people for a living? It's not the movies.

Gabriel bows his head, his shoulders slumping. 'Look, this man killed my pregnant wife and his only punishment has been a pitiful fine. He's got away with it. And worse than that, he's back on the roads. Who's going to be next? A mother crossing a road with her pushchair? Another cyclist? A group of schoolchildren? I have to do something.'

I try to keep a straight face, but I can't stop the corners of my mouth turning up into a grin. Which becomes a smile, and suddenly I'm laughing.

Callum shoots me a filthy look. He obviously can't see it.

'That's very funny,' I say. As if we'd fall for something so outlandishly stupid. Although for a moment, I almost swallowed it.

I thought the woman in the photos looked like a model. I should have trusted my gut. I guess

Gabriel's an actor too. A pretty good one. He certainly had me fooled for a moment.

Gabriel stares at me, his eyes narrowing. He's not laughing, I notice.

'What's so funny?' he asks.

'This.' I wave my hand around as I sink into the sofa, relaxing. 'It's brilliant. The house looks so real. And you. You totally had me going for a minute there.'

'Jade?' Callum's face clouds with confusion.

'Come on, Cal. Don't be so naïve. Can't you see? This isn't real. We're being set up.'

He stares at me as if I'm mad. He throws Gabriel an uncertain glance.

'This is no joke,' Gabriel says with a catch of irritation in his voice.

'I wasn't born yesterday.'

Gabriel drops his head into his hands.

'Gabriel? Is she right? Is this some kind of weird prank?' Callum asks.

'Of course it's not a fucking prank!' he snaps, his head shooting up, his eyes blazing. 'Do you think I'd joke about something like this?' He jumps out of his chair, startling me with the quickness of his movement. 'Look, I'm sorry. I've obviously made a massive error of judgement. I thought you'd understand. I should never have written that letter.'

The smile slips from my lips as a chill shoots through my veins.

I thought I had Gabriel all figured out. That I'd seen through his lies. But now I'm not so sure. I'm not sure about anything. My cheeks flush. I need to get out of here. I want to go home.

'Let's not be hasty,' Callum says. 'I'm sorry. Jade didn't mean to be rude. It's just we weren't expecting this. Please, carry on.'

As Gabriel sits back down, the armchair groans.

What is Callum playing at, telling Gabriel what I did or didn't mean? We're going to have words when we get home.

'Thank you,' Gabriel says. 'Everything I've told you is true. Here, see for yourself.' He finds a mobile phone that's slipped down the side of the cushions, prods at the screen and thrusts it at me, encouraging me to look.

He's called up an article from a local news website. I take the phone with a trembling hand and hold it so Callum can read it too.

Van driver fined £350 after death of pregnant cyclist, the headline screams.

I scan the story, my eyes blurring as the words leap out at me.

...dragged several metres under Greenwood's van...

...four months pregnant with her first child...

...blamed poor visibility for the accident...

...a driving ban would cause undue hardship...

... Mrs Salt's widower left without speaking to reporters...

'You can find the story online for yourselves if you still don't believe me,' Gabriel says.

I should have looked for myself before we came and checked out Gabriel's story, but I'd been so caught up in the intrigue of his appeal, it never occurred to me.

I hand the phone back, bowing my head in shame.

'I - I'm sorry. I thought...'

'I don't blame you. I appreciate I'm asking a lot.'

His story may be true, but he's still asking the impossible. Apart from any ethical and moral considerations, what he wants us to do is illegal.

'You're asking us to fund a hit on the man who killed your wife?' I say.

'My life's not worth living without Tilly. What am I supposed to do? Just carry on while Lee Greenwood's living it up, laughing behind my back about how he got away with it?'

'I can't believe this is what your wife would have wanted.' I bite my bottom lip, desperately sorry for this poor, grieving man, but this isn't right. And I doubt it's going to help him come to terms with Tilly's death, either. It's just revenge. Pure and simple. And I don't want any part of it.

'You think she would have wanted that evil bastard still out there on the roads, thinking he can act with complete impunity? On the day he was sentenced, and the courts let him off with a fine, I was in the public gallery. D'you know he actually turned to me and grinned. He thought it was funny. It was like he was laughing at me. He might as well have spat on Tilly's grave.'

I shudder at the thought. It must have been unbearably painful, but it doesn't mean Lee Greenwood deserves to die.

'Maybe you should talk to someone about how you're feeling,' I suggest. 'A bereavement counsellor, perhaps.'

Gabriel draws in a deep breath and lets it out slowly, like he's trying to control his temper, frustrated he's not getting through to me.

'I don't need to speak to someone. I need Lee Greenwood dead,' he shouts.

I've heard enough. I didn't come here to be shouted at or to spend my money on funding murder. How could he even think we'd contemplate such a thing? I jump up. 'I'm sorry, we can't help you. Come on, Callum, I want to go home.'

'Would you at least think about what I've asked?' Gabriel says, his eyes rimmed red.

'I'm sorry.' I glance at Callum, but he remains resolutely sitting on the sofa, his brow hooded. And when I try to drag him to his feet, he brushes my hand away.

'Hang on a minute,' he says. 'I think we should listen to what Gabriel's got to say.'

'Callum! Are you mad? You know what he's asking could put us all in jail?'

'You said you wanted to do something worthwhile with the money. So here's our chance. What could be more worthy than this?' he says. 'Gabriel, how much do you need?'

'Fifty grand,' he says.

'Fifty thousand pounds?' I splutter.

Callum shushes me quiet. 'Let's just listen to the man.'

I can't leave without Callum, so, with a sulky huff, I sit back down, folding my arms defensively across my chest.

'The guy I found needs the money in cash, but he'll take care of the rest,' Gabriel explains. 'The problem is, I don't have fifty thousand. To be honest, I don't have fifty quid to my name right now. But while Greenwood's still alive, I can't sleep. I can't work. I can't do anything.'

Callum glances up to the ceiling, twiddling his thumbs. 'And if we agreed to help you, there'd be nothing to connect it back to us, right?'

'Nothing whatsoever,' Gabriel assures him. 'Nobody knows I've even reached out to you. All the risk would be mine.'

We drive home in a brooding, uncomfortable silence. At least we're in Callum's old BMW and he didn't insist on bringing the Ferrari. I'd hate to be seen in it, with everyone staring at me.

I'm furious we've been duped. If I'd known what Gabriel was going to suggest, there's no way I'd have agreed to meet. And as for Callum, I can't believe he's seriously contemplating giving Gabriel the money.

'You know we can't do it, don't you?' I say as Callum settles into the fast lane, driving too fast as usual. He's going to end up killing himself one of these days.

'Why not?'

'Callum! We're not paying to have someone murdered. And can you slow down a bit? You're not at Brands Hatch now.'

He eases off the accelerator, but only a fraction. 'You heard him. There's no way it could ever be traced back to us, especially if we paid in cash.'

'And you believe him? Anyway, that's not the point.'

'I thought you wanted to use the money to help people.'

'Not like this. I thought he wanted us to pay for a lawyer.' I stare out of the window, picking out pinpricks of light from houses in the distance.

'What else is he supposed to do? He's the victim of a massive injustice and nobody cares. You heard him, the man was laughing at him in court because he'd got away with it.'

'But it's —'

'And we can afford it. Where else is someone like him going to lay his hands on fifty grand?'

'He could sell his house.'

'And have nowhere to live?' Callum shakes his head. 'There isn't a bank in the country that would give him fifty grand in cash without asking some difficult questions. But nobody's going to question it if we withdraw that kind of money. We've just won the lottery. It's pocket money to us.'

'It's not going to happen. I don't want to discuss it anymore.'

'At least sleep on it. You might feel differently in the morning,' Callum says, recklessly undertaking a car hogging the outside lane.

'I'm not going to feel differently, Callum. I've made my mind up. This isn't the way to help him.' I grip my seat under my thighs as I press an imaginary brake pedal with my foot.

'You know, this is the only way he's going to get justice.'

'It's not our place to interfere.'

Callum glances at me. I wish he'd keep his eyes on the road. 'The courts let him down. And what if this Greenwood bloke ends up killing someone else? How are you going to feel then?'

'Please, Callum, will you just drop it? I've made up my mind and we're not getting involved.'

'Jade —'

'Phone Gabriel in the morning and tell him we're not giving him any money, and not to contact us ever again.'

Chapter 9

If anything, my mind's even clearer after a good night's sleep. There's no way in hell we're going to fund a professional hit, no matter how worthy the cause. What was Gabriel thinking? Did he really imagine we'd stump up the cash for something so reckless?

I feel for him. He must be going through absolute turmoil. His life's a wreck and he's clearly not come to terms with Tilly's death. But paying for the murder of the man who killed her isn't going to magically make all his hurt and pain go away.

And so, after we've eaten breakfast and cleared our dishes away, I make Callum sit down at the kitchen table and call Gabriel.

'Why can't you call him?' he asks huffily. It's like talking to a five-year-old sometimes.

'Because you promised him we'd think about it.'

'I still think you're wrong.'

I shake my head and sigh. 'I'm not arguing about it anymore. Call Gabriel and tell him.'

'Fine. Give me the number.' I stand over him while he dials and waits for the call to connect.

'And tell him not to contact us again,' I whisper.

'Gabriel, it's Callum,' he says, scowling at me. 'Listen, we've talked things through overnight and come to a decision.'

Callum holds his head in his hand with his elbow propped on the table.

'Yeah, yeah, I know, but look, I'm really sorry. We can't get involved. We can't give you any money.'

Callum chews his lip as he listens. I guess Gabriel's not taking it well.

'No, I do understand — '

He jumps up and paces up and down our tiny kitchen. I can't wait until we can find a new house with decent-sized rooms.

'We can't, Gabriel. I'm really sorry. I know you're desperate, but what you're asking is impossible. Jade's made up her mind.'

'Don't make it out it's my fault,' I hiss at him.

'No, that's our final decision. You can't do anything to change our minds. I'm really sorry.'

After an agonising five minutes, Callum finally hangs up and tosses his phone on the table with a long sigh. He runs a hand over the back of his head, looking drained.

'I take it the news didn't go down well?'

'No, it didn't,' he barks at me, his jaw tight. 'He said we're no better than the courts and he hopes we both rot in hell.'

'He said what?'

'I'm going out.' Callum sweeps up his phone and marches out of the kitchen.

'Where?' I ask, following him into the hall where he's pulling on a pair of brand-new white trainers.

'For a drive.'

Great. Another day on my own. So much for the lottery changing our lives for the better. I've never been so lonely. Callum's hardly ever here these days. Maybe I will go out shopping and treat myself for a change. I might even buy myself lunch out. In a decent restaurant. And get my hair and nails done while I'm at it. Callum keeps reminding me we can afford it, although I'm still finding it hard to come to terms with the idea that money is no object for us.

'When will you be back?'

'I don't know,' he says. 'I'll see you when I see you.'

He grabs a jacket, snatches up his keys and walks out without even a goodbye.

Charming.

I know he's cross with me, but it's for the best. We can't go around paying for people to be murdered, whether or not we can afford it. We've won the lottery, not turned into barbarians. Gabriel needs to process his anger and his grief and stop obsessing about the man who killed his wife. Although, if I was in his shoes, I'd probably feel the same. A three hundred and fifty pound fine doesn't seem much of a punishment for taking a life, even if it was an accident. Lee Greenwood was behind the wheel of that van and should have been taking more care. And if he was on the phone, even if they can't prove it, it's unforgivable.

I run upstairs, run a brush through my hair and put on a little make-up. Then I call a taxi. I'm not catching the bus into town. It's only a small extravagance and hopefully some retail therapy will take my mind off Gabriel Salt for a while.

At least he should have got the message loud and clear. We're not paying to have Lee Greenwood killed, and if Gabriel knows what's good for him, he'll leave us alone and not pester us again.

Chapter 10

I've tried pushing Gabriel Salt out of my mind, but my thoughts keep circling back to him, wondering whether he's given up on this idiotic idea of paying to have Lee Greenwood murdered or if he's still trying to raise the money from some other poor, unsuspecting fools.

Several times over the last few days, I've caught myself looking up the case online. And every time, I wish hadn't.

It's heartbreaking. The reports from the inquest are the worst, detailing how Tilly Salt's body had become caught up under Greenwood's wheels, her body broken and her skin literally torn from her flesh, while witnesses screamed at him to pull over. And then there are the obituaries, illustrated with pictures of Tilly, her beautiful long hair cascading over her shoulders, her green eyes sparkling. Anguished quotes from Gabriel about his soulmate being snatched from him too soon. A request for donations, instead of flowers, to be made to a small charity supporting ovarian cancer, a cruel disease that had taken Tilly's mother's life too soon. Glowing testimonies from senior doctors at the hospital where she'd worked and where they'd fought so hard to save her life.

Every kind word, every expression of shock that her life had been stolen so young, brought tears to my eyes. That she was pregnant, and she lost the baby, made those reports even harder to read.

I even found a photo of Lee Greenwood in a few of the reports on the court proceedings. He's older than I imagined. In his fifties, with a shiny bald head, a leathery-skinned face and chillingly cold eyes. It's a picture I suspect was grabbed from one of his social media accounts. In it, he's holding a can of beer, laughing, one arm sheathed in tattoos and his stomach bulging over the top of his jeans beneath his football shirt.

All I could think about when I saw it for the first time was how he'd stood in the dock as he was sentenced, smirking shamelessly at Gabriel. It made my stomach roil with nausea. It's no wonder Gabriel wants him dead.

Gabriel is on my mind again tonight as Callum pulls out a chair for me at a candlelit table in a fancy restaurant we could have only dreamt about eating at only a few weeks ago.

'You look nice tonight,' he says.

'I thought I ought to make an effort, now we're millionaires.' I lower my voice, still a little embarrassed by our newfound wealth.

I've finally bought myself some new clothes. Tonight, I'm wearing a black body-sculpting dress with cap sleeves, matched with a wickedly expensive pair of killer Louboutin high heels. I've had my hair styled, my eyelashes fixed, and my nails done. I feel like a million dollars and something of a fraud. I can't shake the feeling I should be attending the tables, not being waited on, especially when a waiter approaches us with a friendly smile and asks what we'd like to drink.

Callum orders a bottle of champagne without a second thought. He doesn't even look at the wine menu. In our old lives, we'd have agonised over ordering even the cheapest bottle of house white, worried we couldn't afford it. He's already adopted a completely different mindset while I'm still struggling to adjust.

Callum insists we order the most expensive dishes on the menu. Lobster it is, then, although neither of us has had it before and we make a terrible mess eating it, scraping chunks of meat out of the claws and tails with our forks, reducing ourselves to hysterical fits of laughter in the process.

I don't suppose Gabriel will be eating lobster and drinking champagne any time soon.

'You've spilt some down your shirt,' I say, spotting a telltale trail of fatty spots down Callum's front.

'It doesn't matter. I'll buy another one.'

I think he's joking, but I'm not sure. It would be a crass indulgence if he threw the shirt away when it would probably wash out.

The waiter clears our plates and returns with dessert menus. I'm stuffed but Callum pores over his with wide eyes.

'You not having anything?' he asks. 'A nightcap? Coffee?'

'I'm full. I'm ready to go home.'

Callum's about to call for the bill when his phone rings. He's left it on the table for the duration of the meal, which annoyed me. We're in a restaurant, for pity's sake. But it's the fact he's not switched it to silent that drives me crazy. It's embarrassing.

He doesn't even have the grace to dump the call. After checking the screen and frowning, he answers it.

'Hello?' His eyes flick guiltily towards me. 'Gabriel?'

I roll my eyes. What the hell is Gabriel playing at, phoning Callum at this time of night? We made it perfectly clear, we didn't want him contacting us ever again. I'll have to get Callum to block his number.

'Slow down a bit,' Callum says. 'You did what?' His face creases with concern.

I glower at my husband, willing him to hang up. If he's calling to ask for money again, I've a good mind to call the police and tell them everything.

Eventually, Callum finishes the call and places his phone on the table, worry clouding his face.

'What did *he* want?' I snap. Trust Gabriel to call in the middle of our meal and ruin the entire evening.

Callum pushes his tongue into his cheek. 'He's at the house,' he says.

'*Our* house?'

He nods. 'He's in trouble. He says he went around to Lee Greenwood's house and attacked him. He's been arrested by police.'

Sure enough, Gabriel Salt is sitting on our doorstep when we return from the restaurant. At least I think it's Gabriel. His face is a mess, all blood-ied and red, his bottom lip split open and his eyes puffed up like he's gone ten rounds in a boxing ring.

'Gabriel?' I gasp, rushing to him as Callum pays the taxi. 'What's happened?'

He shrugs. 'I fucked up,' he says.

'Come on, let's get you inside and cleaned up and you can tell us everything.'

A mug of tea later, his wounds cleaned and patched up, he sits on our sofa with his head bowed and his glasses slightly askew.

'I did a really stupid thing,' he says. 'I paid Green-wood a visit at home. I thought it would make me feel better, but, unsurprisingly, he wasn't pleased to see me. Especially when he saw I had a knife.'

'What?' Callum says. 'You didn't tell me you went armed.'

He shrugs. 'I figured I needed some protection from a thug like him.'

He took a weapon to *threaten* Greenwood, more like. I knew he was desperate, but I didn't think he had it in him to tackle Greenwood head-on. What a stupid thing to do.

'Did you hurt him?' I ask.

'I didn't get a chance. He wrestled the knife out of my hands, then knocked the living daylights out of me, as you can see,' he says, pointing to his face.

I can only imagine. The thought of the two men squaring up to each other would be laughable if it wasn't so tragic. Gabriel, who looks like a strong gust of wind might knock him over, and Greenwood, the archetypal bald-headed thug. It's not exactly an even match. What the hell was he thinking?

'And then he called the police. They arrested me, held me for a few hours for questioning, and then charged me,' Gabriel says.

'With what?' Callum asks.

'Making threats to kill and possession of a bladed weapon. If they find me guilty, the lawyer says I'm looking at a prison sentence.'

'Prison? That's not fair,' I protest. Someone like Gabriel wouldn't last five minutes in jail. They'll make mincemeat out of him. 'What about Greenwood? Did they charge him for attacking you?'

He shakes his head, pouting. 'They said it was self-defence, and that I provoked him by turning up at his house.'

'We'll pay for a lawyer. A decent one.' It's the least we can do.

'Thanks,' Gabriel says, but his appreciation is half-hearted. Even a decent lawyer's unlikely to get him off those charges.

'Do you want to stay the night?' Callum asks. 'There's not much room, but you're welcome to the box room. The bed's made up.'

'That's kind, but no. I'd better get back. I'm sorry to turn up unannounced. I just needed someone to talk to. I couldn't face going back to an empty house.'

Really? There's no one else he could have asked for help? I glance at my phone. It's almost midnight.

I don't suppose there are trains running back to London at this time of night.

'How will you get home?' I ask.

'I don't know.'

'Then you're staying. That's settled.'

He tries to protest, but neither of us think it's a good idea for him to leave and eventually he agrees, somewhat reluctantly. I find him a clean towel and a toothbrush and point him towards the spare room. He trudges off, looking like he's carrying the weight of the world on his shoulders.

'What the hell was he thinking?' I hiss at Callum as he pushes the kitchen door closed and helps himself to a whisky. 'He could have got himself killed.'

'I dunno,' Callum shrugs. 'I'm not sure he even knows himself.'

'And then to turn up here, as if we can help.'

Callum winces as he takes a sip of alcohol and swallows. 'We *can* help, though, can't we?'

'What?'

'We can help him put this all right.'

'Callum, no. We've talked about this.'

'Lee Greenwood killed Gabriel's wife and child and got away with a small fine. But it's Gabriel who's facing jail. It just doesn't seem fair.'

'But what he's talking about is murder,' I remind my husband. 'If we go through with it, and pay him that money, we're all liable to end up in jail.'

'At least Greenwood would be dead. Look, all I'm saying is that the money he's asking for is a drop in the ocean for us. Pocket money. But it would make the world of difference to him.'

'For what?' I ask. 'Revenge? Because he thinks it's going to make him feel better?'

'It's not revenge. It's justice.'

Is it though? The case has been through the courts, argued over by lawyers and people far cleverer than us. That's what justice means. But I agree, it doesn't seem fair. Gabriel's lost everything, maybe even his freedom now. And Lee Greenwood continues to laugh in his face.

'It's too risky,' I say.

'Is it? Even if the police were suspicious about Greenwood's death, and they somehow traced the money back to us, which is all highly unlikely, we could say we knew nothing about it. We'd tell them Gabriel asked us for a loan, but we had no idea how he was planning to use the money,' he says.

He makes it all sound so easy.

'What if they didn't believe us?'

'It wouldn't come to that. You heard Gabriel. The man he's found is a professional. He'll make it look like an accident.'

'What kind of accident?'

Callum blows air out of his cheeks. 'I don't know, do I? That's down to him, but even if the police thought it was murder, they'd be hunting for him, not us. But I'm sure he knows how to cover his tracks. It's extremely unlikely any link to us could ever be proved.'

I wish I had his confidence.

Is it justice? Or is it revenge? Would we be doing something worthy? Or simply enabling murder? It's such a fine line. And yet, to see Gabriel on our doorstep tonight, mentally and physically broken, was tough. He didn't ask for any of this. He certainly doesn't deserve to go to jail while Greenwood's allowed to get on with his life. I twirl one of my rings around my finger. I thought winning the lottery was all about buying the house of your dreams, splashing out on friends and family. Never having to worry about anything again. Not this. I can't ever remember being in such turmoil.

'The way he was talking tonight,' Callum says, 'it wouldn't surprise me if he ended up doing something silly.'

I swallow hard. Surely not. It's not that bad, is it?

'He's got nothing to live for, has he?' he continues. 'He's lost everything and now it looks as if he's going to prison over something that was completely out of his control, while the two people who could have helped him get justice have turned their backs on him.'

'That's not fair,' I splutter.

'Isn't it?' Callum raises an eyebrow.

'We're not responsible for Gabriel.'

'No, but we have a chance to do the decent thing and to help him put everything right.' Callum plucks his phone from his pocket. 'Did you see this picture?' he asks, turning the screen towards me so I can see. 'I found it when I was looking for news coverage of Greenwood's case. It was taken on the day he was sentenced.'

I have seen the photo before. It shows Green-wood apparently outside the court, flanked by two other men, laughing. It actually looks as though he's on a lads' night out rather than on trial for the death of an innocent woman. It's disrespectful. Contemptuous. But what's worse is that while the two men he's with are walking with their hands in their pockets, looking straight ahead, Greenwood is looking directly at the camera, flicking a middle finger at the photographer, an arrogant sneer written across his face.

'It makes my blood boil,' Callum says.

'Yeah, I know.'

'So?'

A heavy silence falls between us, the air electric. This one decision could entirely change the course of our lives, again. It could be the biggest mistake we ever make.

'Okay,' I whisper, lowering my gaze.

'Okay?'

'Okay, let's do it. Let's tell Gabriel we'll pay him the money and help him get the justice he deserves.'

Chapter 11

Callum's trying to act casual, the rucksack filled with bundles of cash wedged under the table by his feet, but I've never seen him look so nervous. He can't stop fidgeting, playing with his fingers, scratching the table, his leg jiggling furiously. A sheen of sweat glistens on his forehead.

It's taken more than a week to organise, but finally here we are in a dingy pub in a part of London I never knew existed. The single-storey flat-roofed building is surrounded by grim post-war blocks of flats, a place where litter swirls across the pavement like tumbleweed caught on the wind, and an air of depression and hopelessness hangs heavy. A forgotten suburb far from the tourist haunts that's ruled by gangs and criminals. Not the kind of place you want to spend any time. But here we are, and I already regret coming.

At first, we'd been adamant we were going to simply pay Gabriel the money and leave him to make the arrangements for the hit. But Callum got jumpy. It's not that he didn't trust Gabriel, but as the reality of what we were doing hit us both, and with Gabriel already in trouble with the law, we agreed it was better to cut him out of the equation. Besides, he'd been behaving increasingly erratically since he'd turned up at our house, rattled that he was facing jail. There was every danger he would make a mistake. One that would come back and bite us all. We agreed it was safer this way.

Gabriel gave us a number to call on a scrap of paper and instructed us not to use our mobile phones. Instead, we had to find a phone box. A line that couldn't be traced back to us. It was all very cloak-and-dagger and was fun and exciting at first. Like we were spies in a top-secret Cold War operation. Until the reality set in. Even finding a phone box proved to be a nightmare, since we discovered most of them have been decommissioned or ripped out.

Eventually, we found one still in operation a few miles from home, near the train station. It was covered in graffiti and stank of stale urine, but, undeterred, Callum made the call, neither of us really sure what to expect.

The guy with a thick Eastern European accent who answered didn't say much, but gave us instructions to meet him in this pub, and to bring details and a photograph of our victim, or mark, as he called him. That's when it started to feel real. Dangerously real. I'm still not sure we're doing the right thing, but we've come too far to back out now.

It's the most terrifying thing I've ever done, and yet I've never felt more alive. It's exhilarating and horrifying all at the same time. I have to keep reminding myself why we're doing this. It's for Gabriel. And for justice.

My hands are icy cold, my palms damp with sweat, as we sit in the corner of the pub trying to look inconspicuous, which is difficult when we clearly don't belong here. This isn't our world. We couldn't look any more out of place if we tried.

There's a TV on the wall tuned into Sky Sports, showing a golf tournament, the volume up too loud, and a few weathered old men dotted around at tables and propping up the bar, nursing pints of beer and tabloid newspapers, while a heavy-set barman busies himself polishing glasses.

Our faces don't fit. The regulars stare at us like we're aliens newly landed from Mars. It's not the sort of establishment you just pop in for a drink. It's a local boozer, for local people. People who know each other. People hardened by life, who've grown up on these streets and survived. It's the kind of place where I imagine all sorts of shady deals have been made and dirty money changed hands.

Callum asked me not to come. He was worried it wouldn't be safe, but I insisted, against my better judgement. We're in this together, and, anyway, as a couple we're less likely to attract trouble than if Callum had come alone.

The waiting is the worst part. We arrived early, not wanting to be late, but that feels like a mistake in hindsight. It's given us too much time to think, to imagine everything that could go wrong. Of course, we could get up and leave. Walk out with our money and never look back. Every part of my logical brain is screaming at me to do just that, but I can't. Now we've come this far, we owe it to Gabriel to see this though. Even if, right now, it seems like the stupidest idea in the world.

As if sensing my unease, Callum puts a hand on my thigh and squeezes my leg. He shoots me a thin smile of reassurance, but it does nothing to quell my rampaging heart, which is beating hard and fast against my ribs.

Oh god, this is really happening. We're really going to do this.

Have we been naïve walking into a dive bar in one of the roughest parts of London with a bag full of cash? What if someone tries to rob us? Or worse, murder us for our money? I have a suspicion the barman wouldn't even raise an eyebrow.

It's too late now. We're here, waiting to meet a man who's promised he can kill Lee Greenwood. We have no idea what he looks like or what the protocol is when he gets here. This is so fucking stupid.

I knock back my gin and tonic, savouring the buzz of alcohol on my empty stomach. Callum's hardly touched his pint. Too nervous to drink, I guess. I'm about to ask him to buy me another to steady my nerves when a shadow falls across the table.

I hadn't noticed the tall man with grey, almost white, hair approach us from the rear of the pub. Has he been here all this time, watching us? Or has he come from another hidden entrance through the back?

'Follow me,' a gruff voice growls. We both jump up, almost knocking the table over. Beer spills from Callum's untouched pint as he scrabbles under the table for the rucksack.

The man is already walking away. He's stocky with broad shoulders and a confident swagger. Unlike us, he most definitely looks like he belongs here.

As Callum throws the rucksack over his shoulder and I feel eyes around the room watching us, he gives me a look, as if to say, 'So, this is it, then.'

My legs are shaky as I push my chair back and step into line behind Callum, following the man towards a corridor at the rear of the pub.

I have no idea where he's taking us or whether I should be worried. What if it's an elaborate scam to steal our money, and he's not a hitman at all? I've no idea what a hitman is supposed to look like, beyond what I've seen in films. They always seem to dress in dark suits and have black, gelled-back hair. Nothing like the guy we're following.

If this is a scam, how many other hapless fools has he lured to the pub under the pretence of arranging people's deaths, only to take their money and send them packing? Is that what this is? An elaborate, terrifying racket? Why didn't we think about that before? We have no insurance. No protection. We've put ourselves entirely at the mercy of this stranger.

The corridor is dark, save for a single flickering light recessed into the ceiling. All the rest have blown and not been replaced. We squeeze past a pile of metal beer kegs piled up against a wall and stop in front of a door, which the man unlocks with a key he produces from his trouser pocket. He slips inside, flicking on a light as he enters.

It's a storeroom with metal shelving on all four walls, stacked with cardboard boxes and cleaning products. There's a strong smell of bleach. Four chairs have been set out in the middle of the room, facing each other in a circle.

'Sit,' the man instructs, waving us inside.

It's the first chance I get to look at him properly. He's not what I imagined at all.

There's no dark suit or slicked-back hair. He's wearing an olive-green T-shirt under a loose-fitting khaki fleece top as if he's about to embark on a ten-mile hike through the mountains. With his bulging shoulders, thick neck and muscular chest, he looks more like a mercenary than a hitman. Apart from his size, there's nothing about him that would make you look twice if you passed him in the street. Just an ordinary bloke.

I take a seat next to Callum, my throat dry and damp patches growing under my arms. My breath, which comes fast and shallow, sounds unnaturally loud in my ears.

The man pulls up a chair opposite and sits with his legs crossed, one hand resting casually on his knee as he picks at his thumb with a finger.

'We're Callum and Jade,' Callum says, pointing to his chest and then to me, as if it's our first week at Alcoholics Anonymous.

'I know who you are,' the man growls, his cold blue eyes penetrating through me. 'Do you have the money?'

Callum fumbles with the rucksack, resting it on his knees as he struggles with the zip. Eventually, he opens it wide, revealing the wrappers of cash stuffed inside.

It was far easier to get hold of the money than I thought it would be. I never imagined the bank would allow us to draw out so much in cash so quickly, but nobody even questioned it. I guess we have so much deposited, and it's such a tiny amount of our total funds, it didn't raise suspicion.

The man snatches the rucksack from Callum's hands, takes out one of the wraps of money, and flicks through the notes. As if we'd be as stupid to attempt to swindle him. It's crazy enough that we've come here. An innocent young couple with no idea what we're doing, all in the name of getting some kind of justice for a man who, until a week or so ago, we'd never even met.

Someone remind me what we're doing here again?

This guy could kill us, take our money, dump our bodies, and nobody would ever know. It's not as if we told anyone we were coming here. We haven't even told Gabriel the details of the meeting.

The man counts out the cash in a pile on the chair next to him.

'You can call me Henry,' he says. It's obviously not his real name. Not that I care what he's called. I just want to do this thing and get out of here.

'It should all be there,' Callum says, gripping his knee as he leans forwards with a forced smile.

Henry glances up, pauses what he's doing, and glares at him.

'Sorry,' Callum mutters and bows his head.

Seemingly satisfied, Henry shoves the cash back into the bag and pushes it under his chair. 'You have details of mark?'

'Sorry?' Callum says, frowning.

'Mark? Target? You have details of victim like I asked over phone?'

'Oh, right, yes.' Callum holds his hand out towards me.

I almost forgot I have the envelope with all the information in my bag. I dive into it and pull out a brown, unmarked A4 envelope. I hand it to Callum, who passes it to Henry, like we're at a children's party playing a jolly game of pass the parcel.

Henry rips it open and pulls out a sheet of paper we prepared earlier with Lee Greenwood's name, his address, age (which we found out from the court reports), height (which we guessed), description, distinguishing marks (we didn't know of any), place of work, family details (which we cribbed from his social media pages), regular haunts and hangouts (which we didn't know), details of vehicles owned (we assumed he still has his white van), and registration numbers (which Gabriel was able to help us with).

We typed them out on the computer, printed it off and destroyed the electronic file, just as we'd been instructed.

Henry pulls out a pair of glasses and perches them on his nose. They look ridiculously small on his face, and in any other circumstance, I'd have burst out laughing. But it doesn't seem appropriate. Henry doesn't appear to have much of a sense of humour.

He glances at the piece of paper and nods. As he reads, I take a good look at him. He must be edging sixty, if not older. His hair has lost all its colour and is thinning badly. Thick, deep-set lines run from the corners of his eyes, and his nose is flattened and crooked, as if it's been broken at least once, if not more.

He flips the page over, but it's blank. We managed to fit everything we know about Lee Greenwood on one side. Then he pulls out the photos we've printed from the web. The picture I found of Greenwood in his football shirt, drinking beer, and the one where he's leaving court, flicking his middle finger at the camera. Plus another couple we discovered on other news websites, stolen from who knows where.

'Good,' Henry says, finally gathering the printouts together and shoving them back into the envelope.

'So you can do it?' I ask breathlessly.

'Da,' he says. 'Of course.'

'How?' I ask.

He just looks at me and raises an eyebrow. 'It's best you don't know.'

'But you'll make it look like an accident?'

He lets out a long breath that whistles through his nose. 'I will make it look like accident. You can be sure. No one will suspect.'

I'm dying to ask how many hits he's carried out. How many people he's killed. How he got into the business. Whether he's ever been caught. If he enjoys his work. But none of that's appropriate. Any idiot knows those aren't the sorts of questions you ask.

'How long before it's done?' Callum runs a hand over his mouth and chin.

Henry shrugs. 'A week? It depends.'

I want to ask on what, but I sense it's another one of those questions you don't voice.

'How do we know when it's done?'

Henry uncrosses his legs, leans forwards and ferrets in the pocket of his fleece jacket. He pulls out a phone. A small, black mobile, and passes it to Callum.

'Burner phone,' he says. 'I will send message when it's done.'

Callum examines the phone, studying it like he's never seen a mobile before.

'Can I call you on it?'

'Only in emergency. My number is programmed into it, but only call if urgent. And then get rid of phone,' he says.

'So we'll wait to hear from you, then?' Callum slips the phone in the pocket of his jeans.

'You wait to hear from me,' Henry confirms.

And then it's over.

Henry stands, picks up the rucksack and indicates for us to leave.

He lets us out of the pub through a back entrance that opens up into a rear courtyard, and hurries off with his head down, disappearing into one of the nearby housing estates.

We watch him go. Callum grabs my hand. It's cold and clammy.

And then it hits me like a jackhammer to my head.

We've just ordered the execution of a man. One week and Lee Greenwood should be dead.

What have we done?

Chapter 12

For six long, agonising days I've hardly slept and barely eaten. The guilt is eating me up inside, while the anticipation of hearing from Henry with confirmation the deed is done and Greenwood is dead has been building up inside me like a pressure cooker until I'm ready to explode. Every time there's a knock at the door with yet another delivery for Callum, I've convinced myself it's the police come to cart us away.

Callum is in the throes of slaying a horde of brain-dead zombies on a new games console he's rigged up to an enormous TV that's far too big for our tiny lounge when the black burner phone on the table buzzes.

We both freeze.

This is it. The moment we've been waiting for.

We stare at the phone then at each other as Callum pauses his game.

My pulse quickens. It's the text I've been waiting for. The one I hoped we'd never receive.

Callum takes a sip of beer from a bottle, then slowly reaches for the phone. He glances at it. Holds it up for me to see.

It's done

The bottom of my world falls away like I'm in an elevator in freefall. I gasp, clamping a hand to my mouth.

So that's it. Lee Greenwood is dead. And we're at least partly guilty of his murder. I think I might be sick.

Callum jumps up off the floor unsteadily, almost knocking over half a dozen empty beer bottles he's worked his way through this evening. He's been drinking more and more in recent days, I've noticed. 'We should crack open another one of those bottles of champagne left over from the party with my parents,' he says, grinning.

Oh my god. He's actually pleased. A man's dead because of us and he wants to crack open the champagne?

'No, Callum. We're not celebrating.'

'Why not? It's what we wanted, isn't it?'

'Yes. No. I don't know,' I wail, so many emotions running amok around my head. Regret. Remorse. Guilt. Anger. Disgust.

'Lee Greenwood was a scumbag,' Callum says. 'Just remember what he did and how he laughed at Gabriel in court. He deserved to die. He brought this on himself.'

I've tried so hard to tell myself we were acting for the greater good. Correcting a wrong and bringing some balance back to the universe. I've tried focusing on everything Gabriel told us about Tilly. Picturing her joyous, smiling face. Imagining her terror and pain as she was hit by Greenwood's van and dragged along the street under his wheels while he was on the phone texting his wife. Reminding myself of that little bean of a baby in her womb, a creature that never had a chance to live. And yet I'm still plagued by all these feelings that we've done the wrong thing. That we've gone too far.

I wish we'd never met Gabriel Salt, and that we never found out anything about Tilly or her horrific death. I wish Callum had never talked me into going along with Gabriel's plans, that I'd been stronger and stuck to my instincts.

But once we'd met Henry and made a pact with the devil, there was never any turning back. The text is merely a confirmation of the inevitable.

'A man's dead because of us,' I scream in frustration. Why can't Callum grasp the seriousness of what we've done?

He shakes his head. 'Not because of us. Because of what *he* did. He had it coming. He deserved it, Jade. I'd better tell Gabriel. He'll want to know for sure.'

As Callum makes the call, I tune out, lost in my own thoughts and inner turmoil. I don't hear his words, but it's hard to filter out the elation in his voice. The euphoria. The jubilation.

I wish I could feel it too. But all I feel is hollow and sick.

My only hope is that it isn't true.

It's a two-word text message. That's no proof of anything.

While Callum's distracted talking to Gabriel, I google Lee Greenwood's name on my iPad. If he's dead, surely there'll be something about it online.

But all I can find are the stories about his court case.

It doesn't mean anything, of course. If he's only died this evening, it's probably too early for the information to have been made public.

I try again, typing 'man killed' into the search bar and filtering the results to show only news stories from the last twenty-four hours.

All that comes up is a story about a driver losing control of his car and hitting a tree in Surrey, another about police trying to identify the body of a man pulled from a harbour in Cumbria, and something about a court case involving a gang of thugs who kicked a thirty-year-old man to death outside a nightclub in Cardiff.

Nothing that looks remotely like it could be about Lee Greenwood.

'That's one happy man,' Callum says, hanging up his call and slumping onto the sofa. His breath is stale with alcohol. 'Gabriel's absolutely delighted. He couldn't thank us enough. It feels so good, doesn't it?'

'No, Callum. Not really.'

'It's like there's electricity running through my body. It's better than drugs.'

I can't believe he's being like this.

'Don't you have a shred of remorse?'

He stares at me like I'm crazy. 'Of course not. He had it coming to him. He took a life. Actually, two

104

lives. And he didn't even have the decency to show any guilt. Good riddance, I say.'

I can't be with him while he's acting like this. I don't recognise him anymore. 'I'm going to bed,' I announce.

'What? Why?'

'I'm tired,' I grumble. And I need some time on my own to process my thoughts. I can't be around Callum when he's in such high spirits and my head is a fog of regret.

'It's like being a superhero, isn't it?' He's not even listening to me. 'Like Batman or something.'

'You know Batman's not real, don't you?'

'You know what I mean. We're shadowy heroes fighting against evil and bringing the bad guys to justice when the law's failed.'

'Seriously, Callum? Can you hear yourself?'

He laughs and grabs another beer bottle. 'There must be hundreds of others out there.'

'Hundreds of other what?' I snap, hauling myself wearily to my feet.

'Hundreds of other people who've been let down by the courts. We can do something to help them, now we have the contacts.' He holds up the burner phone like it's a sacred sword.

Is he suggesting what I think he's suggesting?

'You can't be serious?'

'Why not? We've done it once. We can do it again.'

'Absolutely not. This was a mistake. We shouldn't have been dragged into Gabriel's problems, let alone be contemplating doing it again,' I say, horrified. 'Promise me you're joking.'

105

'You said yourself you wanted to use the money to help people. What better way could there be than this? Helping people who really need it. The underdogs who've been let down and forgotten by the police and the courts.'

'No way. I'm deadly serious, Callum. Get rid of that phone and I don't want to hear any more talk like this again.'

He raises his arms in mock innocence. 'Talk like what?'

I grind my teeth to stop myself from saying something I might regret. 'I'm going up. I'll see you later.'

I climb the stairs on heavy legs and get myself ready for bed on autopilot. I'm a bundle of nerves, and predictably, when I climb into bed and switch off the light, I can't sleep.

I lie there with gritty eyes, curled into a fetal ball with the duvet pulled up to my chin, my thoughts racing almost as fast as my pulse.

If only I could turn back the clock to the day Gabriel posted that letter through the door. I should have listened to the advice of that man from the lottery and thrown the letter away without a second thought. I couldn't have been thinking straight. But then, I had no idea what Gabriel had in mind at that point.

What if the police don't believe Greenwood's death was an accident and discover we've funded his execution? We might not have physically killed him, but that's hardly going to stand up as much of a defence in court. And if we're convicted, how long are we looking at in jail? Twenty years? Thirty? More? I'd be an old woman by the time I was free.

When Callum climbs into bed a few hours later, he immediately falls into a deep slumber, snoring loudly in my ear. Any hopes I'd had of dropping off evaporate.

I give up. I head downstairs, make myself a cup of chamomile tea and curl up on the sofa in my dressing gown to pore over my iPad again. Jefferson, pleased to see me awake, joins me, curling his body into a tight coil at the opposite end of the couch.

There's still nothing on any of the news websites or social media about Lee Greenwood being found dead. But I keep looking, re-reading all the old reports on Tilly's death and Greenwood's trial.

Eventually, my eyes grow heavy, and my iPad slips out of my hands and falls into my lap.

The next thing I know, Callum's waving a mug of coffee under my nose. I blink and rub my eyes. Light's streaming through the curtains and Delilah's panting in my face, her hot, stinky breath making me recoil in disgust. I push her head away.

'What time is it?'

'Half nine,' Callum says. 'I was worried when I woke up and you were gone.'

'I couldn't sleep.'

'Greenwood?'

I nod as I wrap my hands around the coffee mug, savouring its warmth.

'I know you're upset.' Callum sits by my feet in the space where Jefferson had settled for the night. His hair's all mussed up, and he needs a shave. 'But it's for the best. We've done the right thing.'

'Have we?'

'Of course. Greenwood never showed any regret for Tilly's death. He just saw it as a big joke. He didn't care about Tilly, or her baby.'

'It doesn't mean we had the right to take the law into our own hands.'

'The law let Gabriel and Tilly down.'

'We shouldn't have done it.'

Callum shrugs. 'I'm certainly not losing any sleep over it.'

I can't understand how he can be so dispassionate. I'm a bag of nerves and regret, but he's revelling in what we've done.

He kisses me on the head. 'I'm going to take a shower.'

As soon as he's gone, I jump back on my iPad.

Still nothing new about Greenwood.

It gives me a glimmer of hope that Henry's nothing more than a fraud who's stolen our money and never had any intention of doing Greenwood any harm. I don't care about the money. It might be a lot of cash for some people, but it's a pittance to us. We can afford to lose it. In fact, I'd happily give it away if it meant Lee Greenwood didn't die.

But that hope is finally dashed an hour or so later when I stumble across a small snippet of information that's been recently uploaded onto a regional news website.

A man's been found dead in a remote woodland car park on the outskirts of London.

A chill spikes through my veins.

He was discovered in a white van. Initial indications suggest he died from a drug overdose. Traces of cocaine were found in the vehicle. Toxicology tests are to be carried out.

It has to be him.

A drug overdose made to look like an accident?

They've not identified the victim yet, but I know in my bones it's Lee Greenwood. It has to be.

My stomach flips. My chest tightens. And I just about make it to the bathroom before I'm violently sick.

Chapter 13

Callum's trying to install a ridiculous, profession-al-looking coffee machine in the kitchen. It arrived in a huge box a few days ago, but he's decided he finally wants to get it working. It takes up half the length of one of the counters, all chrome and dials and fancy knobs.

'Everything okay?' he asks as I stand in the door-way, watching. 'I thought I heard you being sick.'

I'm still in my pyjamas and dressing gown, my hair tied back in a ponytail and my stomach tender.

'Not pregnant, are you?'

'No.' At least I hope not. Now really doesn't feel like the right time to be starting our family. We've not even had the chance to look at houses yet, with everything else going on.

'So, what's wrong?' he asks.

I hold up my iPad and show him the story about the man who's been found dead in his van. 'I think it's Greenwood,' I say, as he reads the brief details.

He shrugs and returns to poring over an instruc-tion manual for his new coffee machine. 'Yeah, probably.'

'Henry's made it look like an accidental drug overdose.'

'Yup.' He tears open a bag of coffee beans and pours them into a plastic hopper.

'You don't seem terribly interested.'

'He's dead. That's all I care about,' he says.

I never knew my husband could be so cold. So dispassionate. I've been able to think about nothing else since our encounter with Henry in that horrible pub in London, but he's behaving as if nothing's happened. Or worse, that we've done a good thing. Something to be commended. Has he lost sight of the fact a man's dead?

'What?' he asks in all innocence, as he catches me staring at him in disbelief.

'Nothing, Callum. It doesn't matter.'

It takes another twenty-four hours for confirmation to come through that the dead man is Greenwood, although I can't find any further details about how he died. The report on the web is brief and to the point.

Drug death driver found in woodland identified

A man found dead in a car park near Gravesend on Tuesday has been identified as 62-year-old Lee Greenwood from Ilford.

Police confirmed they were not treating Mr Greenwood's death as suspicious.

It's believed he died from a drug overdose and that traces of cocaine were found in his vehicle.

An inquest is expected to be held later in the year.

Mr Greenwood, a grandfather who was married with two children, had been convicted of careless driving following the death of pregnant cyclist Tilly Salt, in central London last year.

He was fined for the offence but escaped further sanction after the court ruled Mrs Salt's death had been 'a tragic accident that had deeply affected everyone involved.'

I didn't even know you could die from a cocaine overdose until I looked it up online. There haven't been many cases, but it does happen. And then I discovered you can inject it if you mix it with water. Was that how Henry killed him? Did he inject Greenwood with a massive dose of cocaine that stopped his heart and then left evidence in the van to make it look like an accident? A bag of powder? Some traces dabbed around his nose and mouth? I'll probably never find out, and to be honest, it doesn't matter. Greenwood's dead. That's the only detail that really concerns me.

At least the police don't seem to be treating his death as suspicious. Not that it makes me feel any better. We're still responsible for murder, and if that's not bad enough, I now know more about Lee Greenwood. That he was a family man, with a wife and grandchildren.

I'd never thought about it before. I'd only ever thought of him as a van driver. One of those thoughtless couriers more interested in his phone and meeting his targets than keeping his eyes on the road.

From the pictures I'd seen of him, and from what Gabriel had told us about the way he behaved in court, I imagined him as some kind of football thug, with his thick, bald head and bulging beer belly. Probably a bit racist. Almost certainly a misogynist. A dinosaur who struggled to find his place in an ever-complicated liberal world.

I never once thought of him as having a family of his own. That he could be someone's husband. Someone's father. A grandfather.

It puts a completely different spin on my perception of him.

A grandfather, for pity's sake!

With kids. And grandchildren. And how are they coping with the news?

We've not only taken a man's life, but we've almost certainly destroyed a family. That was never the plan, but I never thought about the consequences of what we were doing. We just bowled right in, riding on the surf of Gabriel's tragic story, consumed by a sense of injustice because of what had happened to Tilly.

But what kind of justice is this for the people who loved Greenwood? Who depended on him. They're all innocents who've been dragged unwittingly into this mess.

We should have left well alone. This was never our battle to fight. We should be enjoying our winnings. Planning exotic trips abroad and buying a new house. Instead, I'm wracked with remorse and regret so intense it cuts like a knife. I can think of nothing other than the suffering we've put that poor man's family through. I was happier when I was working in the restaurant with no money to my name.

My mind goes round and round in circles, thinking about the pain and anguish we've caused. It grows in my gut like a cancer, slowly, insidiously blooming until it's verging on an obsession. I remember when my father died, it was almost as if he'd taken a little piece of me with him, and my heart was left aching and hollow. Like Greenwood, he'd been taken too soon. A massive heart attack while he was at work. He collapsed in the office and was dead long before he ever made it to hospital. That was more than fifteen years ago, but I don't think I've ever come to terms with it. The loss still hangs heavy on my shoulders, and I still think about him every day.

I can't find out anything about Greenwood's family online, no matter how deeply I dig. Not even on social media. However, a few days after Greenwood's death, a news alert I set up on my phone brings some new information.

A funeral date has been set, and a death notice on a local newspaper website not only has the date and location of where it's going to be held but reveals some new names. A fresh insight into the real Lee Greenwood and those closest to him.

Lee Stanley GREENWOOD
Passed away unexpectedly on April 14th, 2023, aged 62 years. Beloved husband of Coral, much-loved father to Bianca and Paige, dearly

loved grandfather to Ashley, Kiera, Kyle and Elliot. A funeral service will be held at the County Crematorium in Ilford on Thursday, April 27th at 2:30pm.

The notice is accompanied by a picture of Greenwood I've not seen before. It's much more flattering than those used by the press. It was obviously taken a few years ago. He's not so fat around the face and there's a twinkle in his eye instead of that cold, unnerving stare. He looks quite normal. Like he could be anyone's father or grandfather.

My gaze fixes on the date. The funeral's next week in Ilford. That isn't far from here. Just over the Dartford Crossing and into Essex. And in an instant, my mind's made up.

Maybe it's just self-torture or a crazy need to understand the fallout of our actions, but I've never been more certain that I have to do this.

I'm going to attend the service.

Chapter 14

There are far more people at the crematorium than I imagined there would be. At least a hundred, if not more, huddled in small groups in the car park, murmuring quietly to one another as they wait for an earlier service to conclude and the chapel of rest to become free.

At least it means I should blend in more easily, and the presence of a stranger less likely to cause raised eyebrows.

It's a stupid idea, though. I should never have come. But it was a long journey and I'm here now. I might as well stay and observe. After all, that's all I ever planned to do. Maybe it'll make me feel better. It can't make me feel much worse.

There are a lot of young men in ill-fitting black suits, their ties loose around their necks, standing around looking uncomfortable. Hard-looking men with tattoos and short haircuts, broken noses and missing teeth, accompanied by women with fake tans, long eyelashes, plumped up lips and wearing inappropriately tight, short dresses, skin goose-pimpling like they're freezing to death. It's the end of April, but it's unseasonably cold.

I hang back and busy myself on my phone, trying to look inconspicuous. If Callum had any idea what I was up to, he'd go mad. Fortunately, he took himself out for the day again. Off in that stupid sports car, driving around with nowhere to go. I couldn't think of anything more boring, but at least I've not had to lie to him about where I am or what I'm doing. If he asks about my day later, I'll tell him I went shopping. It's only a little white lie.

The doors of the chapel crank open and mourners from the earlier service spill out, wiping away tears and hugging each other for comfort.

Like a conveyor belt of grief, Lee Greenwood's mourners replace them, shuffling solemnly into the chapel with heads bowed, greeting each other with stoic smiles and pats on the arm.

I daren't rush in and risk getting caught up in an awkward conversation with someone from the family, asking how I knew the dead man and having to wing it. I've already decided that if anyone does ask, I'll tell them I knew him from work and keep it vague, but I'd rather not find myself having to lie. Lies have a habit of coming back to bite you when you least expect it. It's easier if I can avoid conversation altogether.

I watch everyone disappear inside but continue to hang around outside until the hearse arrives.

And that's when it hits me hard.

A big black car, polished to a reflective gleam and with Greenwood's casket on show, swings through a pair of ornate gates at the top of the drive. But it's not the coffin that brings tears to my eyes. It's

117

the enormous wreath of white and blue flowers arranged to spell 'DAD', sitting next to the casket, that sends my emotions racing. A cruel reminder that Lee Greenwood wasn't just the man who killed Tilly Salt and got away with it. He was a father with a family who loved him. And we've stolen him from them.

I need to see this. To face up to my crime. It's the only way I'm going to find closure and put what I've done behind me. Otherwise, it's going to consume me for the rest of my life. If I can experience the grief, listen to the laments and eulogies, and understand the consequences of what we've done, then hopefully I can box it away and move on. It sounds crazy, but I don't know what else I can do other than confess to the police. And I'm not going to do that. I have too much to lose.

Ahead of the hearse, two black Range Rovers with darkened windows pull up outside the chapel. I watch intently as several people climb out. Most notably, there's an older woman in a knee-length black dress, who is dabbing her eyes with a tissue. She looks bowed with grief. Greenwood's wife, Coral, I'm guessing. She's accompanied by two younger women, who flank her protectively, supporting her by the arms. It must be her daughters, Bianca and Paige.

They're a similar height and build to their mother and have the same gait, tottering and unbalanced, as if unused to wearing heels and dresses.

There's also a man and a couple of older kids, who I guess must be grandchildren, allowed the day off school to attend. They huddle together under a wide porch where they're greeted by a vicar in flowing white robes. The hearse rolls to a halt, blocking my view of the family.

It's not too late to walk away. I could call a taxi and be back at the train station and on my way home in twenty minutes. But I can't. I'm drawn to this family and now I've had a brief glimpse of them, I can't drag myself away.

And if I'm going to go inside, it's now or never.

With a deep breath, and pressing my wide-brimmed black hat down on my head, I hurry across the car park. I nip behind Greenwood's wife and daughters with my eyes, hidden behind a pair of dark glasses, fixed on the ground, hoping they don't notice me, but their attention is focused on the coffin being lifted from the back of the hearse by a team of pallbearers in frock coats, and I think I get away with it.

I slot into a spare seat at the back of the chapel next to a brutish, broad-shouldered man with enormous, callused boxer's knuckles, who's wearing a solemn, sulky expression. He reeks of stale cigarette smoke, which sticks in my throat and makes me nauseous, but I can't change places now. I nod politely but, before he can say anything, an organ strikes up, playing a dirgeful piece of classical music I half recognise.

Everyone rises to their feet and a low murmur of voices fades.

Coral and her daughters take their seats at the front. Six pallbearers follow with slow steps, car-

119

rying Greenwood's coffin on their shoulders, the 'DAD' wreath now balanced precariously on top. They carefully place the casket on a plinth draped in dark blue silk, alongside burning candles on tall brass sticks and a wreath of blue and white flowers.

As the organ falls silent, the chapel is filled with the sound of sobbing and sniffing.

I stare at my clenched hands and bite my lower lip to quell my tears. Funerals always make me cry. And this one is no exception, especially as Greenwood is only dead because of us.

The vicar invites everyone to sit. My face flushes hot and cold. I'm taking a big risk being here. If any one of the mourners in this chapel knew the truth of what I've done, they'd probably lynch me.

My hand noticeably trembles as I pick up an order of service left on the back of the chair in front. Greenwood's smiling face stares back at me above his date of birth and the date he died. A date that will also stick in my mind.

Suddenly, it feels incredibly hot. A prickle of sweat breaks out on my forehead.

I take a calming breath and try to settle my nerves. I need to keep my head if I'm going to get away with this.

For the next forty minutes, I sit through what feels like an unending litany of hymns, prayers, and tributes. Even laughter, as one of his Greenwood's friends recalls his lust for life, his family, and his beloved Chelsea Football Club, reciting a series of coarse anecdotes which don't strike me as particularly funny or appropriate for a funeral.

Of course, nobody says a word about how he died, apparently overdosing on illegal drugs while parked up in a remote car park in his van. Nor that he'd achieved a minor level of notoriety in the press when he'd knocked a woman off her bike and killed her while distracted by his phone.

If you'd walked into the service off the street and knew nothing about Lee Greenwood, you'd go away believing he was a saint whose life had been cut tragically short.

I can't stand it anymore. The atmosphere is oppressive and my head feels as if it's filled with helium, liable to float off my shoulders at any moment. It doesn't help that the man next to me keeps glowering at me. He's probably wondering why I'm still wearing sunglasses indoors.

As the casket disappears behind a pair of curtains that swish slowly closed and the familiar, and rather predictable, strains of Sinatra's *My Way* strike up, I grab my bag and rush out, my heels clattering noisily on the tiled floor.

The cool air hits me like a tonic. I breathe in deeply, trying to take control of my senses. I should have eaten something before I came, but I couldn't face it. I was too nervous. And it's all been a bit overwhelming. I just need to sit down for a moment. And then I'll go. I've seen what I wanted to see. Faced down my demons.

My Way is already coming to an end. The stirring last line reaches a crescendo that I doubt will have left a dry eye in the place. I glance around, looking

121

for a refuge. They'll all be coming out at any moment and I don't want to get caught here.

But where do I go?

There's a path that disappears around the back of the chapel. Nobody's going to find me there, surely. I can wait there until everyone has left and make my way back home. I'm in no rush.

The path leads to a secluded patio area where I'm grateful to find a wooden bench overlooking a valley of fields and woodland. Brass memorial plaques have been set into a concrete border around the flagstones, and there are bunches of flowers dotted here and there. It's such a tranquil setting, if a little cold, exposed to the biting wind. Apart from that, it's the perfect place to hide until I can make my escape.

I perch on the bench with my bag on my lap, and button up my coat to my throat, listening to the babble of voices and shuffling feet from inside the building as people start to leave.

'What did you think of the service?'

The voice makes me jump. I thought I was alone. A woman has appeared from the opposite side of the chapel holding an unlit cigarette in one hand and a lighter in the other.

Shit. It's one of Greenwood's daughters. One of the women I saw earlier with his widow, Coral.

This is bad. Really bad.

'It - it was beautiful,' I stammer, getting up to leave.

'Don't go on my account,' she says, waving at me to sit down.

She perches on the opposite end of the bench and lights her cigarette, inhaling deeply and blowing out a grey stream of smoke as she looks wistfully across the valley.

'I'm sorry for your loss,' I say.

'Thank you.' She taps a crust of ash onto the ground and folds her arms across her chest as she shivers with the cold. She's only wearing a thin dress that plunges at the front, exposing a little too much flesh for a funeral, especially her father's funeral.

I wish a hole would open up and swallow me. I can't get drawn into a conversation with this woman, but nor can I leave without appearing rude.

'How did you know Dad?' she asks.

In my panic, my mind goes blank. What was my story again? I'd gone over it repeatedly on the train, but I wasn't expecting to have to explain myself to Lee Greenwood's daughter. 'I used to work with him,' I splutter.

'Oh, yeah?' she raises an eyebrow. 'Where?'

Now what am I supposed to say? I don't know anything about Lee Greenwood's employment history, other than that he was a courier who drove a white van around London.

'Well, when I say worked with him, I mean he used to pop in for coffee. I have a little coffee shop,' I say, praying she'll buy the lie and not ask me for details.

'And you came to his funeral? That's thoughtful,' she says. 'I'm Bianca.'

'It's the least I could do. I was very fond of your father.' I bite the inside of my cheek, focusing on the needle of pain. 'Sarah,' I say, grabbing at the first name that comes to mind. 'Pleased to meet you.'

Bianca turns her head to look me up and down, running her tongue thoughtfully over letterbox-red glossed lips. My heart is hammering so hard in my chest, it's a wonder she can't hear it.

'He was only sixty-two,' she says, her cigarette dangling precariously between two long fingers. She has long red nails and hands heavy with gold and silver rings. 'It's no age, is it?'

'No,' I agree. 'It's not.'

She shakes her head and picks a hair out of her mouth. 'Mum's distraught. You know, they tried to tell us it was an overdose. Can you believe it? As if Dad would have gone anywhere near drugs.'

'Right,' I nod sagely.

Bianca takes another drag from her cigarette and tilts her head back to exhale. 'He loved a beer, but he couldn't be doing with drugs. He hated them, and anyone who did them. Which is why it don't make any sense.'

'No,' I say. She obviously wants to talk about it, but I've no idea why she's picked on me to unburden herself. Maybe because I'm a stranger.

'He didn't even like taking aspirin. But that's the story the police want us to believe.'

'I'm sorry, I didn't know,' I lie.

'We tried telling them, but they weren't interested. They said it was an open and shut case, but that's bullshit.'

I'm shocked by the venom in her tone.

'He wasn't a junkie,' she continues, finishing her cigarette and crushing it into the ground with the toe of her shoe. 'But they wouldn't listen.'

'Oh,' I say, trying to feign surprise. 'So what do you think happened?' I cross my legs and fold my hands on top of my bag, trying to give off a casual vibe and hide how uncomfortable I'm feeling. If she doesn't believe her father died of an overdose, Callum and I have a big problem.

Bianca snorts, then coughs. A proper hacking smoker's cough. I gaze at her through the dark lenses of my sunglasses, which I'm glad I kept on. It's at least a partial disguise.

'Well, obviously someone set it up to make it look like an overdose,' she snaps, as if I'm stupid.

'Seriously?'

She shrugs. 'Of course. There's no way Dad would touch drugs, so what other explanation is there? Someone killed him. I'm certain of it.'

'What?'

'He was murdered,' she says. 'I don't care what the police say.'

I let my hand fly to my mouth in a pretence at being shocked while my stomach turns over on itself.

'Murdered? But who would do that?'

Her eyes narrow as she stares at me, and for a horrible moment, I'm convinced she's going to point the finger at me and tell me she knows everything. I snatch a breath and hold it as she fiddles with an ugly signet ring on her right hand.

'I don't know yet, but I'm going to find out,' she says eventually. Her face tightens into a determined scowl.

'And then what?'

'We'll take care of it.'

Take care of it? A shiver catches me by surprise, shaking my whole body.

'You're cold,' Bianca says. 'You should go and get warmed up.'

'Yes, you're right,' I whisper, the words snagging in my throat. I leap to my feet and straighten my coat, my mind reeling. 'It was nice to meet you.'

'And you, Sarah. Take care.'

I'm about to walk away, my legs like jelly, but there's a burning question I have to ask. I don't want to hear the answer, but I need to know what's going through her mind.

'What will you do when you find out who killed him?'

She blinks rapidly. Chews her bottom lip. 'I've always believed in an eye for an eye,' she says with a menace that chills my blood. 'I'll find whoever did this, and then I'll have them killed.'

Chapter 15

On the Tube across London, my mind's in such turmoil I almost miss my stop. In fact, my entire journey home is a complete blur. Surely there's no way Bianca could ever find out Callum and I had anything to do with her father's murder? We didn't fake his overdose and, as far as she knows, we don't have any motive for killing him. We've never even met Lee Greenwood. All we did was finance his execution...

Oh god.

Gabriel must be high on her list of suspects, especially as he'd recently turned up at Greenwood's house armed with a knife. I'd better destroy that letter from him. That's a key piece of evidence linking us if she or the police started to dig deeper. And of course, there are the phone records. Callum and I have both used our mobiles to contact Gabriel. We can delete the call histories, but the police can access old records through the phone companies, can't they?

But even if they did, it doesn't prove anything. It's just circumstantial. They can't prove what we talked about or that we agreed to fund a hit on Greenwood. Mind you, what if one of Gabriel's neighbours saw us at his house? That would be tricky to explain away.

At least we paid Henry in cash, so there's no financial paper trail back to us. But it's a small mercy. Besides, Bianca doesn't need to prove anything. She just needs to suspect our involvement and then...

My breath comes too fast, too shallow, but I can't seem to bring it back under control. Panic rises from my core, swirling around my body like poison.

I'll find whoever did this, and then I'll have them killed.

Maybe it was an empty threat. People say things like that all the time and don't mean it. Bianca was upset. It was her father's funeral. Emotions were running high. Women like her don't go around killing people, even if she is angry and upset. It's just words. Although the way she said it... That cold, steely look in her eye.

I swallow a lump in my throat.

I'm overreacting. Bianca's not going to come after us. She doesn't even know who we are.

Unless she gets to Gabriel and he tells her we put up the money.

Would he do that after what we've done for him? If he thought it would save his neck, he might.

What do I do? Warn Gabriel? I can hardly go to the police for protection.

What an absolute mess. I should never have gone to the funeral in the first place. What was I thinking?

Callum's already home when I get in. He's plugged into another video game, eating pizza out of a box on the floor, surrounded by beer bottles. The bitter stench of garlic fills the house. He has the volume on the TV up so loud, every gunshot and scream from the game reverberates through our tiny lounge.

'You're back,' he announces unnecessarily. 'Where've you been?'

'Shopping.' The lie trips easily off my tongue. I should tell him the truth and confess my stupid mistake, but I need to build up to it first. Get his full attention and wait until he's in a good mood.

He glances away from the screen and looks at me. Frowns. 'All dressed up like that?'

I dumped my hat on the stairs as I came in and shoved my sunglasses in my bag, but there's no mistaking it looks like I've been to a funeral. I'm wearing a wraparound black midaxi dress and heels, paired with a long, dark overcoat with a faux-fur trim.

I shrug. 'Since when did you take any notice of what I wear?'

I shouldn't take it out on Callum. It's not his fault I've fucked up.

'I've been shopping too,' he says with a sheepish grin. 'I've ordered a new car.'

My heart sinks. 'What new car?'

'A brand-new Aston Martin. In black. It looks super smart. Unfortunately, there's a three-week delivery waiting list, but you're going to love it,' he says, his grin widening.

I doubt it. 'And where do you plan to keep that?' I snap. What a complete waste of money. It's as though our winnings are burning a hole in his pocket and he feels the need to spend them as quickly as he can. We should be looking at new houses. Or investing our money. Not squandering it on polluting supercars.

'I'll hire another lock-up in town. Don't worry, I'm not stupid. I'm not planning on keeping it on the drive.'

'Right,' I sigh. 'Whatever.' I should tell him where I've been and that I've spoken to Lee Greenwood's daughter. That she knows he was murdered and that she's looking to find his killer.

But I'm tired and irritable. I don't want to have that conversation right now. It's going to have to wait. 'I'm going to have a bath.'

'You want me to save you some pizza?' Callum asks, his attention firmly back on the video game. 'Or I can order in fresh?'

'I'm not hungry.'

I leave him to it, lost in his own fantasy world where the biggest problem on his mind is how to reach the next level of his game. I head upstairs and run a bath, my brain replaying the conversation with Bianca over and over, trying to convince myself there's nothing to worry about, and failing.

I drop one of my effervescing bath bombs into the steaming water and strip out of my clothes. Travelling by train always leaves me feeling grubby.

I top the bath up almost to the brim and slip in, wincing as the water burns my feet. I hesitate, letting my skin become accustomed to the temperature, and then submerge my whole body. The tension immediately releases from my muscles, but it does nothing to calm my tortured mind. Usually, a bath works wonders for my anxiety. But not this evening. And soon, my body gets too hot. I need to get out again.

I'll find whoever did this, and then I'll have them killed.

I clamber out, dry myself with a fluffy towel, and slip into my comfiest pair of pyjamas.

It's no good. I need to tell Callum what I've done. I can't put it off. He needs to know I may have inadvertently put us in danger. And anyway, I can't deal with this on my own. I need to talk to someone. I need to talk to Callum. I'm sure he'll be cross with me, but he'll know what to do. It's best to come clean.

I pad back down the stairs and stop to pay some attention to Delilah and Jefferson, who are both curled up on their beds under the stairs. Their tails thump the ground loudly as I scratch their heads and chuck their chins.

I can't put it off any longer.

Callum's still glued to his game with a crust of pizza hanging inelegantly from his mouth.

'Hey, can I speak to you for a minute? It's important,' I say.

'Yup... hang on a second.'

'Callum, please. Can you turn that off?' I raise my voice to be heard over the gunfire as his on-screen character looks about to be overwhelmed by a marauding mob of half-dead monsters.

Callum frowns, shocked that I've shouted at him. I rarely raise my voice. He pauses the game.

'What's up, babe?'

'Turn it off. I need your full attention.'

Now he looks really worried. The silence comes as a welcome relief to my ears.

He leans forwards and flicks a button on the games console. The TV screen turns black. I sit on the sofa, wrapping my dressing gown around my legs.

'It's about Lee Greenwood,' I croak, the words catching in my dry throat.

Callum rolls his eyes like I'm making a fuss about nothing. 'You still going on about that? I told you, forget it. It's done.'

I shake my head and lower my gaze.

'It's not that, it's... it's...'

'Look, there's nothing to worry about, okay? All we did was help Gabriel get justice for his wife's death. What's so wrong about that?' he says, as if funding someone's murder is a completely natural, everyday thing to do.

'No, you don't understand,' I mumble. 'There's something I have to tell you —'

'Yes, me too,' he says, jumping off the floor and joining me on the sofa. He grabs his laptop, which has been shoved out of the way under the coffee table, and flips it open. 'I've been doing some research.' He's grinning again. Why is he always so happy about everything?

'What research?'

'I was saying, wasn't I, that there are probably loads of cases like Gabriel's. You know, cases where people have been let down by the courts and the police. Well, I was right. There *are* loads of cases.' He spins the laptop to face me. 'Look, I've found all these.'

I shake my head in disbelief as I run my eye down a long list of names and dates he's compiled into a spreadsheet. Next to each entry is a brief description under a heading he's named 'Crime'.

'What the hell is this, Callum?' I ask, bewildered.

'This woman, here,' he says, jabbing his finger at the third name on his list. It's someone called Jamelia Humphries. I've never heard of her. 'She's a victim of domestic violence, but her husband was never convicted because of an administrative cock-up by the police.'

But before I can read the details, he's pointing to another name, further down the list.

'And this bloke framed a friend of his for murder. What he'd done only came to light after his mate killed himself in prison, but the courts said there wasn't enough evidence to prosecute him, so he was never punished. And this one. He's a rapist who was never prosecuted because he claimed diplomatic immunity and disappeared back to Algeria before the police could arrest him.'

'I - I don't understand,' I stammer. 'Why've you done this?'

'It's research.' He looks at me blankly, as if it's obvious. I just hope it isn't true. That it's not what it appears to be.

'But why?'

'Because these are all people we can help,' he says.

'Help?'

'Yeah, like Gabriel needed our help.'

'No,' I gasp. 'You can't be serious.'

'Why not?' He closes the laptop and puts it behind him as he swivels to face me, taking my hands. 'These are all people we can help get justice for.'

'More hits?'

He pouts. 'Yeah. We have the money now. We can afford it.'

'But we've been through this already. You promised me Lee Greenwood would be a one-off. It was a mistake. We should never have got involved with Gabriel Salt. And now, here you are, going behind my back and plotting more.' I snatch my hands out of his, my blood boiling with anger.

'Why are you being like this, Jade?' he says, scowling. 'We could make a real difference to these people's lives.'

'I said no more, and I mean it.'

He stares at me, his jaw stiff and the veins in his forehead popping. But I'm not arguing about it. We are not using our money to pay for any more people to die.

'I don't believe you. You were the one who said you wanted to use the money to do some good,' he says, twisting my words again.

But this isn't about helping people. For Callum, this is about something else. It's about power and control. It's got a grip of him. Its talons embedded in his flesh. If he'd really wanted to do something worthwhile with the money, he'd have offered to make a donation to charity.

'It's not going to happen, Callum. So drop it,' I warn him.

He stares at me for a moment, his eyes blazing. I think he's going to carry on arguing, trying to change my mind, but instead he jumps up. 'I'm going out,' he announces.

'Where?'

'I don't know. But I can't stay here. I'm going to end up saying something I'll regret,' he says. 'You're totally unbelievable. You know that?'

He marches out of the room. The front door clicks open and slams shut. The house falls silent.

Fine, let him sulk. He'll get over it, and when he comes to his senses, he'll thank me.

Although, I'm grudgingly impressed. I never knew my husband had it in him to be so resourceful. I didn't even know he could put together a spreadsheet. He's always claimed never to be any good with computers, but I guess there are all sorts of things we don't know about the people who are supposed to be closest to us.

The laptop is still sitting on the cushion where Callum dropped it. A red light on its edge flickers on and off like a beacon. I can't help myself. I pick it up, flip it open. The screen blinks into life and opens on the spreadsheet again. I count at least twenty cases Callum's listed. Presumably, he's found all the details online. News stories and court reports. I don't know when he's found the time, but he's certainly done a thorough job.

Not that it matters. We're not getting involved with any of these cases, whether Callum likes it or not. It's not right. It's not ethical. And, worse than that, it's illegal. I'm not putting my freedom at risk for a bunch of strangers, no matter how deserving they are.

I'm about to switch the computer off when I have another idea.

I open an internet browser and search for 'Bianca Greenwood'.

I've tried looking her up before, when I first found the death notice, but it didn't turn up anything useful. Nothing's changed. There are half a dozen social media profiles for women who share the name Bianca Greenwood, but none of them is the woman I met earlier.

Of course, it's entirely possible she's married now and has changed her name. Her fingers were covered in rings. I didn't notice a wedding ring, although I wasn't looking for one specifically.

I clear my search and try a new one, typing 'Bianca nee Greenwood' into the search bar.

Nothing.

Finally, I type 'Bianca married father Lee' and, to my surprise, I discover a brief entry on a local news website from five years ago announcing Bianca Greenwood's marriage to some guy called Tomas Kezmar at a church in Essex.

That sounds more promising. It's in the right area, at least.

With nothing to lose, I try a different search. This time on the name 'Bianca Kezmar'.

There are a few Bianca Kezmars with social media profiles, but none of them is Lee Greenwood's daughter.

There's only one thing left to try. I type 'Tomas Kezmar' into the search bar, more in hope than expectation.

To my surprise, the internet has plenty of information about Tomas Kezmar. In fact, there are pages and pages of results.

With my hand shaking nervously, I click open the first result. It's a newspaper report dated almost three years ago. I take a deep breath and begin to read, wondering what the hell we've got ourselves into.

Chapter 16

I pore over page after page of information about Tomas Kezmar with a knot tightening in my stomach. If it's all true, we're in trouble. Really deep trouble. As if things weren't bad enough already.

I stay up well beyond midnight, waiting for Callum to return home. There's no point going to bed. I'd never be able to sleep, but more importantly, we need to talk. Urgently.

I've resisted calling him because even though I've been desperate to speak to him, it isn't a conversation to have on the phone. We need to sit down and thrash out what we're going to do next. How we're going to stay safe. At least we have money. Maybe we can disappear. Buy ourselves new lives. New identities. It would be a radical thing to do, but I'm all out of other ideas.

Callum seems surprised to find I'm still up, propped up on the sofa in my dressing gown. When I'm not working, I'm usually in bed by half ten.

'Jade?' he says, his brow furrowing as he stands in the doorway, still wearing his jacket and shoes. Delilah sniffs around his knees, bleary-eyed. 'Is everything okay?'

No, everything is most definitely not okay. 'Sit down,' I say softly, patting the cushion next to me.

'Sorry I stormed out,' he says.

'Where did you go?'

'Just driving around, thinking.'

'There's something I need to tell you,' I say. 'Something you really need to hear.'

His eyes widen, his pupils growing black. 'Now you're worrying me.'

'I tried to tell you earlier, but you weren't listening.' I wring my hands, trying to find the right words to explain. 'I've done something stupid.'

Callum tosses his keys on the side and sits, angling his body to face me. 'Go on,' he says. 'I'm listening now.'

This is worse than when I had to confess to my father that I'd scratched his car trying to negotiate my bike out of the drive when I was nine.

'I didn't go shopping. I'm sorry, I lied to you. I went to Lee Greenwood's funeral.'

I expect him to shout and rant. To tell me what an idiot I am. But he stays silent, staring at me. And somehow it's worse.

'Why?'

'I don't know. I know I shouldn't have done it, but I couldn't help myself. It's like I was drawn there.' I can't even explain it to myself, so how can I hope to make Callum understand? 'While I was there, I found out some information. It's not good news.'

Callum sucks in a breath and continues to stare, saying nothing. Waiting for me to continue.

'Greenwood's family knows it wasn't an overdose. They know he was murdered.'

His head drops, his chin falling onto his chest. 'How?'

'Because he's never touched drugs in his life. They say it's totally out of character and think it was set up to look like an accident. Not that they can prove anything, of course.'

'Who do they think did it?'

'They don't know, yet. But they're not going to let it go.'

'How do you know all this?' Callum glances up, his eyes narrowing. 'Who've you been speaking to?'

'Greenwood's daughter, Bianca.'

'What?'

'I didn't mean to. She caught me by surprise.'

'Oh, Jade, how could you have been so stupid?' He looks genuinely disappointed in me. I wish he'd just shout and yell.

'I said I'm sorry. I made a mistake.'

'Yes, you did.'

'She said she's going to find who was responsible for her father's death... and kill them.'

Callum's head jolts upwards as if he's been hit in the stomach. 'She said that?'

I nod. 'And I think she meant it.'

He bites his lower lip. 'I'm sure she didn't.'

'That's what I thought, at first. People say stuff like that all the time and don't really mean it. But then I found this.' I pick up Callum's laptop and show him one of the web pages I've been browsing.

'What's this?'

'A news story. You'd better read it.'

Callum falls silent as his eyes flash across the screen, scanning an article I found from three years ago. I've read it so many times tonight, I know it almost word for word.

Human trafficking gang jailed for exploiting hundreds of women

A gang who trafficked hundreds of women from Hungary into the UK has been jailed for a total of 75 years by a court.

An investigation by the Metropolitan Police identified more than 300 potential victims who had been brought illegally into the country and forced to work in brothels and massage parlours across London.

Isleworth Crown Court heard the women were often kept in squalid conditions, had their passports seized and lived in fear of violence and brutality under the control of the gang, which included eight men and two women.

The gang was only caught and their smuggling operations uncovered after a commercial truck was discovered, apparently abandoned in an industrial park in Essex last year.

A passer-by raised the alarm after hearing noises coming from the vehicle.

When police investigated, they discovered eight women locked inside, barely clinging to life, with just one bottle of water to share between them.

They were all suffering from hypothermia and only survived by huddling together for warmth on what had been one of the coldest February nights on record.

Callum glances up and shakes his head. 'I don't understand,' he says. 'What does this have to do with anything?'

'Keep reading,' I urge him. 'Here, look.' I point at a few paragraphs further into the story.

Tomas Kezmar, 36, from Ilford in Essex, was jailed for twelve years for his role in the operation.

Police said he was a key member of the organisation with responsibility for controlling the women.

The court was told Kezmar would often mete out violent beatings and cruel abuse.

He was said to be particularly feared because of his violent temper and unpredictable nature.

One witness gave evidence that on one occasion, Kezmar had hammered pins into the tips of another woman's fingertips after she'd tried to claim she was too ill to work.

'I still don't get it, Jade. What does any of this have to do with Lee Greenwood?'

'I've been doing some of my own research,' I say. 'This guy, Kezmar, is Bianca's husband.'

'What?'

'They were married five years ago. I found a wedding announcement and looked him up.'

'It's definitely the same man?' Callum asks, his face leaching colour.

'I'm pretty certain, yes.'

'Shit.'

'What the hell are we going to do, Callum?'

He closes the laptop and falls back into the sofa with his hands on his head. 'He's still in prison, I take it?'

'I assume so. He was only jailed three years ago, and I'm pretty certain he wasn't at the funeral. He definitely wasn't with the family. I'd have remembered.'

There was a man with Bianca and her sister, Paige, when they arrived with their mother and what I assumed were some of Lee Greenwood's grandchildren, but I don't think it was Tomas Kezmar. His picture's plastered all over the news websites I've been trawling through, a police mugshot where he's scowling into the camera, wearing a week's worth of stubble, his hair close-cropped. He has mean, narrow black eyes, and thin, cruel lips. It's the sort of face I'd remember if I'd seen it before. And I'm sure I haven't.

'Okay, so that's good news,' Callum says, his eyes darting left and right as if his brain's processing all this new information and working overtime. 'He can't do anything if he's inside, can he?'

I shake my head, but I'm not so sure. Someone like Kezmar is bound to have connections with the criminal underworld. If he wanted to do us harm, I'm sure he'd find a way.

'And you're certain Bianca has no idea who you are?' Callum asks.

'I told her my name was Sarah and I owned a coffee shop in London,' I tell him.

Callum frowns.

'I didn't know what else to say. I told her that her father used to pop in for coffee.'

'Well done. That's good,' Callum says, rocking back and forth. 'So she has no reason to suspect we had anything to do with her father's death?'

'Not unless Gabriel opens his mouth. She's bound to suspect it has something to do with him. He's the one person with an obvious motive.'

'Gabriel won't say anything,' Callum says.

'How can you be so sure?'

'Because I trust him, okay? Look, there's absolutely nothing to connect us with Lee Greenwood's death. We're going to be fine.'

I wish I shared his optimism. If we're going to be fine, why do I feel so scared? I've read what Tomas Kezmar is capable of and we know he has a history of violence. If the family finds out we're involved, I can't even imagine what's going to happen to us. The one thing I am sure of is that they'll take matters into their own hands and it won't be the police we need to worry about.

And all it would take is one word from Gabriel.

'Don't you think we should move out of the house?' I say. 'As a precaution. We're already planning to move, so why don't we ditch this place and find another short-term let, somewhere quiet, until we buy somewhere?'

'But we have another three months to run on our contract.'

'So? We could afford to carry on paying the rent here and somewhere else. Somewhere they can't find us,' I plead.

Callum glares at me, and then his face softens. 'We're not on the run from the mafia,' he laughs. 'You always were such a worrier.'

'Just as a precaution.' I can't understand why he's being so blasé about it. If the Greenwoods find out we funded the hit, they're going to kill us. 'Perhaps we could book into a nice hotel or a B&B for a few weeks? You know, just until the dust has settled.'

'And what about all our stuff? And the dogs?'

'I don't know. I don't care, but I don't feel safe here. Maybe we should think about buying ourselves some new identities and disappearing.'

He laughs again. 'Disappearing? You've been watching too many crime dramas. Nobody's coming after us, okay? Now come on, it's late. Let's get to bed. Everything will seem brighter in the morning.'

But, of course, it won't. A good night's sleep isn't going to deter the Greenwoods from coming after us. We need to act now. Make some plans to protect ourselves before it's too late.

Sure, they don't have any idea who we are right now. But what if that changes? What if they do find out who we are and what we've done? That would change everything.

Chapter 17

Callum tosses a ball in a looping arc, sending Jefferson and Delilah scrambling across the park with their tails wagging. Jefferson wins the race, jumping on his hind legs to catch the ball as it bounces off the hard ground. He comes tearing back, but despite Callum's reasoned pleas, he refuses to give up his prize and Delilah quickly loses interest, heading off to sniff around a clump of tall grass instead.

It's a momentary distraction from my worries, but my mind quickly returns to darker thoughts.

It's been four days since the funeral and we've heard nothing more from Bianca or Gabriel. Four days I've shut myself inside, too fearful of stepping out of the door. But today, Callum insisted we should get out of the house for some fresh air, if only for an hour or so.

He wouldn't take no for an answer, and so, as it's a bright day, we agreed to take the dogs for a long walk. But it's not been the tonic I thought it might be. I've found myself watching everyone who comes close suspiciously, my mind turning every stranger into a potential threat.

At least we're doing something together for a change. Although we've been living under the same roof, we've hardly spent any time together since our win. It's been such a whirlwind, I'm worried we're neglecting our relationship. The last thing I want is for the money to drive a wedge between us and split us up. That would be a tragedy, especially with everything else going on.

'Fancy a coffee?' Callum nods towards the cafe at the edge of the park next to a kids' play area.

'Thanks. I'll keep walking with the dogs. Catch us up?' The thought of being in close proximity to other people right now leaves me cold.

'Alright, I won't be long.'

He hands me the dogs' leads and the tennis ball, wet with slobber, that he's finally managed to prise from Jefferson's jaws. I grimace and throw it. Delilah races after it and snatches it up before Jefferson's even noticed, while I meander along a path that rises gently up an embankment, lost in my thoughts.

Callum's been in a surprisingly good mood today, so maybe I'll broach the subject of moving out of our rental with him again later. Maybe I am being overcautious, but it's better to be safe than sorry. And what's the point of taking the risk in staying and Bianca finding us when we could be holed up in a lovely country hotel somewhere, being waited on hand and foot? Never mind all this tech Callum keeps ordering for himself online. That's what we should be spending our money on.

In the meantime, I've been trying to keep my mind off the Greenwoods by immersing myself in property ads. But the choice is overwhelming. We could afford to buy anything we want, but there's almost too much to choose from.

Do we stay local, near to Callum's family, and my mother? Or do we look further afield where we'd get more for our money? We could buy a Scottish castle if we really wanted. I've seen at least two on the market we could afford. Or a twelve-bedroom mansion in the Cotswolds. But what would we do with twelve bedrooms when there's only the two of us? Maybe we'd be better off looking for somewhere smaller but in a fabulous location with amazing views. I don't know, and Callum's not been much help. He's more interested in playing video games than helping me look seriously. It's as if all this money has turned him into a thirteen-year-old boy again.

As my mind wanders, a rustle in the bushes behind me makes me jump. A bird darts out of the foliage with a cry of alarm, and I clamp my hand to my chest.

It's nothing.

My imagination running off on its own course again.

I take a deep breath and let it out slowly, calming my frazzled nerves. I thought lottery jackpot winners were supposed to be happy and carefree. Right now, I'm neither.

Then, as I turn back to carry on my way with the dogs disappearing ahead, a figure springs out of

148

nowhere in front of me, pointing a camera in my face. Taking photos of me.

I squeal, freezing on the spot.

What the hell is this? Some kind of pervert?

'What are you doing?' I snap, waving a hand to shoo him away. But the camera keeps clicking.

The photographer, a scruffily dressed man in loose-fitting jeans and a leather jacket, lowers his camera and checks his work on a small screen.

'Jade Champion?'

The voice from behind makes me spin around. There's a second man. He's approaching slowly. He's better dressed than the photographer, but his suit, worn with a tartan scarf wrapped around his neck, makes him look overdressed for the park.

'Giles Middleton, from the *Post*,' he says with a cheesy smile. 'Could I grab a quick word?'

I look around in a panic. Where's Callum?

'Wh - what's this about?' I stammer.

'Well, firstly, congratulations.' He holds up a note-book in front of his chest, a pen poised to write. 'You must be delighted?'

'What? Yes, thank you.'

'So, it's true? You *did* win the jackpot? The whole fifty-one million pounds?'

Oh shit.

'How did you find out about that?' I have the urge to run, but my legs are heavy and refuse to move. I'm trapped, stuck between a journalist and a photographer, ambushed like a defenceless gazelle surrounded by hungry lions.

'Social media,' he says with a knowing grin. 'There's been lots of speculation about there being a local winner. And then we had a tip-off in the newsroom that it was you and your husband. Callum, isn't it?'

'I'm sorry, I have nothing to say.' I bury my hands in my pockets and hunch my shoulders, marching onwards. The dogs have already vanished out of sight.

Grudgingly, the photographer steps out of my way.

'Mrs Champion, wait! Just a quick quote for our readers,' the reporter hollers after me.

'Go away,' I scream, walking faster, my heart pounding.

Where *is* Callum? Is he actually roasting the coffee beans himself?

I shouldn't have said anything. Or denied it. Told him he had the wrong person, but I didn't. I confirmed his story and now it's going to be all over the papers, with my picture.

Fuck. Fuck. Fuck.

How could I have been so stupid?

But they can't print my picture without my permission, can they? That's an invasion of my privacy.

My phone rings. It's Callum.

'Where are you?' he asks. 'Do you want to walk back this way and I'll meet you at the cafe?'

'There was a journalist,' I wail, tears bubbling up in my eyes. 'And a photographer.'

'What journalist? What photographer?'

'They know about us, Callum. About the lottery.'

Callum's breathing heavily above the sound of children playing in the background. 'Are you sure?'

'They just fucking asked me about it, so yes, I'm pretty fucking sure!'

'Alright, no need to raise your voice.'

'They took my picture and now everyone's going to know,' I say.

Everyone. Including Bianca and her violent husband, Tomas.

And if Bianca sees the story, she's going to recognise my face and remember me from the funeral. She'll know I lied to her. She'll know I'm not called Sarah and I don't own a coffee shop in London. And then she's going to ask herself what the hell I was doing at her father's funeral.

Fuck. Fuck. *Fuck.*

'Calm down,' Callum soothes. 'We'll sort this out. Don't worry.'

That's easy for him to say. It's not his face that's going to be all over the news.

'They can't print it, can they?'

'I don't know. I don't think so. Not without your permission. Did you say anything to them?' Callum asks.

'Of course not,' I cry.

Well, I didn't give them an interview, if that's what he means.

'Let me call Marco at the lottery. He'll know what to do. He can probably get the story stopped.'

Yes, of course, Marco. He was brilliant at the beginning when we'd just found out we'd won. He'll know what to do. I'm sure he'll be able to talk to the paper and tell them they can't publish the story.

At least I hope he can.

Otherwise, we're going to have to accelerate that house move and disappear sharpish.

Chapter 18

Every day it feels as if my world is spinning faster and faster out of control. First it was Gabriel's begging letter, then Lee Greenwood's death, Bianca's threats and now this. We've tried so hard to keep a lid on our win and now it's about to blow up out of all proportion.

I'm slumped low in Callum's old BMW with my head down, warming my hands on my coffee cup. At least Callum didn't insist on bringing the Ferrari. It wouldn't have been practical with the dogs, anyway.

Is that how the news has spread? Has someone spotted Callum out and about in it and joined the dots? How else would someone on a mechanic's wages be able to afford a car like that? Maybe one of the neighbours has seen him. The problem is, it's such an ostentatious car, it attracts attention. It's no wonder rumours have been flying around.

The only other people who know about our win are Callum's parents, his sister, and her husband. But I trust all of them implicitly. There's also Gabriel, of course. But why would he go to the press? It doesn't make sense.

Not that it matters now. The secret's out. What really matters is getting a lid on it, and fast.

Callum dials Marco's number, puts his phone on speaker, and holds it between us as it rings.

'Marco? It's Callum Champion. We need your help.'

'Callum, great to hear from you. Sure, I've got five. What's up?'

'A journalist from the *Post* has been sniffing around. He and a photographer pounced on Jade while we were out and took some pictures,' Callum explains.

'Right, that is unfortunate. I'm sorry, but that's always the danger. It's hard to keep the cat in the bag when there's so much money involved.'

'Can't you do something? Talk to them and tell them they can't run the story?'

Marco sniffs and his chair creaks. I imagine him sitting in a palatial office with grand views over London, his feet up on his desk. 'Where did they photograph you?'

'In the park,' I say, leaning closer to the phone so he can hear. 'We were walking the dogs. Callum had gone to get coffee.'

'Hmmm,' he murmurs. 'It's a public place. There's not much I can do.'

'But you can at least speak to them?' Callum says. 'Explain to the editor that we don't want our names and faces published?'

'My mother doesn't even know yet,' I cry.

'I'm afraid it's not my place to tell newspaper editors what they can and can't print.' It sounds as if

Marco's trying to suppress laughter. 'It doesn't work like that.'

Callum shakes his head, frowning at me. 'But we were very clear when you came to the house that we didn't want any publicity.'

'I know, and we respected that, but if the press has found out because someone's tipped them off, then really there's nothing you or I can do. People love a good story about a big lottery win. It makes everyone believe it's possible. But, look, you want my advice? You need to take back control of the narrative and that means going public with your news before the newspaper has a chance to publish.'

I stare at Callum in astonishment. That's the last thing either of us wanted to hear.

'Go public?' Callum says. 'No, we can't.'

'I know this was something you were keen to avoid, but the alternative is much worse. As soon as one paper publishes, the rest will more than likely pile in, desperate to play catch-up. You'll have them on the doorstep offering to pay for exclusive access. Or digging in the bins for dirt. Harassing your family. Your friends. Is that what you really want?'

'No, of course not,' I say. When he puts it like that, it's obvious we're over a barrel. Damned if we do. Damned if we don't. We can't win.

'The way to prevent all that is to come clean now. Hold a press conference. We'll invite all the papers and broadcasters, get you to pose with a giant cheque, pop a champagne cork or two, answer a few banal questions, and it's done. Your problems go away,' Marco says cheerily.

If only he knew. The moment our names and my face appear in the news, it's only going to be the beginning of our problems.

I know exactly what he's proposing. I've seen it often enough. Happy couples and syndicates of work colleagues posing for the cameras and speculating on how they'll spend their winnings. I was just like everyone else. I loved watching those stories and dreaming what it would be like if it was me. How I'd spend my money. How it would change my life for the better.

How naïve. The truth is, I'd return all the money in a heartbeat if I could bring Lee Greenwood back to life.

Callum's staring at me, as if he's waiting for me to make the decision.

Why me? Why does this have to fall on my shoulders?

What does it matter anyway? Either way, the story's getting out. And then we're dead. It's just a matter of how long it takes for Bianca to find us.

'Are you sure there's nothing you can do to stop the *Post* from publishing the story?' I plead. 'It's not fair.'

'I would if I could, Jade,' Marco says, but it's his job to promote the lottery and in his interest for stories like ours to make it onto the news, to encourage more people to play in the hope that one day they could be in our shoes.

I wouldn't wish that on anyone.

'Just give me the word and I'll get straight onto it,' he continues. 'We'll set it up in a nice hotel near you, get some champagne on ice and issue a press notice.'

I groan. 'When would it be?'

'The sooner the better. Certainly within the next twenty-four to forty-eight hours if the papers already have a whiff of the story.'

I bury my head in my hands. That really doesn't give me much time at all. Before we announce it to the press, I need to deal with one of the problems that's been giving me a headache. I need to tell my mother. I've been putting it off, but I can't avoid it any longer.

'Fine,' I say. 'Do what you need to do.'

Chapter 19

The smell is rancid, like overflowing bins that have been left out in the sun all day, and it hits me the moment my mother opens the door. She looks far older than her fifty-seven years. Her skin is grey and blotchy with thread veins, and she's wearing her thinning hair pulled up into a rough, messy bun on the top of her head. Her eyes are sunken and glazed, her thin lips cracked and sore. She might be my mother, but she looks a wreck.

'Hello Mum.' I force a smile as she stands staring, hunched over, cigarette smouldering between her long, bony fingers. Her whole body tremors uncontrollably.

If she's pleased to see me, she doesn't show it. She doesn't hug me. Or even smile. All the things I imagine other mothers do when they're reunited with their daughters. She does at least invite me in, which is something, I suppose.

The smell inside is even stronger, even more stomach-churning. The house an absolute state. There's rubbish everywhere. The carpets don't look like they've seen a vacuum cleaner in months and when I stick my head around the kitchen door, the sink is piled high with dirty dishes.

She's getting worse. At least she used to keep on top of the chores. Now it looks like she doesn't bother, and worse, she doesn't seem to care.

I came early, but clearly not early enough. As I follow her into the lounge, there's a can of strong lager open on a low table in front of the sofa, next to an overflowing ashtray. The TV is on in the corner blasting out some mindless daytime drivel. She struggles to sit, using her arm to lower herself slowly back into her crumb-peppered seat.

'How are you getting on, Mum?' I ask, clearing a space on a threadbare armchair to sit down.

It breaks my heart to see her living like this, but nobody can help her until she accepts she has a problem. I've tried in the past and it's been a waste of time. Rightly or wrongly, I've given up. I don't have the emotional bandwidth for it.

'Yeah, alright, love,' she croaks, her voice hoarse. 'Can't complain.'

She brings her cigarette up to her mouth but her trembling hand struggles to find her lips.

'Are you eating properly?'

'Don't fuss. I'm fine.'

She's always had a difficult relationship with alcohol, but it came to a head when we lost my father. One minute he was here. The next he was gone. We all thought he was fit and healthy. Certainly, he didn't have medical problems I was aware of. He was carrying a little extra weight, but so do a lot of people. I never imagined his heart would just

AJ WILLS

stop working like that. That he'd drop down dead with no warning. It was such a shock to us all. But I suppose everyone expects their parents to live forever, don't they?

It hit my mother particularly hard. She coped the only way she knew how, finding solace at the bottom of a bottle.

You'd never think it, looking around the house, but she's not short of money. Dad's pension provides her with a reasonable income and these days she's on disability benefits because of her mobility issues. Not that it stops her pleading poverty. I've felt sorry for her and given her money in the past, hoping she'd use it to put food on the table, but she just spent it on Benson & Hedges and cheap vodka.

'How's Callum?' she asks, the faintest glimmer appearing in her eyes.

'Yeah, he's good,' I say, nodding.

'Still working hard in that garage?'

'Actually, he's thinking about leaving,' I say.

She looks surprised, the heavy lines on her forehead and around her dark eyes deepening. 'I thought he enjoyed it there?'

'Yeah, he did, but it's time for a change.' I glance down at my hands. 'I'm thinking of jacking in my job at the restaurant too.'

She hesitates in the process of stubbing out her cigarette, glancing at me suspiciously. 'Why? It pays good money, doesn't it?'

'Yeah, but I have to work most evenings, which means Callum and I don't get to spend much time together.'

160

'What are you going to do? I thought you were saving up to buy a house.'

I chew my lip. I can't put off telling her any longer. It's going to be everywhere in the next few days.

'Actually, Callum and I have some news.'

'You're having a baby?' she wheezes, her face lighting up.

'Oh, no, not that kind of news.' My cheeks flush hot. There's nothing more my mother would love than for me to fall pregnant and give her the grand-child she's always craved. 'It's the reason we're giving up our jobs.'

Her face falls with a mixture of disappointment and worry. 'You're not moving away, are you?'

'No, although we're finally going to be able to buy a place of our own. Mum... we've won some money on the lottery.'

'The lottery?' She's caught by a wracking cough that doubles her over and leaves her struggling for breath.

'Mum? Are you okay?'

She sits up straight, her dull eyes wet, and thumps her chest. 'I'm alright,' she says.

'It's quite a lot of money. Enough for us both to be able to quit our jobs and buy a house without having to worry about working.'

She stares at me, as if she's not sure whether I'm winding her up. 'How much?'

'A few million.' I glance at the TV, unable to look her in the eye. It's my own mother, but I'm still embarrassed by the size of our winnings and can't bring myself to tell her the true amount.

'What? Are you joking with me?'

I shake my head. 'No, Mum. It'll be all over the news in the next few days. We wanted to keep it quiet but one of the papers found out, so now we're going to have to go public.'

A smile creeps across her lips and the glaze across her eyes fades. Now she's interested.

'Darling, that's wonderful news,' she gushes, coughing again.

'Thank you.'

She picks up the can of lager and takes a swig. How she can drink beer at this time in the morning is beyond me, but I've learned the hard way not to say anything. She'll only fly into a fury and tell me to mind my own business.

'Obviously, we'd like to use the money to help you out.' I lick my lips, carefully picking my words. I don't want her to think she's getting a handout of cash to drink herself into oblivion. 'We're going to help Callum's parents with a new house. We said we'd do the same for his sister and her husband.'

'A new house? Wow,' she says.

'We wanted to share our good fortune,' I explain. 'We'd like to do the same for you, if that's okay? We could do this place up, put it on the market and move you into somewhere a bit nicer. How would you like that?' It's more than she deserves, and I doubt she'd look after it, but I feel I have to make the offer.

She shakes her head. 'No, I'm happy where I am,' she says. 'I don't need a new house.'

'It's no more than we promised Callum's parents.' I'm not giving her money, but it's not fair that she misses out. She's family too. She's my mother.

'What would I do with a new house? All my memories are here. It's the house I bought with your father. It's the house you grew up in,' she says.

Looking at it now, it's hard to believe it's where I used to call home. She's let it get into such a state, it's almost unrecognisable. My father will be turning in his grave. He was always so particular about it being kept clean, nagging my mother if he came home and found any mess.

'I don't want to argue about it, Mum. And it wouldn't feel right if we didn't give you something to help you out.'

'Well, I am a little short this month,' she says, finishing her can. 'I could do with a bit extra, you know, just to get me through.'

Oh god. This is what I was afraid of.

'No, Mum, not cash.' I take a deep breath. 'We'll help get you set up in a nice new house. Or maybe we can get you some things for here. A new bed? Some new curtains? We could get the back garden landscaped for you. How about that?'

She screws up her eyes and purses her lips in frustration. 'What do I want with any of that?' she snaps. 'I don't need a new bed and the garden's fine. What I need is a little extra money. Not too much to ask, is it?'

'For what?' I snort, letting my rising irritation get the better of me. 'Another couple of bottles of Smirnoff? More fags?'

'Why do you always have to be like this?'

'Like what?'

'Difficult.'

'Me?' I jab a finger into my own chest. 'I'm not the difficult one.'

'Always so selfish. You were always the same. You never change.'

I know it's the alcohol talking and I should rise above it, but she knows the buttons to press and I can't help myself.

'Me, selfish?' I snort. 'You're a fine one to talk.'

'And what's that supposed to mean?'

'Oh, Mum, come on. Look at yourself. Look at this place.'

'Don't you talk to me like that.' She reaches around the side of the sofa, produces another beer and cracks it open angrily.

I breathe in deeply through my nose and close my eyes, trying to centre myself. 'I didn't come here to argue with you.'

'No, you came here to gloat.'

'That's not true —'

'You couldn't wait to tell me, could you? I haven't seen you in weeks and now here you are, bragging about all your money. And yet you can't even bring yourself to put your hand in your pocket to help out your own mother with a few measly quid.'

'That's not fair. I just offered to buy you a new house.'

'I told you, I don't want a new house,' she yells.

'Alright, I get it. You don't want to move. Fine. If you're short this month, I'll take you out shopping.

We can fill the cupboards with as much food as you want.'

'I don't want to go shopping with you. I'm quite capable of shopping on my own, thank you.'

'So what then, Mum? Why do you need cash?'

'I told you, I'm a bit short this month, that's all. And the gas bill is due.'

'Fine. Give me the bill. I'll pay it.'

'No, no, no.' She's getting really agitated now, balling her hands into fists and rocking backwards and forwards, her face crumpled in distress.

I hate seeing her this upset. It would be the easiest thing in the world to give her what she wants. I could transfer ten thousand pounds into her account right now and tell her to do with it what she wants. But I might as well sign her death warrant. I can't have that on my conscience.

'Mum, you need help,' I say gently. 'I can't stand seeing you like this.'

'Then help me,' she pleads.

'I want to help you.' Tears prick my eyes. 'But you know I can't give you money.'

'Selfish slut,' she hisses.

I close my eyes, trying to block it out, telling myself she doesn't mean it. But her words sting like a slap across the face.

'Let me pay for some therapy,' I suggest. 'I'll look into some addiction clinics. Some private ones. It'll be like staying at a fancy hotel, but they'll be able to help you there.'

'I don't need anybody's help.'

'I think you do and deep down, you know it too,' I say, although I know she'll never listen to me.

'Get out,' she yells. 'Get out. Get out. Get out.'

'Mum —'

'Didn't you hear me?'

There's no point talking to her when she's like this. Stupid me for thinking this time it would be any different, that money could change things.

'Please, let me help you, Mum.'

'Go.'

I stand up and wipe the tears rolling down my cheeks. 'Fine, I'm going. But think about what I said.'

She tips the rest of the can of beer down her throat, belches and fixes her attention on the TV, as if I'm no longer in the room.

'Mum?'

'Fuck off.'

'Right,' I cry, 'well you know how to get hold of me if you change your mind.'

Chapter 20

Flashing bright lights blind us as we emerge, blinking uncertainly from inside the hotel. It feels like a hundred pairs of eyes are all staring at us as we approach a large huddle of photographers, TV cameramen and journalists who've assembled in the courtyard garden, watching us as if we're a circus act expected to perform tricks. I've never been one of those people who enjoys being the centre of attention, even among friends, and this whole charade makes my insides squirm.

Marco, smiling like *he's* won the lottery, guides us towards a fountain where a table's been set out with a pair of champagne bottles in an ice bucket next to two glasses.

He makes us stand awkwardly, facing the media horde, as they continue to take photos and shoot footage. I grasp Callum's hand for reassurance. I couldn't have done this on my own. No way.

Marco introduces us, telling the reporters that Callum works in a garage as a mechanic and that I'm a waitress. Or at least, we were.

I force myself to smile, hoping it doesn't look like a grimace, and look at all the cameras, remembering what Marco told us a few minutes ago when we'd gathered in a private room to prepare.

'Just be yourselves. All they want is to hear your story and how it's changed your lives. And don't forget to smile.' He exaggerated a cheesy grin, drawing an upward arc over his mouth with his fingers.

So many strange faces. So many pairs of eyes staring. I wish I could dive into the fountain and swim away. There's not an atom in my body that's enjoying this, but as Marco keeps telling us, the alternative, having journalists camped on our doorstep, going through our bins, poking long-lens cameras through our windows, would have been much, much worse.

A glamorous blonde woman in a sparkly dress and with fulsome false eyelashes and a smile as wide as Marco's appears from nowhere carrying a cheque the size of a large suitcase. Callum takes one end. I take the other, as instructed by Marco. The camera clicks become a continuous buzz as Marco pops open one of the champagne bottles, pours, and hands us each a glass. I'm tempted to down mine in one to calm my nerves, but how would that look? I could just imagine the headlines. Instead, I hold up my glass and contort my face into what I hope is a grin of delight.

Eventually, Marco takes the cheque from us and invites us to sit. I pull my chair up close to Callum's and hold on to his arm tightly, fearing I'll drown if I let go. Marco sits to the side, his chair angled towards us, as if we're a celebrity couple appearing on his TV chat show.

And then he starts asking questions.

'Tell us where you were when you found out you'd won,' he says, still grinning. His jaw must be aching. That smile hasn't slipped once.

Callum glances at me as if to check whether I'm happy for him to answer. I lower my head, fix my gaze on my shoes, and give his arm a squeeze.

'I'd been out playing football and forgot to check our ticket,' he chuckles. 'Jade reminded me after I'd picked her up from work. I couldn't believe it when I saw the numbers matched. I thought it must be a mistake. I ran screaming into the kitchen to find her, waving the ticket above my head like an idiot.'

My head jolts up. What? That's not what happened.

'And presumably this kind of money is going to change your lives beyond recognition?' Marco asks.

Callum nods enthusiastically. Takes a sip of champagne. 'Well, we won't need to work again,' he laughs nervously.

A titter of polite laughter comes from the press pack. Marco said they'd all be pleased for us and they weren't here to catch us out. Even so, I can't relax.

I took ages choosing what to wear in the hope that if I felt good about myself, it would make it easier to face the cameras. Eventually, I decided on an asymmetric Victoria Beckham midi dress. Smart but understated. I figured we needed to look well turned-out for the cameras without appearing to be flaunting our new wealth. That would have been crass.

I've also applied far more make-up than I'd usually wear. A shield to hide behind, but also a mask to cover up the dark circles around my eyes, my pasty skin, and the spots that have erupted on my face at the worst possible time.

'Jade, many people can only imagine how it feels to win more than fifty million pounds. Tell us, what has it been like for you?'

Me? What's he asking me for?

'Ummmm...' I mumble. 'Yeah, it's amazing. Really good.' Even I can hear how flat my voice sounds, completely devoid of emotion.

But what's there to be happy about? Within hours, our names and faces are going to be splashed across the news and there's every chance Bianca is going to recognise me. And she'll know I lied to her.

Marco quickly moves his attention back to Callum, who's had his hair cut in a fashionable tousled French crop and has gone too heavy on his aftershave. It's overpowering. Even outside, it fills my nostrils and claws at the back of my throat.

'What does your family think about your good fortune?'

'Obviously, they're delighted for us.' Callum casts a sideways glance at me. 'And it's nice we can finally give something back to my mum and dad, my sister and her husband.'

'That's grand. So they're winners too, in a way?'

'We're buying them each a new house, so yeah, I guess they are.'

He doesn't mention my mother, of course. I specifically asked him not to. I didn't want him telling the world that she's a washed-up alcoholic who turned down our offer of a new house because she'd rather have the cash to piss away.

'And the million-dollar question, which funnily enough is a question you can afford now,' Marco says, almost falling off his chair with delight at his own joke, 'is what are you going to spend the money on? I mean, it's nice to treat your family, but what about you two?'

'We're in rented accommodation at the moment, so obviously we're looking to buy somewhere,' Callum says. 'Maybe somewhere with a pool and a home cinema. A man-cave, perhaps.'

'Ahh, I heard you liked your tech, Callum. So, a man-cave, is it?'

'You know, somewhere to hang out with the lads. A few games consoles. A bar. A pool table. Beanbags. That sort of thing.' Callum beams with delight. I can't believe he's actually enjoying this.

'What about you, Jade? What's on your shopping list?'

'I don't know, really,' I mutter. 'A new house, of course. Somewhere private.'

'Anything else?' Marco prompts.

My mind's a blank. 'Ummm, not really.'

'Callum, you must have spent some of your winnings already? A petrolhead like yourself, I bet you've at least had your eye on a nice motor?'

Callum looks down at his hands in his lap. 'I might have hired a bright red Ferrari,' he smirks. 'And bought myself a brand new Aston.'

My insides twist. Does he realise how smug he sounds?

'Good man. Well, you can certainly afford it.'

'And Jade, all that money has to be burning a hole in your pocket. You must have spent some of it by now?'

A solitary camera flash fires, a burning, phosphorous bright light that momentarily blinds me. In that flash, I see Lee Greenwood's face. It's the smiling, happy image of him from the order of service at his funeral. I can even hear the sobs and the grief, and feel Bianca's sorrow. A family ripped apart. A husband, father and grandfather murdered in cold blood on our orders. Paid for *our* money.

My stomach tightens and churns. Acidic bile rises up my throat and I have a compulsion to confess how we handed over fifty thousand pounds of our winnings, stuffed in a rucksack, to a man in a pub we'd never met before with the instructions to kill a man and make it look like an accident.

The blood rushes in my ears and I have the strange sense of drifting out of my body, floating up into the trees and watching from above. It's peaceful up there, but I know it won't last. I can't escape from reality forever.

As soon as the news is out, Bianca is going to know. Or at least, it's going to make her suspicious. I was wearing a hat and sunglasses at the funeral, but surely she'll recognise my face. My voice. How could she not? And then what? If she thinks I have anything to do with her father's death, there's no knowing what she'll do.

172

'Jade?'

Marco's voice brings me hurtling back into my body with a jarring thud.

I blink and glance around at the surreal scene. Me and Callum sitting with a big cheque, glasses of champagne and the attention of the media focused on us.

I can't do this. It's all wrong.

My mouth is like sandpaper. My head humming. My arms and legs heavy.

'I'm sorry,' I say. 'I'm not feeling well.'

I jump out of my seat and scurry across the grass towards the safety of the hotel, bowling through a set of double doors, into a lobby and back to the room where we've left our coats and bags.

The door slams shut and I collapse into a tub chair, trying to catch my breath. I'm breathing too fast. Too heavily. My head's wheeling. My heart's racing. Everything in my vision is too bright.

Someone comes into the room.

Kneels by my chair.

'Jade? Are you okay?' It's one of the women assisting Marco with running the press conference.

'I think I'm having a heart attack,' I pant, pressing my hand to my breastbone while I gasp for air, remembering how my father died. Is this how it was for him in his last few minutes?

'Deep breaths,' she says. 'In slowly and out slowly. You're having a panic attack, that's all.'

A panic attack?

'It's a big deal having to face all the cameras, but you did really well.'

173

She has absolutely no idea.

'Is Callum coming?' I wheeze.

'A few of the broadcasters want to do interviews with him first,' the woman says. She has a kind voice and a warm manner. She must be used to dealing with women like me who find it all too much. 'Now, breathe in, one, two. And out, one, two.'

My breath gradually comes back under control. My heart stops trying to fight its way out of my chest and my panic subsides.

The woman brings me a glass of water which I sip.

What would she think if she knew the truth? That we'd used our winnings to have a man killed? I doubt she'd be here rubbing my back and telling me everything was going to be okay.

But we can never tell anyone.

It has to be a secret we take with us to the grave.

And that means a lifetime living with the guilt and the shame.

A lifetime that could be short-lived if Bianca decides to come after us.

Chapter 21

The lottery team invited us to stay the night at their expense at the hotel, their way of thanking us for agreeing to do the press conference, Marco said. But I was embarrassed I'd made a fool of myself in front of the cameras and just wanted to get home. Anyway, we couldn't leave the dogs on their own overnight. So instead, I'm sitting with Callum on the sofa at home, Jefferson and Delilah at our feet, flicking through pages and pages of coverage on his iPad together. The story is everywhere, all over the internet and running on almost every radio station and news channel. I guess it's what they call wall-to-wall coverage. To a casual observer, I suppose it looks like a good news story.

Some of the articles have made a big deal out of me fleeing from the press conference, speculating that the occasion was too much for me to handle. Others have politely overlooked my sudden departure and focused on Callum's assertion he's going to buy a fleet of fast cars with his winnings. Yeah, right. Over my dead body.

'I didn't think there would be this much coverage,' I say.

'Must be a slow news day,' Callum murmurs.

'And when Bianca sees the story? What then?' I rub my hands across my face.

'She's not going to do anything,' he says.

'But what if she does? I know you think I'm being a coward, but please, let's just get away for a few weeks.'

'We're not going into hiding like a pair of fugitives,' he says. 'You're over-reacting. Even if she suspects we had something to do with her father's death, what do you think she's going to do?'

'I don't know. Maybe kill us?' I snap, recalling with a chill the conversation we had at the funeral.

'It's just words. It's what people say when they're upset.'

'Alright, well what if she goes to the police?'

'They can't prove anything,' Callum asserts, but I'm not so sure. There must be phone records showing we were in contact with Gabriel around the time of the hit, for a start. 'Are you hungry?'

'Sure,' I say, although I don't have much of an appetite. My stomach's a shredded ball of nerves, knotted and tight with anxiety.

While Callum flicks through his phone, deciding what takeaway to order, I absentmindedly start browsing through my social media. Lots of news organisations have shared our story, and they've garnered hundreds of likes and comments. I know how spiteful people can be online, but I can't stop myself checking out what people are saying.

It starts with some lovely congratulatory messages. Clapping hands and party popper emojis.

People who seem to be genuinely thrilled for us. Strangers saying how amazing it is and how happy they are for us. Plenty of other comments from people discussing how they'd spend the money if they won fifty-one million pounds.

And then there are the others. The nasty, bitter comments from the keyboard trolls who resent our luck.

FraggleRock1994 Dont no why they gloating - they should give the money to charity

MissTCup Cant believe they stupid enough to go public. If that was me I wouldn't tell noone

Johnno She's fit. Dunno what she's doing wiv him tho. Bet shes gonna leave him

Madmickey What does anyone need £51m for? you will end up lonly and divorced

JS15639 People like them dont deserve to win

PaulaS Don't know how they can sleep at night. People who win the lottery and don't use the money to help worthwhile causes are an utter disgrace.

The remarks become progressively worse. More vitriolic. More personal. Lots of people think we're mad to have gone public. As if we had a choice.

My low mood grows gloomier. Anyone who thinks winning the lottery makes you happy has no idea. I've never felt more anxious, more depressed, more uncertain of the future than I do right now.

I switch back to scouring the news in the vain hope the agenda may have miraculously moved on in the last five minutes. No such luck. My attention's caught by an awful picture of Callum and me on one of the sites. My eyes are half closed, making it look as if I'm drunk. I'm sure they've done it deliberately.

Why do some people have to be so spiteful?

My eye drifts down the page and is drawn to a teaser headline for another story. Something far more gruesome and interesting.

Missing man plunged 21-floors to his death

I shudder at the thought. I've never had a head for heights and the thought of falling from a 21-storey tower block leaves me feeling queasy. But, of course, I have to know more now. It's perfect click-bait. I click on the headline and the story opens up.

It's dominated by the image of a high-rise block of flats but inset into the picture is another photo. A photo of a familiar-looking man.

I sit bolt upright, not sure if my eyes are playing tricks on me.

With a growing unease, I skim-read the story.

Missing man's death from tower block 'not suspicious'

Police say they're not treating the death of a man who'd been reported missing as suspicious after he apparently fell from a 21-storey block of flats in Waltham Forest in London.

The body of the 39-year-old was discovered by a street cleaning team in the early hours of Wednesday morning.

Although the man has not yet been formally identified, it's believed to be missing Gabriel Salt.

Mr Salt had been due to stand trial on charges of attacking the van driver who killed his pregnant wife in a traffic collision.

Tilly Salt had been cycling to work when she was struck by a van driven by Lee Greenwood. Her body was dragged several metres along the road before Greenwood stopped.

Although Greenwood was prosecuted for careless driving, he was fined only £350 after claiming he'd not seen Mrs Salt because he'd been blinded by the sun as he turned across her path.

At the time, the sentence was described by Mrs Salt's widower as 'unduly lenient'. He's alleged to have confronted Greenwood at his home in Essex earlier this month.

Mr Salt went to Greenwood's house armed with a knife but Greenwood escaped without injury after a brief altercation.

The family of Mr Salt reported him missing three days ago after he vanished from his home in West London.

An inquest into Gabriel Salt's death is due to be held at a later date.

The words swim in front of my eyes, and an involuntary gasp slips from my lips.

Gabriel Salt is dead.

'Everything alright?' Callum glances at me and frowns.

'Have you seen this?' My voice quivers.

I pass my phone to Callum and watch as he reads, his eyes growing wide.

179

'Oh my god.'

'When did you last speak to him?'

Callum shakes his head as he runs a hand through his hair. 'I don't know. A few days ago. A week, maybe. It was after I had that confirmation text from Henry.'

'And how was he?'

'Over the moon.'

'Not sounding suicidal?'

'Far from it,' Callum says. 'He was jubilant. God, I can't believe it. That's awful.'

'They've made it sound like he jumped.' My whole body is shaking.

'You don't think he did?'

'Why would he?'

'So what then?' he asks, eyebrows raised.

'Bianca. I told you she was dangerous.'

'You think she lured him up there and pushed him?' Callum asks sceptically.

'Not on her own, no. She must have had help.'

'Fuck.' Callum buries his head in his hands. 'Which is why you should never have gone to the funeral. What were you thinking, Jade? This is really bad.'

'You think I don't know that?'

'We need to do something.'

At last.

'Let's get out of here while we can. We'll find somewhere to lie low until it all blows over,' I say, grateful Callum's finally come to his senses, because if Bianca is capable of killing Gabriel, she's not going to think twice about coming after us. And with all the coverage of our win, it's only a matter of time before she works out our involvement and where we live. For all we know, Gabriel may already have told her we bankrolled her father's murder.

'I have a better idea.' Callum digs in the pocket of his designer jeans and pulls out a small, black mobile phone. The burner phone Henry gave him.

'What are you still doing with that?' I splutter. 'Didn't you get rid of it?'

He shrugs. 'I thought it might come in useful, you know, in case we needed Henry's services again.'

'Are you insane?' I scream. Jefferson lifts his head, looking worried, and whines. 'We should never have had anything to do with Henry in the first place. That's why we're in this mess.'

'We're in this mess because you went to Greenwood's funeral and started chatting with his daughter, who just happens to be the wife of a dangerous criminal,' he fires back.

I guess he has a point, but I'm not the only one at fault.

'I wouldn't have gone to the funeral if you hadn't talked me into helping Gabriel,' I hiss.

'Which you readily agreed to do.'

'Only because you convinced me to. I always thought it was a stupid idea,' I say.

Callum sighs. Arguing about it isn't going to change anything.

'Look, all I'm saying is it would be easy to call Henry and pay for him to arrange a little accident for Bianca, if you're that worried about her,' he says. 'Then she'd be out of our lives for good.'

181

My jaw falls open. 'You have to be kidding? You think you can make this mess go away by having Bianca killed?'

He shrugs. 'Yeah, why not?'

'And how do you think her husband's going to react to that? We know he's a violent man and he's bound to have people working for him on the outside.'

'Henry'll make it look like an accident.' Callum sounds so sure of himself, I think he actually believes it's a good idea.

'Like he made Greenwood's death look like an accident?' I arch my eyebrows. 'That didn't exactly pan out too well, did it? And how long before the police start to get suspicious? First Greenwood and a matter of weeks later, his daughter. No, Callum. Having Bianca killed doesn't solve anything.' I can't even believe I'm saying the words.

'Alright,' he says, throwing his hands up in the air. 'It was just a suggestion. Keep your knickers on.'

'It was a stupid suggestion. Get rid of that phone, and I don't want to hear any more about Henry or hits or killing people, do you understand?'

'Fine,' he huffs. 'What are we supposed to do then?'

'I know you don't want to, but we have to hide. It's the only way to guarantee we can stay safe. We have enough money to disappear for a while,' I suggest again, hoping Callum is finally coming around to my way of thinking. It's the only way.

'And how's that going to work? In case you haven't noticed, our faces are all over the internet.'

182

'Let's get out of the country,' I say, an idea form-ing in my mind as I speak. 'We could go trav-elling. It's the perfect opportunity to go to all those places we've talked about visiting in the past. Italy. Switzerland. Spain. We could go anywhere we liked. Or maybe Canada. Asia. Anywhere but here.'

Callum pushes his bottom lip out and nods. 'That's not a bad idea,' he says. 'But what about the dogs?'

'We'll have to leave them in kennels until we get back. It's not a big deal.'

'I'm not doing that. It's not fair on them.'

Jefferson lifts his head, and looks at us with sad eyes, as if he senses he's being talked about.

'Then what do you suggest?' I ask, 'because we can't risk staying here.'

'Alright, I agree, it's probably safer if we move out for the time being.' He throws up his hands in submission. 'But let's not rush into anything. Why don't you go and pack some things and I'll see if I can find a dog-friendly B&B somewhere in this country until we can work out something longer term.'

I don't wait to be asked twice. I vault off the sofa and charge for the stairs.

'I'll call Mum and Dad and let them know we won't be around for a few days. Are you going to speak to your mum?' Callum shouts after me.

I roll my eyes. My mother couldn't care less whether I'm at home or in Timbuktu these days. 'Yeah, I'll call her later when we're on the road.'

I've never packed so quickly in all my life. I just want to get out of this house and to somewhere Bianca can't find us.

Maybe I am worrying unnecessarily. Maybe Gabriel wasn't pushed and decided to take his own life after finally achieving justice for Tilly. Maybe Bianca's not looking for us, but it's best to be safe than sorry. Getting away for a few days will probably do us good, especially after all the stress of the last few weeks.

I manage to fit everything I need into one large suitcase. If I've forgotten anything, we can always buy new. I guess that's the joy of having a bulging bank balance. It takes the worry away.

'I've found a nice place in the New Forest which has rooms free,' Callum says, standing at the bottom of the stairs as I struggle down with my case. 'They're expecting us in a few hours.'

My heart soars. I've always wanted to go to the New Forest.

Fifteen minutes later, we're finally ready to leave. The car is packed and the last job is to shepherd the dogs out of the house. They climb onto the back seat of the old BMW where Callum's laid out a rug for them and they soon settle down.

I lock the front door and take a moment for myself in the front garden. It's possible we may never be back if we decide to go travelling or finally manage to buy a place of our own. We've been renting the house for the best part of three years and have created so many happy memories in our time here.

184

But it's only bricks and mortar, and I'll always have the memories.

'Come on, let's go,' Callum yells at me, jumping into the car.

I take one last look at the house and slip the keys into my pocket.

It feels like the end of an era.

Callum fires up the engine. Headlights blink on.

He starts to reverse out of the drive, but slams on his brakes as another vehicle tears down the road, appearing out of nowhere and travelling far too fast, its lights blazing in the gathering gloom of the early evening.

Tyres squeal. Engines roar. Another two cars screech to a halt at the foot of the drive, inches from Callum's bumper, blocking him in.

What the hell?

The cars are all the same make and model. Black Range Rovers with darkened privacy glass. Doors fly open. Heavily built men in dark clothing jump out.

I'm so shocked, I don't move, my mind trying desperately to process what's going on.

One of the men marches purposefully up the garden path towards me. He has unkempt shaggy dark hair and a vaguely familiar face. I've seen him before, although I'm not sure where.

'Come,' he orders.

'What?' I've no idea what's happening.

'You need to come with me. Now!' he shouts.

Another man approaches Callum's car. He pulls open the driver's door and physically drags Callum out by his arm.

'Stop! What are you doing?' I scream, my panic building.

The man looming over me snatches my elbow. I try to fight him off, but he's too strong, his grip too powerful. He pulls me down the path towards the waiting cars.

'Get in,' he orders, shoving me roughly into the back of one of them.

I'm too scared to argue. Whatever's going on, it's futile to resist. And it's so unexpected, so far beyond the realm of my normal, boring life before we won all this money, that it's totally disorientating. I don't know what to do. How to act. What to think.

As I'm bundled into the back seat, I catch a glimpse of two men wrestling Callum into one of the other cars.

This is Bianca's doing. It has to be. I remember now why I recognise the man who grabbed me. He was at Greenwood's funeral. Just a face in the crowd at the time, but obviously one of her henchmen.

'Don't forget the dogs,' a heavily accented voice commands. 'Make sure you bring them.'

As I scramble to sit up on the slippery leather seat, turning my head towards our car, I see two men manhandling Jefferson and Delilah into the back of the third vehicle.

'Don't hurt —' I begin to yell, but my words are cut short as someone yanks a hood over my head and my whole world goes dark.

Chapter 22

The car rocks on its suspension as men clamber in, filling the space all around me. I can feel them. Sense them. Crowding me. Doors slam shut. The engine growls and we're pulling away. Accelerating sharply. I'm pressed against the bodies of two strangers. Their firm, muscular thighs pressing against mine. Shoulders bumping. They don't speak, but I can hear them breathe and there's no mistaking the sour notes of body odour, alcohol and garlic seeping out of their pores.

I whimper, too afraid to speak. Blinded and disorientated.

At first, the driving is erratic. We slow down and speed up through tight corners and junctions, stopping and starting, but I soon lose any sense of where we are, my perception of space and time lost along with my sight.

Eventually, our speed picks up and remains more constant. We're cruising along steadily now, which I guess means we're on the motorway. But I have no idea where they're taking me.

It's not cold in the car, but I begin to shiver as fear takes a grip of me. I try to swallow but my throat's so dry. I bite my lip, pinning it between my teeth and focusing on the needle of pain. Anything to take my mind off what's happening and what's coming.

I wish Callum was with me. Being separated from him is a cruel torture. At least if he was with me, it would be some comfort. But I don't even know where he is. In a car behind? In front? Are they even taking us to the same place?

When the car finally slows and makes a sharp turn, pitching my body against the man next to me, I've no idea whether we've been travelling for ten minutes or sixty. Time is a blur.

Smooth tarmac becomes bumpy ground. My body bounces violently up and down in the seat as we trundle along at a snail's pace. It's darker here. There's less light permeating through the thin material of the hood over my head. I guess we're somewhere remote, then. A forest, maybe?

When the car finally slows to a stop, it doesn't come a moment too soon.

A spike of adrenaline sends my heart rate racing. What now?

Is this where I'm destined to die, alone and afraid with a bullet in the back of my head or my throat slit open?

A blast of cold air fills the car as the doors are thrown open and the men spill out.

This is it.

Should I try to make a run for it? If I can catch them by surprise, maybe in the confusion I can get away. Hide in the undergrowth. If they're going to kill me anyway, I have nothing to lose. I have to do something.

'Get out,' a husky voice orders.

I shuffle to the edge of the seat and swing my legs out of the car. They hang in mid-air and when I step out, I completely misjudge the distance to the ground and stumble.

Someone grabs my shoulder, yanks me unceremoniously onto my feet and whips off the hood.

It takes a moment for my eyes to adjust. I stand blinking, waiting for everything to come into focus. We're not in a forest at all. The only trees I can vaguely make out are in the distance, their branches silhouetted by the silver light of a crescent moon. We're on a patch of rough scrubland, apparently in the middle of nowhere. I don't recognise it at all. In the distance, I catch the twinkle of lights against the night sky, but it's impossible to tell whether they're coming from housing, office blocks or industry. Not that it matters. The point is there's nothing and no one around for miles. We're far from any prying eyes and there's no one to hear if I screamed for help, and nowhere I can run to escape.

Another car pulls up, crunching over the uneven earth and through the vegetation, its headlights casting long shadows from our feet across tangled mounds of grass and thistles.

Doors open. Another cohort of scary-looking men fall out. One of them reaches into the back and drags Callum out. He collapses to the ground, shouting and swearing, for which he's rewarded with a swift kick in the ribs. I wince, but keep my mouth shut. They stand him up, face him forwards and remove the hood from his head.

He looks up, dazed. Blinks. Runs a hand through his hair. Then he spots me standing a few metres away and smiles weakly.

Nobody stops me running to him. I throw my arms around his neck and hug him tightly as he kisses the top of my head.

'Are you okay?' he asks. 'Did they hurt you?'

'No, I'm fine.'

He glares at the men surrounding us, as if he'd kill them given half a chance.

He grabs my hand and holds it tight. 'Stay close to me. Everything's going to be alright.'

'What's going on?' I hiss.

'I don't know.'

'I'm scared.'

'Me too,' he says.

'It's Bianca, isn't it? I thought I recognised one of the men from the funeral. Do you think they've brought us here to... to kill us?'

'Look, I don't know, but don't say anything and do exactly what they ask, okay? We're going to get out of this. I promise.'

I wish I had half his confidence. I glance at the men crowding around us. There isn't a friendly face among them. All broken noses, chipped teeth and five o'clock shadows. The kind of men you'd cross the street to avoid at night. The sort you'd expect to find hanging out in some backstreet bar knocking back cheap vodka over ill-tempered games of poker. Tough men. Brutal men, with calloused knuckles from who knows what kind of barbarity.

'I want to go home,' I whimper.

'I know. But stay strong. It's going to be okay. Did you see where they took the dogs?'

'I think they're in that car,' I say, nodding at a third Range Rover parked a short distance away that I'd noticed when they first removed my hood.

'If they hurt them, I'll kill them.'

I appreciate the sentiment, but Jefferson and Delilah's safety is the least of our worries. I'm more concerned about how we're going to get out of this alive.

I'm about to whisper to Callum asking if he thinks we ought to make a run for it, when the rumble of an engine diverts our attention. Headlights cut a swathe across the scrubby ground. And another car shows up. A smart saloon. Dark coloured. A Jaguar, possibly.

The headlights dim as the engine dies.

A hush descends, all eyes fixed on the new arrival.

At first nothing happens, like whoever has just turned up is deliberately making us all wait. Building the tension.

Finally, a rear door cracks open. A pair of slim, long legs slips out. A woman straightens her skirt and flattens her hair with one hand.

Bianca.

I knew it.

She stumbles inelegantly across the uneven ground in an unsuitable pair of high heels, making a beeline for us. Her hair is pinned off her brow, and she's wearing thick, black eyeshadow which gives her face a hollowed-out, sinister look.

She comes right up to me. 'Sarah,' she says with a cheery smile as if she's greeting an old friend. 'Or should I say, Jade?' Her smile fades and her face hardens into an unpleasant scowl.

'Bianca.' My voice is no more than a whisper, my skin goose-pimpling with fear.

'And this must be Callum,' she says. She looks him up and down, a sneer set on her face. 'You looked younger on the TV.'

'That was my twin brother,' he says. I don't know whether he's trying to be clever or making a joke, but she just stares at him with disdain.

'Why did you come to my father's funeral?' she asks, turning back to me.

I swallow the hard lump in my throat. 'I wanted to pay my respects.' I lower my gaze, trying not to be confrontational. There's still a chance we can talk ourselves out of this hole.

'But you didn't know him. So why would you possibly want to be there?'

'I - I don't know,' I stammer.

'You'd never even heard of him until you met Gabriel Salt, did you?'

My head jolts up at the mention of Gabriel's name and an image flashes through my mind of him being manhandled off the top of a tower block, arms flailing as he fell, screams echoing through the night sky. It was probably one of these men surrounding us who threw him off.

'Who?' I croak.

'Oh, come on, Jade. Don't play clever with me.'

'I don't know who you're talking about.'

'He's dead now, of course. But I expect you knew that. Such a waste of a life. But after losing his wife and with nothing to look forward to apart from a stint in jail, it's not surprising he took the coward's way out.' She's standing so close, our noses are almost touching and I can smell her distinctive perfume. It's sickly sweet. Overpowering.

'You pushed him,' I snarl.

Her eyes open wide. 'So you do know him. How interesting.'

'You killed him because you thought he'd murdered your father,' I hiss. 'You're evil, Bianca.'

She holds a hand to her heart, as if my words have wounded her. 'How can you say such a thing?'

'So it's not true?' I challenge.

'Jade,' Callum warns. I know, I know. He wanted me to keep my mouth shut. But I'm not going to stand idly by and listen to Bianca's lies.

'Why would I want Gabriel dead?' she asks, her face a picture of innocence.

'Because you thought he was responsible for your father's death.'

'Wasn't he?' Her over-plucked, thin eyebrows shoot up.

I clamp my mouth tightly closed. I've said too much. Callum was right, I shouldn't be saying anything. Arguing with Bianca isn't going to help us.

'What I couldn't understand was how he'd done it. He'd made it look quite convincing, like Daddy had taken himself off somewhere quiet to get jacked up and miscalculated the dosage. Except my father would never touch drugs. Never in a million years. He despised them and what they did to people. The police couldn't see it, but it was obvious to me. The question was, *how* had he done it?'

Callum squeezes my hand. It's cold and clammy but I'm glad of the reassurance. It would be so much worse if I was here on my own.

'He couldn't have done it on his own,' Bianca continues. 'It was sophisticated. Whoever set it up knew the police were highly unlikely to treat a co-caine overdose as suspicious and that they'd rule out anyone else being involved pretty sharpish. Plus, someone had to get my father to that car park in his van, kill him and make his death look like an overdose.'

I shrug. Is she hoping we'll confess to something? Is that what this is about? Maybe she doesn't know the full story after all.

Bianca takes a step back and turns away from me with a sigh. 'It didn't seem to me to be the kind of thing Gabriel Salt was capable of pulling off,' she says. 'Of course, he admitted everything, eventual-ly, right before he died. It's amazing what someone will tell you when they're dangling by their feet twenty storeys above the ground.' A barbaric smile creeps cross her face, setting my blood throbbing at a canter through my veins.

'To be fair, he held out for a while. I was even beginning to wonder if I had it all wrong. But they always talk in the end. He told me how he'd hired some professional help. Someone he'd found on the dark web. It cost him fifty grand. That's a lot of money. Although not much for my father's life. Afterwards, I started wondering how he could have afforded it, and then everything fell into place when I saw your picture on the news. It was like finding a missing piece of a jigsaw.'

'I don't know what you're talking about,' I mumble.

'Of course, if you hadn't come to the funeral and we'd never met, I probably would never have worked it out. So I guess that was a bit of a mistake on your part.'

'Bianca —'

She shushes me quiet. 'Congratulations on the win, by the way. When I saw the pictures of the two of you, all smiles for the cameras and your big cheque, I had a niggling feeling I recognised you, but I couldn't for the life of me work out from where. They say things come to you in a flash sometimes, don't they? And it did. Completely out of the blue. I realised we'd met at the funeral. Except you'd told me your name was Sarah. Obviously that was a lie. Now I can see why.'

'Please, let me explain —'

'Shut up! I'm not interested,' she says, raising her voice to cut me off. 'What I couldn't work out at first was why you'd come to the funeral, pretending to be someone else. I wondered if you had a weird kink, someone who gets a kick out of attending funerals of people you don't know. But no, there was a more logical explanation, wasn't there, Jade?'

'I - I – ...' I stammer.

'What's wrong? Cat got your tongue? Let me help you out. You came to the funeral because you used your winnings to help Gabriel Salt fund the hit on my father, didn't you? And you felt guilty for what you'd done and thought if you came and paid your respects, that would go some way to atoning for what you did. Am I right?'

My gaze slides to the ground. What can I say?

'Or did you come to see how we were suffering? To take pleasure in our grief?'

'No! Of course not,' I cry. How could she think that? I've regretted everything we've done. If I could turn back the clock and undo it all, of course I would.

'What I still don't understand is why you felt the need to get involved with Gabriel Salt in the first place. Was he a friend? Or did he find out about your winnings and come with a begging bowl in hand?'

'Does it matter? All you need to know is that Gabriel was desperate because of what your father did to his wife, and the fact that his only punishment was a slap on the wrist from the court. It was a travesty,' Callum says, spitting the words out like they're poison in his mouth.

'Shut up, Callum,' I snap. For all we know, Bianca could just be guessing. If he confesses to paying for her father's murder, there's no way we can talk our way out of this. She'll kill us on the spot.

'No, no, let him speak,' Bianca says, holding up a hand to silence me. 'I want to hear what he has to say, don't you?'

197

I glare at Callum, willing him to keep his mouth shut. Our lives could depend on it.

'You can't prove anything,' he says, his shoulders slumping.

'I don't need to prove anything. You've told me everything I need to know.'

Callum's head jolts up. 'What? No, that's not what —'

But it's too late. Bianca's already turned away, heading back towards her car, one of her henchmen at her side.

She turns to him, without breaking stride. 'Kill the dogs,' she orders. 'Then kill them. And make sure you get rid of the bodies where they'll never be found.'

Chapter 23

'Wait!' I scream. 'Please!'

Callum's gone still as he stares after Bianca. Stunned into silence.

A hand clamps my shoulder, pushing me down to the ground as a rough voice commands me to kneel.

Bianca's already climbing into her car. She clearly has no interest in staying to watch our execution. But the moment she leaves, we're dead. There's nowhere to run. There's no way we can fight our way out. Which leaves only one card left to play.

'We'll pay you! A million pounds. Compensation for your loss.'

'Jade, no,' Callum says.

A man behind him forces him to his knees with a blow to the back of his neck. In the corner of my eye, I see the man's produced a handgun. An ugly lump of metal, like something I've only ever seen in films.

'A million pounds,' I repeat, desperate. 'In cash.'

Bianca freezes as she's about to pull her door shut. She glowers at me, eyes narrowing. The man who accompanied her to the car is striding purposefully back towards us, his hand dipping into his jacket. He also pulls out a gun.

'I mean it. It doesn't mean we're admitting anything, but we'll pay you in return for our lives. Please,' I beg.

Callum grunts as the barrel of the gun is pressed to the back of his head.

'Wait!' Bianca holds up a hand and steps out of the car again.

The man behind Callum lowers his weapon and backs away. Callum lets his chin fall onto his chest with a groan of relief.

But we're not out of the woods yet.

'We can get the cash together really quickly,' I say, the words tripping off my lips without really thinking what I'm saying. I've no idea how long it will take to get our hands on a million pounds.

As Bianca walks slowly back towards us, her hips shimmy.

'How quickly?' she asks.

I glance at Callum. He shakes his head. He has no idea either. It wasn't difficult to lay our hands on fifty thousand to pay Henry, but a million pounds is a lot more money. I don't suppose many banks keep that much cash.

'A week,' I guess.

'Jade, we can't —'

'Shut up, Callum,' I snap back. It's our only chance of getting out of here alive. 'But the deal is, after the money's paid, we never hear from you again. Okay?'

'Call it five million,' Bianca says, holding my gaze. Challenging me.

I curse under my breath. I might have known she'd try to negotiate. I should have started lower, although I'm surprised she's not asked for the lot. Five million is an eye-watering amount of money, but it's still only a fraction of our total winnings. There'd still be plenty left for a comfortable life.

'And I want it within three days,' she adds.

'Three days?' I suck the air through my teeth. I've no idea if that's even possible. 'You know we have the money, but you need to give us time to get our hands on it.'

'I never wanted your money. I wanted justice,' Bianca says, lifting her chin and looking at me down her nose as my knees dig into the hard ground. The irony of it would bring a smile to my face if the situation wasn't so serious. Justice was all Gabriel ever wanted for his wife and that's why we're all here in this remote field in the first place. 'But if you want to save your lives, I want five million, in cash, and I want it delivered in the next three days.'

'Fine,' I agree. What other choice do I have? 'But that's it. We're not paying a penny more.'

We're in no position to bargain, and if she wanted, she could have demanded the whole fifty-one million. But she's not stupid. She must know that would arouse suspicion with the bank and everybody else who knows we're supposed to be multi-millionaires. If she leaves us with nothing, how would we possibly explain that away?

Callum's holding his head in his hands in despair, but if it'd been left to him, we'd already be dead.

'Okay,' Bianca says. 'But if you involve the police, I'll know and you'll die. If you tell anyone about this deal, I'll know and you'll die.'

'Of course,' I gasp. 'Thank you.'

'Where are the dogs?' Bianca glances at a man standing behind me.

'In the car, boss,' he growls.

'Get them.'

'Leave them out of this,' I beg. 'This has nothing to do with them.'

But no one listens. The man marches over to one of the Range Rovers and returns with Jefferson and Delilah. They're obviously delighted to be out of the car at last and are straining at their leads, panting and sniffing around curiously, completely oblivious to me and Callum.

'Give me your gun,' Bianca demands of another of her men, her hand outstretched.

A gun lands in her palm with a slap. I wouldn't have the first clue what to do with a weapon like that, but Bianca seems comfortable with it. It's clearly not the first time she's handled a weapon. She glares at me and without shifting her gaze, points the gun at Jefferson's head.

'No!' I scream. 'Please, not the dogs.'

Jefferson gazes up at Bianca with big, droopy innocent eyes and sniffs the barrel of the gun. Stupid bloody dog.

I screw my eyes shut, my stomach contracting.

'I'll be in touch with details about where you can deliver the cash,' she says. 'But if there's any nonsense, or I get any hint you've spoken to anyone about our arrangement, I'll kill your dogs and send you their tongues in the post.'

I have absolutely no doubt she means it.

'Not that I think you're stupid enough to alert the police,' she adds. 'Not unless you fancy a life stretch for the murder of my father.'

I close my eyes and lower my head. She has us over a barrel and she knows it. There's no way we could risk going to the police, so I guess five million pounds is a small price to pay for our lives and our freedom.

'Take them away,' Bianca orders.

A hand grabs me under my arm and yanks me to my feet. Another man pulls Callum up. They shove us towards one of the cars and bundle us into the back. We sit together and don't resist as they pull black cloth hoods over our heads. And then the car's taking off, bouncing across the uneven ground until it reaches smooth tarmac and accelerates.

It's a shorter drive than the journey that brought us to meet Bianca, and after only a few minutes, the car slows and pulls over.

'Get out,' a voice orders us from the front. The engine's still running.

Someone yanks off our hoods. The back door flies open, and we hurry to clamber out. Before we even get a sense of our bearings, the car shoots off, spitting dust and grit from its back tyres.

We stand silently watching the taillights disappear around a corner, abandoned, alone and dazed in the dark.

Callum's breathing heavily. 'You okay?' he asks.

'Not really. You?'

He bites down on his lower lip, looking beyond me. I've never seen Callum cry, but he looks as if he's teetering on the edge of tears now.

'Where the hell are we?' He sniffs and wipes his nose with his finger, pulling himself together.

'I've no idea.'

They've dropped us by a gate at a muddy entrance to a field along a narrow winding country lane.

Callum pulls out his phone. The glow from the screen illuminates his face as he holds it up close to his nose.

'No signal,' he sighs.

I check my phone. 'Same.'

'Why did you offer to pay her?' Callum growls.

Seriously? He wants to have that argument right now? 'Because the alternative was a bullet in the back of the head.'

'I know, but five million, Jade? That's our money you're giving away.'

'You'd have preferred to die, would you?' The way everything's panned out in the last few weeks, I'd have happily given away the entirety of our winnings, the whole fifty-one million, if it meant our lives going back to how they were before.

'Of course not, but it's so much money. Just think what we could have spent it on,' he says.

I can't believe he's quibbling over a measly five million pounds when there's ten times that amount sitting in the bank.

I sigh. 'Never mind that. How are we going to get hold of the cash without raising suspicion?'

He shrugs. 'I already have some. It won't be a problem getting the rest,' he says. 'Although three days is going to be pushing it.'

I shake my head in disbelief. 'What do you mean you already have some?'

'I took some out in case we needed it.'

'For what?'

Callum turns away from me, not able to hold my gaze. 'I don't know. This and that.'

'How much?'

'About half a million.'

'You've withdrawn half a million pounds and didn't tell me?' I can't believe I'm only just finding out.

'What? I don't trust the banks.'

He's certainly never mentioned that before. It sounds like an excuse to me, but why else would he need so much cash? Maybe he was planning something he didn't want me to know about. Or he's looking to leave me. But he's not given any hint he wants a divorce. It's true we've fallen into a bit of rut lately, but don't all relationships go a little flat from time to time? It can't always be champagne and roses.

'Are you planning on leaving me?' I whisper.

'What?' He frowns, staring at me like I'm insane. 'Of course I'm not. Why would you say that?'

I wish it wasn't so dark. That I could see his face better and read his expression. Is he lying to me? I just don't know.

'Where is it?' I ask. Does he have bags stuffed with cash hidden somewhere? What if someone finds it?

Steals it? It should be in the bank. Keeping it in cash is just reckless.

'Don't worry, it's safe.'

'It's my money too, you know,' I remind him.

'And you've just agreed to give five million of it away.'

'Well, if you hadn't talked me into this stupid idea of Gabriel's, we wouldn't be in this mess, would we?' I snap back. I'm not carrying the blame for this. I might have been the one who first responded to Gabriel's letter, but I wanted to walk away the moment he started talking about using our money for murder. It was Callum who wouldn't listen.

'Hang on a minute,' he says. 'We'd have been fine if you'd not gone to Greenwood's funeral. What the hell were you thinking, Jade?'

'I don't know, Callum. But can we talk about this later? In case you hadn't noticed, we're in the middle of nowhere, miles from home, with no phone signal. And in three days, we need to have raised five million pounds in cash for Bianca. Or she's going to kill the dogs, and then us.'

Callum takes a deep breath, in slowly through his nose, and out again. He prods his tongue into his cheek and glances up at a smattering of stars twinkling in the vast inky sky above. 'Of course, there is an alternative,' he says. 'One call to Henry and Bianca will be out of our lives for good.'

Not this again. When is he going to learn? We are never going to use Henry, or any other professional killer for that matter, ever again. It's what got us in this mess in the first place. I shake my head, disappointed he's even thought it was worth suggesting. 'No, Callum. No more hits. No more killing. And besides, if we have Bianca killed, her husband's going to come after us twice as hard.'

'And you think paying her off is going to stop her? When she realises how easy it is to squeeze us for five million, she'll want more. And more after that. She's never going to stop coming for us. She knows we can't go to the police, and she also knows we're sitting on more than fifty million quid. She's never going to be out of our lives until we're bankrupt.'

'We made a deal,' I say. 'I trust her.'

He snorts. 'Then more fool you.'

'No more killing, Callum. I mean it. The only real alternative is that we call her bluff and involve the police. We tell them everything and hope that we get lighter sentences for co-operating.'

Callum spins around. Even in the dark, I can see the flash of anger in his eyes. 'You wouldn't dare,' he growls.

'Right, well, we'd better start walking then.'

Chapter 24

The house feels desperately empty without Jefferson and Delilah, like a big hole has been carved out of our lives. I hope they're being looked after. That someone's feeding them and taking them for regular walks. If anything happens to them, I'll never forgive myself.

Unfortunately, raising so much cash has proved every bit as difficult as I anticipated. It's our money, and you'd think it would be the easiest thing in the world to withdraw it. But it's not. You have to jump through hoops. And it all takes so much time, not least because the banks apparently don't have big underground vaults of cash and gold, like in the movies. It's all done digitally these days. Money moved around by computer. Not in hard currency, but in flashing digits on a screen.

I've left Callum to sort it out. He's spent most of the last two days on the phone arguing with them. It was only when he threatened to shut our account, withdraw all our money and move it elsewhere that things started moving and the bank agreed to expedite the transaction. They've promised to move heaven and earth, but the clock's ticking. The deadline expires in a little over twelve hours and if Bianca hasn't received her money... Well, I don't know what happens next, but it's not going to end well.

Callum's driven into London to collect the cash from one of the larger branches while I try to keep myself busy around the house, cleaning and tidying. Anything to take my mind off the clock and imagining what Bianca might have in store for us if we miss her deadline.

He's only been gone an hour when an unexpected knock at the door startles me. I peel off a pair of rubber gloves, drop the sponge I was using to clean the bath into a bucket of water, and trot down the stairs. It's odd not to have the dogs barking madly when someone comes to the door, although it's only usually couriers with boxes of stuff Callum's ordered online these days. The silence is a painful reminder they're gone.

I throw open the door with a smile, but it's not a courier.

It's an unshaven stranger in dark clothing, black brooding eyes shaded under the peak of a baseball cap. He doesn't need any introduction. I'd spot one of Bianca's men from a mile off.

He thrusts an envelope at me, his jaw working noisily as he chews gum.

'What's this?'

'Your instructions,' he grunts. 'Read them carefully.'

I wipe my damp fingers dry on the thighs of my jeans and, with a trembling hand, take the envelope.

Like getting hold of physical cash from the bank, it all seems a bit analogue. An old-fashioned way of doing things. Why couldn't Bianca have just sent me a text? I'm sure she could have found my number easily enough.

The man turns and walks away towards a car parked across our drive, engine idling.

It's the first contact we've had with Bianca since she had us abducted from the house and threatened to kill us. We had to walk two miles along an unlit country lane before Callum finally managed to get a mobile signal and work out where we'd been abandoned. They'd taken us north, across the Thames Estuary into Essex, which wasn't a great surprise. It was a long ride home in a taxi though, with both of us lost in our thoughts, silent and fearful.

I watch the man drive off, standing with the envelope clutched tightly in my hand. Across the street, a curtain twitches. It's the old lady with the cats. She never misses a trick. God knows what she must have thought when she saw Callum and me being bundled into the back of those big, black Range Rovers the other night.

I retreat inside, shaking.

The envelope reminds me of the letter Gabriel posted through the door, blank except for our names handwritten on the front. The letter that started everything.

It was the first begging letter we received. Sadly, it's not been the last. Since our win made the news a few days ago, the post has been piling up. There's a huge stack of unopened letters on the kitchen table that I've not had the inclination to open yet. I'm half-minded to throw them all in the bin. I don't have the headspace to deal with any of that right now. Not until we've squared our deal with Bianca and she's out of our lives for good.

My heart's racing again as I collapse on the stairs and stare at the envelope. It's plain white with nothing written or printed on it. I can't put it off any longer. Ignoring it won't make it go away. I slide a finger under the edge of the flap and rip it open.

Inside is a single sheet of white paper. The instructions printed on it are short and succinct. It includes the address of an abandoned brickworks north of London where we're supposed to deliver the money, and a further specific instruction that takes me by surprise. Something I wasn't expecting and which sends a chill through my veins.

They want me to go alone.

Shit.

I can't go alone. Why would Bianca even ask that? Does she think Callum is a threat? Or is this some kind of devilish plot Bianca has concocted to separate us? But for what reason? My mind spins. My stomach tightens. She's playing games again. Trying to unsettle us. Put us on the back foot. But what am I supposed to do? She's still holding Jefferson and Delilah and if I don't do what she asks, I know she'll kill them. And then she'll kill us.

I snatch my phone from my pocket, letting the letter fall to the floor. I need to talk to Callum.

When he answers, I can hear he's driving. Hopefully, he has the cash, and he's on his way home. I really need him right now.

'I've had the instructions for the drop from one of Bianca's men but they want me to go alone,' I cry, with tears in my eyes.

'What are you talking about? Why do they want you to go on your own?'

'I don't know. It doesn't make any sense. They're going to bring a van to the house and I'm supposed to drive that to an old brickworks with the money.'

'That wasn't part of the deal.' Even over the bad line and the hum of the car, I detect the panic rising in Callum's voice.

'What are we supposed to do?'

'I don't know. Let me think.'

'What if it's a trap?' I say.

'Should we tell her we're not doing it?' he suggests.

'How? We don't have any way of getting in touch with her.'

'Or we could ignore it and travel together, anyway?'

'I don't think we can risk it,' I say. 'It's too dangerous. Did you get the cash?'

'Yeah, eventually. I'm on my way home. I should be home soon.'

'Okay, hurry,' I urge him.

'Don't worry, Jade. Everything's going to be fine. We're in this together.'

'Okay.'

I wish I had his confidence, but I don't. I have a terrible feeling about this. Something doesn't add up. I just can't quite put my finger on it.

Chapter 25

When Callum gets home, I show him the letter and we talk through all our options.

We could ignore Bianca's demands and go together in our car. Or we could take the van but Callum comes with me. Or I could go alone without the cash, in case it's a trap.

But ultimately, we concede we have no real choice. We have to follow Bianca's rules while she has the dogs. Neither of us wants to risk them getting hurt.

The concession is that Callum will follow me in his car but he'll pull off the road before we reach the location of the drop, and wait for me. It's far from ideal, but we're in no position to negotiate. I just want this deal done and to get our lives back on track.

With less than three hours before I'm due to meet with Bianca again, a car pulls up outside. We're sitting at the kitchen table, nursing mugs of tea, going over the route I'll need to take and where Callum will wait for me.

We both stiffen at the sound of footsteps. The letterbox rattles. Someone pushes something through the door. It sounds like keys landing on the mat. Keys to the van I'm supposed to drive to the drop-off point.

'I guess this is it,' Callum says, his expression serious. 'Are you ready?'

He heads into the hall and comes back with a key attached to a miniature handgun on a ring. A not-so-subtle reminder of what's at stake if anything goes wrong.

We run through the plan one more time, checking a mapping app on my phone for the best route and traffic conditions. It's going to take us around ninety minutes. Ninety long minutes in an unfamiliar van, with five million pounds in cash stashed in the back, driving on my own. It's not a prospect I'm relishing, but it has to be done. The sooner this is over with, the better.

There are so many variables that could go wrong. I rarely drive these days and I've never been to the brickworks before, so what if I get lost? Or crash? What if Bianca demands more money when I arrive? Takes me hostage? Tries to kill me?

All these questions swirl around my head, leaving me giddy with nerves. But I can't dwell on them. I have to trust Bianca's a woman of her word.

The first thing we're going to do when it's all over is what we should have done a long time ago. We're going to move out of the house and disappear. I don't care where we go, as long as it's far from here. I've already started researching camper vans. We could buy something amazing and travel into Europe to visit all the places we've dreamt of seeing.

Never stopping for long in one place. Living off grid. The thought of it is what's keeping me going.

As promised, Bianca's arranged for a van. It's waiting outside the house. It's white and anonymous-looking, with rusting door sills and dirt splattered over the bodywork. Inside, it's filthy. The floors are plastered with mud, the seats stained, and the dashboard covered in a thick film of dust. Who knows where it's come from. For all we know, it might be stolen. I don't want to think about it. Imagine if I was stopped by the police in a stolen van with five million pounds in cash in the back. That would take some explaining.

I hop in behind the wheel and familiarise myself with the dashboard. The gears. The switch for the lights. And then I check I can see out of the mirrors. Finally, I'm ready. I can't put this off a second longer if we're going to make it on time.

'Okay?' Callum asks, leaning on the door.

'All good. Let's go.'

He's stashed the money at the lock-up where he keeps the Ferrari. So we need to head there first, load up and then we can be on our way.

When I turn the key in the ignition, the engine splutters and rattles like it's on its last legs. A dirty, black cloud belches out of the exhaust. But after a few seconds, the engine settles into a steady rhythm.

Callum hurries off and jumps into the BMW. He pulls out of the drive and flicks on his headlights. I give him a thumbs-up and he pulls away.

I crunch the gear lever into first, lift the clutch and immediately stall the van. Callum's taillights disappear around a corner at the far end of the estate as I turn the engine over again and lurch forward, panicking he's left me behind.

I shift into second, accelerate and crawl along the road until the familiarity of driving finally returns to me like a long-lost friend and I catch up with the BMW. I can't remember the last time I drove. I usually rely on Callum. Or take the bus. It's not something that comes easily to me.

The lock-up is a ten-minute drive away, in the heart of a residential area at the end of a narrow track behind a row of fenced gardens. Callum pulls up in front of a grey metal gate topped with fearsome-looking spikes, jumps out of his car and releases a heavy-duty padlock with a key.

Beyond the gate is a small compound surrounded by flat-roofed brick garages. You'd never know this is where he keeps a car worth more than most people make in a year. But I suppose that's the point. There's nothing flashy about the garages or the compound.

He pulls up in front of a garage at the far end of the yard. It has a white door which slides up and under the ceiling when he unlocks it, revealing his gleaming bright red Ferrari inside. He might not own it, but he's fallen in love with that car. It's certainly seen more of him than I have in the last few weeks.

He flicks on a light and runs his hand along the vehicle's bodywork with a gentle caress like he's stroking a lover. It's pathetic. It's only a lump of metal and rubber.

There's a strong smell of damp inside the garage. It's not really somewhere you want to be stashing large sums of cash, but I can understand why Callum didn't want it in the house. People know where we live and now they know we've come into money, the house is more likely to attract the attention of thieves than the lock-up. It's been such an effort to lay our hands on all this cash, we couldn't risk losing it.

Behind the Ferrari, against the rear wall, there's a battered wooden desk complete with an old, frayed typist's chair. Callum rolls the chair out of the way and drags out an enormous blue canvas holdall. Behind it are several more, all bulging as if they're full.

'Is that the money?' I ask, my eyes growing wide.

'All five million,' he says, shooing me out of the way as he struggles to lift the bag, shuffling backwards with it, careful not to scrape his beloved car.

'Is the van open?' he asks.

I nod. 'The keys are in the ignition, if you need them.'

He grunts and huffs as he toils, finally humping the holdall into the back of the van with a groan.

While he's busy, my attention's caught by a spew of paperwork that's been left messily strewn across the desk. It looks as though he's made a start on some of the post we've received. There are dozens of begging letters, most of them handwritten, alongside a mountain of screwed up envelopes.

I pick up a handful, scanning them out of curiosity while I wait. There are lots of sob stories about serious illnesses and the need for expensive experimental drugs. Some from people just chancing their arm and outright asking for a handout. And others asking for investments in their businesses.

I toss them aside one by one until I come to the last sheet of paper in the pile. It's not a letter but I recognise the handwriting. It's Callum's. He's written out a long list of names, some of which have been crossed out and some have question marks next to them.

'What's this?' I ask, as Callum returns, sweat pouring off his brow.

He blanches, panic washing over his face. 'Nothing,' he mumbles. He attempts to snatch the paper out of my hand, but I'm too quick.

'It's clearly not nothing. Who are these people?'

Some of the names look familiar. Others I don't know.

'It's just a bit of fun. We don't have time for this. Come on, give it back to me.'

Ravi Prakash.

Why does that name ring a bell?

And Aidan Peters?

Wasn't he one of Callum's teachers from school? He used to talk about him sometimes. He didn't like him much. He taught PE, but Callum always claimed Peters bullied him. There were even rumours he used to interfere with some of the boys in the showers. I remember now. They used to call him Pervy Peters.

What about Ravi Prakash? I'm sure he was the landlord who evicted us from that flat we rented in the high street years ago, all because we were a week late with the rent.

And there's a name I'm much more familiar with. Clive Christy. Callum's old boss who sacked him because he falsified an MoT certificate for a mate as a favour. It was a stupid thing to do but Callum was young and naïve. He thought it was an overreaction and never forgave him.

Oh god.

'These are all people you have grudges against, aren't they?'

He shrugs. 'Maybe. Look, we have to get going. We can't be late.'

There are other names on the list that mean absolutely nothing to me.

Matt Dalby.

Harish Chaudhari.

Afia Kingsley.

Junior Tolland.

The list goes on.

'Who are these people?' I demand.

'I told you, they're nobody. I was just doodling.'

'So why does your old PE teacher have a line through his name?' I pray to god Callum's not been that stupid, that he's not done what I think he's done. A shiver runs down my spine and brings goosebumps to my arms. 'Tell me you've not done something you're going to regret.'

'Like what?' he huffs.

'Is this why you kept hold of Henry's burner phone?'

'I don't know what you're talking about.' Callum shoves his hands in his pockets sulkily.

I try to read his face, but he won't look at me, shifting awkwardly from one foot to the other.

Maybe he was just doodling. Of course, there's one way to find out. I unlock my phone and open an internet browser. I type in Aidan Peters' name and wait.

I really hope I'm wrong. That I've jumped to the wrong conclusion. That I've misjudged Callum.

At first, I don't find anything. The initial page of results throws up nothing that remotely appears to have anything to do with Callum's former teacher.

But on the second page, a Facebook post brings my world crashing down.

It's him. Or at least it was him. I don't recognise his profile picture, but he's the right age and his biography confirms he was a teacher at Callum's old school from 1986 until 1993.

The post, with a smiling image of Peters in a rugby shirt and holding a pint of beer, doesn't make easy reading.

It is with great regret and sadness that we have to announce Aidan has unexpectedly and prematurely passed away. Our hearts are torn. Our light has gone out. No words can express how devastated we are at this difficult time. He was a true gentleman. A loving husband. A devoted father. Funeral details will be posted here in due course. Aidan's family x

My lip quivers. My hand trembles.

Please don't let this be what I think it is.

With tears blurring my eyes, I search for another name that's been crossed out on Callum's list. This time one I don't recognise.

Afia Kingsley.

It's an unusual name, and it doesn't take long to discover she's a young mother who was in court six months ago for assaulting her two-month-old daughter. I scan a news report, sickened by what I read.

Drunk mother spared jail after assaulting baby

A woman has walked free from court after subjecting her two-month-old daughter to a cruel attack at home while drunk.

Afia Kingsley was heard by concerned neighbours shouting loudly and banging around the house after spending the evening drinking heavily.

When police arrived at the property, Kingsley's daughter was found unconscious on the floor.

Although it is unclear how the baby was injured, Kingsley admitted full responsibility and pleaded guilty to one count of child cruelty.

She was spared jail by Judge Peter Hallatt who said he was content that Kingsley was in such a state of intoxication she would have been unlikely to have foreseen the consequences of her actions and had shown genuine remorse and regret for her actions.

She was given a two-year suspended sentence.

A two-year suspended sentence for attacking a baby? That's obscene. Another injustice.

Callum watches me, biting a fingernail nervously. The blood sinks into my shoes and my head swims with dizziness.

'These people,' I gasp, waving the sheet of paper under his nose. 'Have you... Did you...?' I can't bring myself to say the words out loud.

Callum blinks rapidly, his tongue darting out of his mouth, wetting his lips.

'Not all of them, no,' he says. 'But they all deserve it, one way or another.'

'This woman who attacked her baby. What did you do to her? Is she dead?'

He stares at me, the whites of his eyes bright in the darkness of the garage. 'She choked on her own vomit,' he says. 'She drank too much.'

He's made it look like an accident. Like Lee Greenwood's 'accidental' overdose. I wonder what happened to her baby.

'And Aidan Peters?' I ask, my legs weak and unsteady.

'An overdose of paracetamol and vodka.'

The bottom drops out of my world. 'Is that what you've been doing all those times you've been out of the house? When you said you'd been driving around?'

'Sometimes, yes.'

223

'But why? Why would you do this when I begged you not to?' How could he have gone behind my back and done this? With our money? Is he insane?

'I've righted a few wrongs, that's all. Is it really so bad?'

My mouth drops open. *Is it really so bad?* 'You realise this makes you a... a serial killer?'

His face clouds with irritation. 'Don't be so melo-dramatic. I didn't kill any of them. I haven't seen Pervy Peters in years and I never even met Afia Kingsley.'

'But you paid to have them killed. It's the same thing.'

'Not really.'

'Don't be so stupid, Callum,' I scream. 'How could you do this? What were you thinking?'

'I wanted to use our money for a good cause,' he says, 'and after Lee Greenwood, I realised how easy it is.'

'You're out of your mind.'

'Don't say that.' He scowls at me. 'You were quite happy to go along with it when Gabriel gave you his sob story.'

'That was a mistake. You know I've regretted it ever since.'

Callum raises his eyebrows, his eyes opening wide. 'It felt good though, didn't it?' His lips twist in a cruel smile.

'No! It didn't, Callum. It was wrong. And so is this.' I flap the sheet of paper in the air. It's such a long list. 'How many have there been?'

He presses his lips together, his jaw tight, and for a moment I don't think he's going to tell me.

'All the names crossed out,' he says.

I count them up. Five in total.

'And the rest? Have you paid Henry to kill them too?'

'Some of them.'

'You have to stop him. I mean it, Callum. Phone Henry and call him off. Tell him he can keep the money, but this has to end tonight.'

Callum laughs. 'What, just call him and tell him I've changed my mind?'

'Yes!'

He shakes his head. 'Can't do that. Sorry, Jade. That's not the way this works.' He checks his watch. 'Can we talk about this later? If we don't get a move on, we're going to be late for Bianca.'

He ducks under the desk again and pulls out another holdall, dragging it along the dusty floor and around the rear of the Ferrari.

So that's why he's already withdrawn a large sum of cash. Suddenly, it all makes sense. Why he's been evasive. Spending so much time away from the house. He wasn't planning to leave me. He was plotting murder.

My feet are rooted to the ground. I can't move. I can't think straight. This is the worst kind of nightmare. The type you can't wake up from. It's so fucked up. Just because Callum has money doesn't mean he gets to decide who lives and who dies, no matter what they've done. It's not up to him. Hasn't he learnt his mistake from what happened with

Greenwood and the mess that's landed us in? And it's only going to take one small slip up and everything's going to come crashing down. The danger is, he's liable to take me with him.

If he's caught, he's going to prison for a long, long time. And me too, especially if they think I was involved.

I watch, mesmerised, as Callum lifts and loads the last few bags into the back of the van and slams the doors shut. I'm not sure what's become of my life.

'Jade, hurry up,' he yells at me. 'We don't have all night. We have to get moving.'

He's right. I'll have to deal with this later. Right now, I have a more pressing concern. I fold up the sheet of paper and shove it in my pocket. But this can't go on. It has to stop before more innocent people get hurt.

If Callum won't listen to sense, he's going to leave me no choice. No one else can die. If he won't stop, I'll have to go to the police and tell them everything. What else can I do?

Chapter 26

We hit the motorway and I drift off into a daze, sticking resolutely to the speed limit as cars and vans and lorries flash past. The meeting with Bianca has become the least of my worries. All I can think about is Callum and that stupid kill list in my pocket.

Five people dead already. Six if you include Lee Greenwood. And who knows how many more there are in the pipeline, innocently going about their business with no idea they're being stalked by a hitman planning their murders.

How many more deaths has he commissioned? And where does it end? The worry is that with every successful hit, Callum's becoming more and more convinced of his invincibility. I think he genuinely believes he won't get caught because Henry is supposed to be a professional who knows what he's doing, and Callum isn't directly involved in the killings. But any idiot can see that, sooner or later, it's going to catch up with him. He's going to get caught out. And when he does, is he going to bring me down with him?

I'm complicit in Lee Greenwood's murder, so it would be foolish to think the police would believe

I didn't know about the rest. But if Callum won't stop, I'll have to do the unthinkable and report my own husband. I hope that's a decision I don't have to make.

I'm so lost in my thoughts, I almost miss the turning for the brickworks. I only notice because Callum, driving close behind me, flashes his headlights as a warning. I have to veer violently off the motorway onto a slip road, chastising myself for not paying attention. It was nearly a stupid mistake and I can't afford for things to go wrong tonight.

The road soon leads onto a quiet lane where traffic is light. When Callum flashes his headlights again, I know we're close. I check the satnav as he pulls off onto the side of the road to wait for me. I'm about a mile away from the brickworks now. I need to concentrate and get my mind back on the job in hand.

My throat is Sahara dry and my palms on the steering wheel damp with sweat as three towering chimney stacks come into view, silhouetted against the night sky like fingers reaching for the heavens.

That must be it. The relics of an old industrial site. I swing through a roundabout, slowing as I try to work out exactly where I'm supposed to be going. I thought it would be obvious, but the site is huge and the instructions about where exactly I'm supposed to meet Bianca weren't specific.

The road eventually ends at a pair of chain mesh gates. There are signs plastered everywhere warning trespassers to keep out. This has to be the right place, but where's Bianca?

Beyond the gates, all the old buildings appear desperately sad and neglected. There's a depressing air of desolation about the collection of vast, empty brick warehouses with their rows upon rows of broken windows. Scrubby weeds, long grass and wiry bushes are pushing up through the cracks in the ground and winding around the old man-made structures as nature slowly reclaims the site. No doubt, it'll soon be a new housing development, swallowed up by developers who'll cram several thousand new homes onto the land. They seem to be popping up everywhere these days.

The van's dim headlights cast eerie shadows ahead as I slow almost to a halt, and when a man appears from the gloom at the side of the road, my heart almost bursts out of my chest.

I don't like the look of him. He's short and squat with a surly expression and hooded eyes. There's no mistaking the bulge of a gun under his jacket. At least, I assume that's what it is.

I shake my head. This is so out of the realms of my normal life, it's surreal. It's as if it's happening to someone else and I'm just a voyeur, watching from a distance.

The man steps in front of the van with a hand raised, indicating for me to stop. I hit the brakes and watch nervously as he wanders up to the gates, removes a chain securing them closed and swings one of them open. He points me towards one of the empty warehouses from where a dim glow of artificial light is coming.

There's no turning back now. I take a deep breath and release the brake. As furious as I am with Callum right now, I wish he was here. I hate having to do this on my own. It's like sleepwalking into a pit of snakes.

I let the van roll forwards and follow the road slowly, crunching over gravel and debris that's accumulated over the years. The front of the warehouse I'm heading for is open to the elements, its roof missing in patches, revealing exposed iron girders that make up the roof struts.

Inside, three dark-coloured Range Rovers are parked in a semi-circle, waiting for me. My pulse thumps noisily inside my head as I approach and spot a number of Bianca's men slipping out of the shadows and stepping out of the cars. I count nine of them in total. Probably the same men as before, but to me they all look the same. Swarthy, unshaven and intimidating. They gather silently, watching me, crossing their hands over their stomachs like some kind of ragtag security detail. Every cell in my body is screaming at me to turn around and drive away. But I'm not leaving without Jefferson and Delilah. I just want to dump the money, grab the dogs and get the hell out of here.

I kill the engine. My headlights go out and I'm left with a residual hum of silence in my ears.

What happens now?

I unbuckle my seatbelt and climb out of the van.

'Put your hands up where I can see them,' one of the men yells, his voice echoing off the old brick walls. 'And turn around. Slowly. No sudden movements.'

I'm too scared to disobey, so I do as I'm instructed, lifting my arms up and turning my back on the assembled throng of heavies.

Another guy hurries over. He pats down my arms, pushes my legs apart and runs his hands up and down my jeans. As if I'd have been stupid enough to turn up armed. I don't have a death wish.

'She's clean,' the guy yells as he retreats.

I take it as an invitation to lower my hands and turn around to face them again.

The rumble of another vehicle approaching fills the warehouse with a new sound. A car appears from the opposite end of the building and pulls up between the parked 4x4s. The same car from our last meeting with Bianca in Essex. Its headlights dim. A rear door opens. Bianca slips out, pulling the jacket of her black trouser suit down over her hips. Her hair is so tightly pulled back from her face it drags her eyebrows upwards, giving her an odd, fixed quizzical expression. She's wearing enormous gold, hooped earrings and bright red lipstick. It's a cheap look but at least she's made an effort, which is more than I have. I didn't think it was an occasion I needed to dress up for.

'Do you have the money?' she demands.

'It's in the back.'

One of her henchmen marches towards the van and throws open the rear doors. Bianca stares at me as we wait, a sneer of contempt plastered across her face as if she's sullying herself breathing the same air as me. But I don't want to be here any more than she does.

The man at the back of the van hauls out one of the holdalls, unzips it and peers inside. He nods at Bianca, and apparently satisfied I've not filled the bag with strips of newspaper and all the money is there, zips it back up and carries it to Bianca's car. The boot pops open and he dumps it in.

More men hurry over to help with the rest of the bags and in a matter of seconds it's done. I've kept my end of the deal and delivered five million pounds in cash right into Bianca's hands, and all within three days, just as she demanded.

'Where are the dogs?' I ask, trying to see through the darkened glass of the three Range Rovers, hoping to catch a glimpse of them. They're going to be so pleased to see me.

Bianca pokes her tongue into her cheek as she looks me up and down. 'The price has gone up,' she says casually.

'I beg your pardon.'

'I've been thinking and five million doesn't seem much to someone who's just won fifty-one million.'

I might have guessed. Never trust a crook. Or a crook's wife, at least.

I shake my head. I'm in no mood for haggling. 'We made a deal,' I say, through gritted teeth. 'The price was five million. We agreed.'

'But you can afford more.'

'The agreement was five,' I say, digging in my heels. If I let her negotiate, she'll keep coming back for more, just like Callum said she would. 'If you've changed your mind, put the bags back in the van and I'll leave.'

'And I'll shoot your dogs,' she says, deadpan. There's not even a flicker of emotion behind those baby-blue eyes. She clicks her fingers and a man standing next to one of the Range Rovers jumps into action.

He pulls open the boot hatch. Jefferson and Delilah poke their heads out, tongues lolling, noses twitching, fizzing with excitement.

My heart melts in my chest and I have to stop myself calling to them as they clearly haven't noticed me. Stupid dogs. They probably haven't even realised Callum and I haven't been around for the last few days.

Jefferson finally spots me and whines. He jumps down, followed by Delilah, but they're yanked back by the man at the car who has a tight grip of their leads.

'It's okay. We'll be going home soon,' I soothe. Jefferson turns in a tight, anxious circle, weaving around the man's legs.

'I want ten million,' Bianca says.

I snort. She has to be kidding.

'I think that's a fair price for my father's life.'

'I'm sorry for your loss, Bianca, but the deal was five million pounds. That's what we both agreed. I've delivered the money exactly as you asked and now I want my dogs back.' I hope she doesn't notice the tremor in my voice.

'I'll give you another three days to get the rest together,' Bianca says.

233

I shake my head and pinch the top of my nose between my finger and thumb. If I give her another five million, how long before she demands another five? And another five after that, until she's bled us dry? 'No, Bianca. I'm not paying a penny more.'

She tuts and rolls her eyes. 'That's such a pity. I'd hoped it wouldn't come to this.' She holds out a hand, palm up, fixing me with a long, hard stare.

The guy holding the dogs steps forwards, reaches into the waistband of his jeans and pulls out a gun. He places it in her hand and, still staring at me, Bianca aims it at Jefferson's head.

The warehouse feels like it's shrinking, the ground spongy beneath my feet. My whole body is swathed in a thin film of sweat.

'Ten million,' Bianca says, steely eyed.

'I - I can't,' I stammer. 'I've brought the money you asked for, now please, give me back my dogs and let me go.'

Her eyes narrow.

She's trying to work out whether I'm bluffing. If I'll hold my nerve. But we can't pay her any more. It would be madness.

Slowly, she raises her hand, lifting the gun away from Jefferson's head.

I let out a long sigh. Thank god. I really thought she was going to shoot him and I'd have to live with that memory for the rest of my life.

Bianca's arm swings towards me, the barrel of the gun level with my head.

I snatch a breath, a hard knot of muscles tightening in my stomach.

'Don't try my patience,' Bianca hisses.

'So, what, you're going to kill me now?'

'I should have done it before,' she says. 'You paid to have my father murdered. It's what you deserve.'

'He killed an innocent woman,' I remind her. 'A pregnant doctor and her unborn baby.'

'It was an accident. He didn't mean to hurt her.'

'He was on his phone, distracted. It was careless, and he was lucky the courts took a sympathetic view,' I say, not sure where this newfound boldness is coming from. But I have nothing left to lose. My husband's embarked on a killing spree with our winnings, and if I get out of this warehouse alive, I'm probably looking at spending the rest of my life in prison. It's hardly the life of luxury I'd planned.

'He didn't deserve to be murdered.' Bianca's eyes turn wet and glassy as if she's fighting tears.

I lower my head.

'You're right, he didn't deserve to die. We didn't have any right to take the law into our own hands,' I say. 'But Gabriel Salt's paid for it with his life and you have five million pounds in compensation. Don't be greedy, Bianca. Let me go.'

'Last time of asking.'

'I can't. I'm so sorry.'

She lowers the gun, and for a fleeting moment I think it's over. I've called her bluff. She doesn't want a dead body on her hands.

'Left or right?' she asks.

I frown, not sure I understand, until I see she's now aiming the gun at my legs.

'Either will be equally painful and you'll probably never walk again. Is that worth five million to you?'

'Stop it, Bianca. You can threaten me as much as you like, but I'm not giving you a penny more.' My heart is virtually clawing its way out of my chest, but I refuse to back down. I'd rather die here than leave myself at Bianca's mercy forever more.

The gunshot is so loud, it almost bursts my eardrums, a sudden explosion of sound and light that reverberates around the warehouse, sending a frightened community of roosting pigeons flapping into flight.

My breath catches in my throat, and I freeze, shock paralysing every muscle in my body. I never seriously expected her to shoot me.

As I wait for the inevitable flood of crippling pain, I lower my head to look for a wound.

But there's no blood. No torn muscle. No pain. Just a numbing ringing in my ears.

When I look back up, Bianca's watching me with a look of bemusement. 'Last chance,' she sneers. 'This time I won't miss.'

I can't do it. 'Five million. That's all you're getting.'

A thunderous silence descends. Nobody moves. Nobody says anything. Even the pigeons have gone. We've reached a stalemate, and it's Bianca's move.

Blood barrels through my veins, a heady mixture of adrenaline and cortisol that makes every nerve ending in my body tingle.

Eventually, Bianca's sour face softens into a smile. She lowers the gun and lets it hang at her side.

'You're not going to give in, are you?'

I shake my head. 'Never.'

And then she laughs. 'I like you,' she says.

I'm not sure what's worse, having her threaten to shoot me or telling me she likes me. It makes my flesh crawl.

She hands the gun back and steps closer.

'Most women would have been begging for their lives,' she says. 'They'd have promised me the world to save their skins, but not you. That was brave. I admire that.'

I assume it's a compliment. I force myself to hold her gaze. I don't want to show any weakness now.

'Alright, we have a deal. I'll take the five million and you can have the dogs back.'

'And that's it? You'll leave us alone?'

'I'll leave you alone.'

The man with Jefferson and Delilah steps forward and hands me their leads. I'm still not convinced this isn't a trick, but I gladly taking the leashes. Jefferson jumps up, resting his front paws on my chest so he can lick my face.

'Now get out of here before I change my mind.'

I don't wait to be asked twice.

I turn away and walk past the van, out into the open, yanking the leads, dragging Jefferson and Delilah behind me. They want to stay and nose around in all the mess on the floor, but I just want to go home.

'Come on, let's get out of here,' I tell them, my legs shaky.

I take one step, followed by another. And another. I don't look back. I keep my eyes forwards. Heading for the main road.

And as I walk, I brace myself, waiting for another gunshot and a bullet in my back.

Chapter 27

I keep walking with the dogs trotting obediently at my heels. There is no gunshot, no bullet in my back or any attempt to stop me. When I reach the gates, the squat man with hooded eyes lets me through without a word.

I can barely believe it's over. The adrenaline that flooded my veins turns into pure, unadulterated euphoria. I've done it. I've faced Bianca down, and walked away with the dogs and a promise that we'll never see or hear from her again. The thrill of it swells in my chest like a balloon about to burst. The feeling is almost as good as the day we found out we'd won the lottery.

Outside the main gates, I hurry along the road with the dogs in the darkness. And with every footstep my shoulders feel lighter and the tight band around my forehead loosens.

I wait until I reach the roundabout, a quarter of a mile from the gates, before I reach for my phone to call Callum, conscious the agreement was that I came alone, and I don't want to blow things at the last moment. I can't wait to tell him what happened. I doubt he'll believe it, that I actually stood my ground and refused to give into Bianca when she was demanding more money with a gun levelled at my head.

I glance back. There's no sign of anyone. So I make the call, head bowed, continuing on my way.

It feels like an eternity passes before the line clicks and I hear Callum's voice.

You've reached Callum Champion. Leave a message.

What? That's odd. Why's he not answering?

I hang up and try again.

But it goes straight to his voicemail once more.

'Cal, it's me. I'm done. I've got the dogs. You won't believe what happened. Can you come and pick me up and I'll tell you all about it.'

He's probably pulled up in an area where there's no signal. I guess I'll just keep walking, heading back towards the motorway in the hope he picks up my message soon.

It's annoying though. We talked through the plan so many times. He was going to wait for my call and be ready to collect me the moment I was done. Instead, I'm going to have to walk in the dark in the middle of god knows where. At least I have Jefferson and Delilah for company.

I keep to the grass verge at the side of the road with my phone in one hand, waiting for Callum's call. Maybe he's popped into a garage for a coffee. Or had to nip to the toilet. I'm sure it's just bad timing. I'll try him again in a minute or two.

Up ahead, blinding headlights approach. It's probably Callum. I pull Delilah off the road and keep both dogs on a tight lead.

As the vehicle comes closer, its lights are so dazzling it's impossible to make out the model, let alone its colour. I've no idea if it's Callum or not, but I wave anyway.

The vehicle doesn't slow down. It shoots past in a blur of light and noise, setting the dogs off yelping and barking excitedly.

I turn and watch despondently as it speeds away. It's not Callum's car. It's a blue van. The driver must have wondered who the hell was waving at him from the side of the road. Oh well. The thought brings half a smile to my face. He probably thought his luck was in.

I try Callum's number again.

It connects straight to his voicemail and I leave another short message out of frustration, not bothering to hide my irritation.

'Callum, where the hell are you? I'm walking back towards the motorway. Can you please hurry up?'

Where is he? He knew I was going to phone the moment I'd finished at the brickworks, so why isn't he picking up?

Crossly, I stomp on, my anger simmering. I was in such a good mood a few minutes ago and now it's evaporated into the cool night air.

Another vehicle approaches from behind. I hear it a few seconds before its headlights wash over us, lighting up the road and the verge, casting long, ragged shadows on the grass and the bushes. My legs appear about three times too long for my body while Jefferson and Delilah look like monsters with huge heads and giant arched backs. I drag the dogs out of the gutter as the vehicle draws closer. I don't want them being run over in the dark.

The vehicle slows down as it passes. It's the blue van that passed us in the opposite direction a few moments ago. Bright red brake lights burn through a light mist like acid through rice paper.

It pulls up a few metres further along the road, directly ahead of us. I grip my phone tightly, willing Callum to call as the van sits at the side of the road, engine idling, exhaust smoking. Now would be a really good time to hear from him, as I have a bad feeling about this. A claw of concern in my gut that something's not quite right.

There's no one around for miles and here I am, a woman on her own, at the mercy of any stranger. I have Jefferson and Delilah with me, but they're so docile they'd probably just lick anyone who tried to attack me.

I slow my pace. Should I cross to the other side of the road? Or am I being overcautious? It's likely to be someone who's just pulled over to take a call or to check a map. I've been so wired and anxious today, it's probably my imagination going into over-drive. There's nothing sinister about the van and there's no reason to suspect I'm in any danger.

Even so, I try Callum's number again but when I reach his voicemail I know there's no point leaving any more messages.

I crane my neck, trying to see in the reflection of the van's wing mirrors who's behind the wheel, but it's too dark. I can't see anything beyond the blazing taillights.

I keep walking, passing the van with my heart pounding. The driver's door opens on the far side of the vehicle, out of my view. Someone gets out. Footsteps crunch along the road, seemingly heading towards the rear of the van. The driver's probably stopped to get something out of the back. Nothing to be worried about. But I keep marching on at a pace.

Any minute now, I'm sure Callum's going to turn up, apologising for being late, and we'll be heading home, laughing about it all.

The footsteps fall silent. I drag the dogs on as they stop to sniff around the van's wheels. A different sound now. The squelch of feet on wet grass. And the sense that someone's right behind me.

I whirl around with my heart in my mouth and a scream strangles in my throat as a ghoulish figure looms over me, two terrifying, unblinking eyes peering through the slits of some kind of mask.

Strong, muscular arms bundle me up as a gloved hand clamps across my mouth, silencing my attempt to shout for help.

It all happens so quickly. I don't know what's going on or what to do.

A door in the side of the van slides open with a rumble and I'm being pushed inside. I stumble, my knees clattering painfully against the metal sill, and

I fall onto a rough, wooden floor, gritty with mud and dirt.

Then he's on top of me. Pinning me down. Restraining my arms. And for one awful minute, I think he's going to rape me.

He pulls a strip of thick sticky tape across my mouth. Then he's wrapping it around my wrists. Binding them tightly. Cutting off my circulation until my fingers start throbbing.

I have to breathe through my nose. Hard and fast. My head spinning. Snot streaming from my nostrils as he grabs my ankles and trusses me like a turkey at Christmas.

The dogs! What has he done with Jefferson and Delilah?

I get my answer a few seconds later, when the man climbs out and the dogs clamber in next to me, slobbering all over me, fussing around with all the new smells in a strange vehicle. At least he didn't leave them here, alone and confused. It's a small comfort.

As the door rattles closed, trapping me inside, I lift my head as if I might be able to find some answers.

My abductor is framed in the doorway, staring at me. He's tall. Taller than Callum, at least. Broad and muscular too. His mask isn't a mask, but a balaclava. Meaty lips and soulless eyes poke through narrow gaps in the wool giving him a grotesque, monstrous look.

As the door closes, my desperate scream is muted by the tape over my mouth. Jefferson licks my face, trying to console me, while Delilah whines and curls up on the floor with her warm body pressed against mine.

I glance around, looking for clues. Anything to identify who this man is and what he wants with me. But the van is empty. There are no tools or work equipment, lengths of wood or reels of electrical cable. So who the hell is he? And what does he want? I tremble with fear, my mind running wild. You hear of women being abducted all the time. I just never thought I'd be one of them. But then again, I never thought I'd win the lottery. It must be my lucky year.

The man climbs back in behind the wheel and we pull away at speed, my body spilling across the floor, unable to stop myself sliding. My head clatters against a metal pillar and I wince in pain.

Maybe this has something to do with Bianca. Is it all part of a larger plan to lay her hands on more of our money? It wouldn't surprise me. Perhaps I should have given her the whole fifty-one million. After all, it's brought nothing but misery and stress since we won.

Or am I being kidnapped for a ransom? We should never have agreed to do the press conference. Now everyone knows who we are and how much we're worth. Are they going to send pictures of me, trussed up and dishevelled, to Callum and demand a huge sum of money for my safe return? Is that what this is? It happens, doesn't it? Just not to people like me.

I used to laugh when people said money was the root of all evil. How could it be evil when it brought so much joy and happiness? But that was before I had any. I'd spent years dreaming about winning the lottery, imagining the amazing life I'd lead. But it's without doubt the worst thing that's ever happened to me. To us. I wish so much that I could return to my boring, old, uncomplicated life, working long shifts in the restaurant, saving up for a deposit on a house. Because none of this would have happened if we hadn't won. Life was tough before, but it was a million times better than this.

I close my eyes and let the tears come flooding out, unable to hold them in. It's been such a crazy day. And now this. I'd have been better off if Bianca had shot me.

I quickly lose track of time but it doesn't feel as though we've been driving for long before we slow down and eventually come to a complete stop. Jefferson, who's been dozing all this time, lifts his head and whimpers.

The man in the balaclava jumps out. The side door slides open. He grabs my wrists, forcing me to sit up. I cower in fear as he produces a small knife and holds it in front of my face.

For a moment, I think he's going to cut me or stab me, and I squeeze my eyes shut. A second later, the tape around my ankles is cut loose, freeing my legs.

When I open my eyes again, I see over the man's shoulder that we're in woodland, surrounded by trees. There's also a derelict-looking house at the end of the dirt track where he's parked. Its roof is riddled with holes. There are windowpanes missing and no lights on inside. Is this where he's planning to keep me prisoner? Is this where I'm going to die?

He grabs my wrists, pulls me to my feet, and shoves me towards the old building, shutting the dogs in the van. I stumble in the dark, but he catches my elbow before I can fall, roughly yanking me up.

My eyes dart left and right, looking for somewhere I can run. But there's nothing around other than trees and the creepy old house. I wouldn't make it more than a few metres before he caught me again.

An owl's hoot carries on the breeze, eerie and foreboding. I have to do something. Put up some kind of fight. If only I could give him the slip or distract him for a second...

But, as if he's reading my mind, he grabs my hair and pulls so hard, pinpricks of light shower my vision and a sharp pain spreads across my scalp. He forces my head down and drags me along, ignoring my muffled yelps of agony.

When my toe catches on a rock protruding from the ground and I lose my balance, he simply pulls my hair harder, urging me to get up. The pain's so intense, I'm close to passing out.

He kicks open the front door, almost taking it off its rusty hinges and pushes me in first. It's dusty and damp inside, the bare floorboards filthy from years of dirt and grime. It must have been empty for ages. It's probably been condemned. But that's the least of my worries.

247

He shoves me along a narrow hall where faded strips of torn wallpaper are a reminder that this once used to be a home. To my left, a staircase is disintegrating, the steps reaching only halfway up to the floor above.

I stumble into a room with a small window. Two wooden chairs have been set up facing each other. The man pushes me towards one of them, grabs my shoulder and forces me to sit.

He pulls a roll of tape from his pocket and binds my ankles to the chair legs, then frees my wrists and attaches them to the arms.

Before taking the seat opposite, he switches on a shadeless lamp in the corner, the naked bulb emitting a harsh light that hurts my eyes.

He leans forwards and stares at me through the holes in his balaclava.

My heart's beating so hard, I'm sure he must be able to hear it.

I lower my chin to my chest, hunching my shoulders, trying to prepare myself mentally for whatever depravity he has in mind. Maybe he'll kill me quickly. Or is he the kind of man who gets his kicks making women like me suffer?

Bile rises from my stomach and burns the back of my throat and for a moment I think I'm going to be sick.

But I can't be sick. Not with this tape across my mouth. I'll choke to death.

The only sound in the room is the whistle of air through my nose, the blood rushing through my ears and my heart pounding against my ribcage.

Why's he just sitting there, staring at me? Doesn't he have anything to say?

I crack open my eyes and lift my head.

'Please, let me go,' I try to plead, but of course he can't understand what I'm saying.

So I gaze into his eyes, the only part of his face that's visible, and try to make him understand.

Now I look more closely, I can see his eyes are brown, flecked with hazel. They're evil, disturbing eyes, that narrow cruelly.

I wish he'd say something. Do something. Instead of just staring.

I try fighting against the bonds around my wrists and ankles, rocking the chair back and forth, but the man puts a gloved hand out and grasps my arms, stilling my motion.

I stop fighting. What's the point? I allow my body to relax.

He takes a deep breath and grabs the balaclava, pulling it off one-handed in a swift motion.

His shakes his head and runs a hand through sweat-soaked grey hair and I stare, stunned, into his face. The familiar cut of his jaw. The slightly crooked nose. His thick neck. Now I'm really confused.

What the hell is this?

Chapter 28

'Don't scream,' the man warns as he reaches for the tape over my mouth. 'Although out here no one's going to hear you.' He rips it off violently in one go, causing me to grimace at the sharp, stinging burn.

'Henry? What's going on? What are you doing?'

I eye him suspiciously. He might be a familiar face but he's no friend. This is a man who kills people for a living, and for some reason, has abducted me. I can't make sense of it. Why would he do that? Unless someone's paid him...

'It's complicated,' he says. He leans forwards, resting his elbows on his thighs, and bows his head. He looks weary. Conflicted about something. About me?

'Has someone... paid you to kill me?' I ask, my voice barely a whisper.

He glances up, his beady eyes searching my face. He runs his tongue over his lower lip as if he's pondering how to reply.

'Tell me,' I hiss. 'I have a right to know what's going on.'

He nods silently.

'You know Callum's looking for me, don't you? And when he finds out I'm missing, he'll call the police.'

'No,' Henry says. 'No one's looking for you, Jade. And police aren't coming.'

'What?' I gasp. 'Of course he is. You don't know what you're talking about. He was about to pick me up when you arrived. Does this have something to do with Bianca?'

He frowns.

'Has she paid you to do this?' She must have done. No one else knew where I was going to be, unless he followed me from home.

'I'm so sorry, Jade,' he says, sounding genuinely remorseful.

'Sorry for what? For god's sake, untie me will you? Let me go,' I beg. 'Callum's going to be out of his mind with worry and when he raises the alarm, how long do you think it's going to be before they come looking for you?' I rattle the chair, fighting my bonds with growing anger and frustration.

'Callum's not looking for you, Jade,' Henry says so quietly I think I must have misheard him. 'He's gone home.'

'What? Don't be stupid. Of course he hasn't. Why would you say that?'

He sighs and runs a hand over his face. He has dark circles under his eyes and a melancholic air I don't remember from when I first met him. 'How do you think I knew where to find you?'

'I - I don't know,' I stammer. 'Bianca?'

251

He shakes his head and looks at me blankly. 'Who?'

'Don't play games with me.'

'I'm not. I'm trying to help you.'

'Help me? Ha! You have a funny way of going about it. If you want to help me, you'll untie me this minute and take me home. I promise, if you do that, I won't breathe a word of this to anybody.'

'Callum wanted you to have accident.' He lowers his head and stares at the ground as he speaks. 'A serious one.'

A shockwave of paralysis descends over my body, stilling my muscles but sending my brain into freefall. The walls of the room crowd in and I have the sensation of plummeting from a great height.

He's not serious. He can't be. He's messing with me. Messing with my head. Trying to get me to believe something that can't possibly be true. Why would he say that? It's an awful thing to suggest.

'What? Don't be ridiculous. You're lying.'

This has to be a wind-up. Callum's idea of a joke. I bet he's put Henry up to it, thinking it's a laugh.

'He told me where you'd be tonight and at what time,' Henry says.

I stare into his eyes, looking for the lie. Some kind of tell that he's not being serious. But I can't find it.

'I don't... I don't understand.'

'Like I said, it's complicated.'

'But if Callum wanted me dead, what's all this?' I ask. 'Why abduct me and bring me here? Why not just kill me?'

I can't get any of this straight in my mind. None of the pieces of the jigsaw flying around my head want to fit together in any semblance of an understandable truth.

'Is it... is it the money?' I ask. 'Is that it? Did he tell you he wants me out of the way so he can keep all the money for himself?' Even as I say the words out loud, they sound ludicrous. There's more than enough money for us to share without either of us going without. And Callum's never been a greedy man. We've always shared everything. A bank account. The bills. It's what we've always agreed. Ever since the day we were married.

'It's not that,' Henry says. He grips the top of his nose and squeezes his eyes shut, as if he's struggling how to tell me something I need to hear.

'Then what? Please,' I beg. 'You have to tell me what's going on.'

'There's someone else. Another woman.'

I feel the curl of my lips stretch into an uncertain smile. 'No.' Now I know he's lying. Callum would never do that to me.

'Callum's been having affair. I'm sorry.'

'No, I don't believe you.'

'I think you know her. Someone from garage where he worked. Victoria? Or Vicky, I think he called her.'

Victoria Etheridge? The girl on reception? Surely not. I've met her a couple of times, although only briefly. I didn't warm to her. She was cold and aloof, although I can't deny she's attractive with her long honey-blonde hair, perfect skin and arctic-blue eyes. She might only be a receptionist, but I'd have thought she was way out of Callum's league. Although I guess that was before he became a multi-millionaire.

Fucking gold-digger.

How could I have been so blind? So naïve? All those days and nights he told me he was out driving, cruising the countryside in that stupid sports car, and all the while he was probably with *her*. I'm such an idiot.

'Are you serious?'

'I'm sorry. I know this is hard.'

'How do you know this?' I demand.

Henry shrugs. 'He told me. I didn't want to know but I guess he thought he owed me explanation.'

My head's so light, it feels as though I could faint. My chest is tight and I'm struggling to draw in enough air.

'Breathe,' Henry says.

'I can't.'

'You can. Slowly. In. And out. Try to calm down.'

'Calm down?' I spit, rattling the chair again. 'I've just been abducted off the street, bundled into the back of your van, tied up, brought to this derelict house and told my husband's ordered a hit on my life. What exactly do I have to be calm about?'

'Well, I didn't kill you,' Henry says. 'And you get to live another day.'

'Did he really pay to have me killed?' I ask. I can believe Callum's eye has been turned by a pretty face and a short skirt, but I thought he loved me.

That he'd never lay a finger on me. 'If what you're saying is true, why didn't he just leave me?'

'He was worried you'd make fuss and try to stop him getting hands on the money.'

'If he really wanted a divorce, I'd have let him have his half.'

Henry shakes his head. 'He wanted it all. He didn't want to share.'

'Bastard,' I hiss. I thought I knew him, but it goes to show, we never really know what's going on inside anyone else's head, even if we share their bed.

'I agree.'

It's not much consolation. 'So what happens now? You still going to kill me?'

I might as well be dead.

'What?' Henry's brow furrows. He has a long scar running from his cheek to his ear I hadn't noticed before. 'Of course not. If I was going to kill you, you'd be dead already.'

'Then why have you brought me here?'

'Because I have offer to make you,' he says.

'What offer?'

'I think you're good person, Jade. You don't deserve to die just because it would be convenient for your cheating husband.'

I laugh nervously. 'I've heard it all now. A hitman with a conscience. You might want to think about a change of profession.'

'Don't mock me, Jade.'

'Right, and you're doing this because? Don't tell me. It's against your hitman's code of conduct?' I'm being spiteful. Taking it out on him when it's not his fault my husband's a pathetic scumbag who can't keep it in his trousers.

'I have proposition for you,' he repeats. 'I've seen news. I know how much you won.'

'So you want money? I might have known. Join the queue.'

'Don't be so cynical. I'm offering you opportunity to square things with Callum. For a price, obviously.'

'Stop talking in riddles. Whatever you've got to say, just spit it out.'

'Callum paid me to kill you,' he says. 'I'm open to... counteroffer.'

'A counteroffer?' I raise my eyebrows. He makes it sound like we're bidding for a house in a closed auction.

'If you were to offer bigger sum, I'd be willing to reverse hit.'

'Reverse? You mean you'd kill Callum instead?' My words form slowly as the enormity of what he's suggesting hits me.

'And spare your life, of course.'

I stare at him, waiting for him to laugh. To tell me it's all a big joke, and that of course he has to kill me. But he doesn't. His gaze fixes on me, waiting for me to make my decision.

'And how much would that cost?' I can't believe we're having this conversation, that I'm even con-templating negotiating to have my husband mur-dered when I've been clear ever since Lee Green-wood died, there would be no more killing.

'I'd do it for a million because I like you.'

'How much did Callum pay you?'

'Usual fee, but this is more unusual arrangement,' he says. 'It's riskier for me.'

'Fifty grand? But you want a million to kill Callum?'

'It's only money, Jade, but I guess it depends on how much you think your life is worth. I'm happy to fulfil my original obligation and kill you tonight. Or we can strike deal and for a million, I can spare your life and take your husband's instead. If you agree, Callum will be dead within the week.'

He makes it all sound so simple. So matter-of-fact. Like it's nothing more than an innocuous business transaction.

'And you'd make it look like an accident?' I can't believe I'm even considering it.

He dips his head. 'Of course.'

I stare into his eyes. The eyes of a killer. How does he sleep at night? Does the blood on his hands haunt him in the small hours? Does he regret any of the deaths? Is he plagued by guilt?

'How many others have there been?' I ask.

He squints at me. 'Others?'

'Hits. Contracts. Murders. Killings. How many others did Callum order? I found a list of names. People he says he'd had killed, by you, presumably. I counted five. Six if you include Lee Greenwood. Were there more?'

He gives a half shrug. A half shake of his head. 'I can't talk about that,' he says.

'More than six?'

'Da, maybe.'

I knew it. Callum wasn't only cheating on me with another woman, he went expressly against my word and has been ordering contract killings with impunity. And paying for them with our money.

This isn't the man I fell in love with.

'What's your decision?' Henry asks. 'Do we have deal? Do you want Callum dead or not?'

Chapter 29

The key clicks in the lock. The door opens a crack and Jefferson noses his head inside, racing into the house with his tail wagging excitedly.

So much for sneaking in quietly.

Delilah plays it much cooler. Almost nonchalant. Nowhere near as excited to be home after our three-day adventure away.

I silently press the door closed behind me and stand in the hall, listening. The house has a hollow, empty feel about it. Callum must be out.

An image flashes across my mind of him curled up in bed in a fancy hotel with that blonde receptionist from the garage, and my blood boils.

I swallow the anger back down. I'll deal with her later. For now, I need to keep a clear head and not let my emotions get the better of me.

Part of me is relieved, but another part is disappointed that Callum's not here. I've spent the last two hours psyching myself up, ready to confront him. And while I've not been looking forward to having the conversation with him, I've not been able to stop imagining his expression when he sees

I've risen from the dead. His face is going to be a picture. I can't wait to see how he reacts.

I wonder if he tried to cover his back, ringing around the hospitals and the police after a suitable length of time when I failed to return home. He probably didn't even think about that. But that's Callum for you. He's never been the shiniest spoon in the drawer.

I shrug off my jacket and hang it on a hook in the hall where it's the first thing he'll see when he gets back. And I might as well leave my shoes at the bottom of the stairs too, roughly kicked off as if I've come home in a hurry. That'll freak the bastard out.

When Henry finally let me go, my first instinct was to head straight home and have it out with Callum on the spot. I was raging with fury. As if seeing another woman behind my back wasn't bad enough, the fact he'd planned to have me murdered so they could run off together with my share of the money left me sick to the pit of my stomach.

Henry talked me out of it. And he was right, my revenge will be all the sweeter with a cool head.

I've spent the last three nights in a quiet guesthouse, where the owners made a fuss of Jefferson and Delilah. Somewhere I could straighten everything out in my head and put some contingencies into place. But now I'm ready to hear what Callum has to say for himself. How he's going to explain what he's done.

It's early evening when he finally returns, just when I was beginning to get jittery, wondering if he was coming home at all. When I hear his key in the

260

lock, I take my place in the lounge and flick off the lamp. I've had the whole day to choreograph exactly how this is going to go, but now the butterflies have taken to the wing in my stomach and my pulse is racing.

Unfortunately, the surprise I'd planned is somewhat spoiled by the dogs, who race to the door, barking, as soon as they hear Callum's back.

'Hey, you two. What are you doing here?' he asks. The shocked tone in his voice gives me a buzz of pleasure. His head must be spinning.

The dogs' tails thump loudly on the floor and I suffer a twinge of disappointment when I hear their whimpers of delight at being reunited with Callum. Dogs are supposed to be perceptive. It's a shame they've not seen through him.

I hear the rustle of clothing as Callum shrugs off his jacket and presumably hangs it in the hall on top of my coat. Then there's a slight hesitation.

'Hello?' he calls out with a definite quiver in his voice. 'Who's there?'

As he steps into the lounge, I flick on the lamp, delighting in the effect it has on him, simultaneously illuminating me, sitting casually on the sofa, and making the point that I'm here in the house and very much alive.

The colour drains from Callum's face and his eyes widen with surprise as he jumps backwards with a start. He looks like he's seen a ghost, which I suppose, in a way, he has.

'Jade?' he rasps.

261

'Hello, Callum.' I force a sweet, innocent smile, enjoying his obvious surprise and discomfort.

'Wh - where've you been?' he stammers, leaning against the doorframe, trying to look casual, like nothing's wrong. But there's no hiding the fear and confusion on his face. 'I was worried about you.'

'I needed a few days away to clear my head,' I say, jumping up and putting my Kindle to one side. I've read the same page about ten times, unable to concentrate on the story, my mind on other things.

I step across the room, reach up on tiptoes and plant a kiss on his cheek. It turns my stomach to touch him. To kiss him. But it's worth it to see him squirm. It's important to make everything seem as normal as possible. For now.

'Is everything okay?' I ask, furrowing my brow. 'You look... tense.'

'I'm fine,' he mutters.

This is priceless. I wish I'd thought to film it so I could watch it back later. Revel in his discomfort in my own time.

'Did you miss me?'

'Yeah, of course I did,' he says.

Liar.

'You didn't try to call me, though?' I say.

'I - I tried... but you know...'

I love watching him flounder, but I need to be careful. I can't afford to box him into a corner and force him into doing something stupid. I should have thought to have grabbed a paring knife from the kitchen to defend myself. I guess I've not really been thinking straight.

'You know why I had to go away, don't you?' I ask.

He swallows hard and blinks rapidly, a sure give-away he's not as comfortable as he's pretending to be.

'No - not really.'

'Come on, Callum. That list I found in the garage. The one with all the names on it. You remember? It made me so angry.'

A sigh of relief whistles from his lips. 'Oh, right, that. Yes, of course.'

'And I was scared. Disappointed you'd gone behind my back when I expressly said I didn't want you contacting Henry again. Don't you see how wrong it is?'

His eyes narrow as he tries to work out what the hell is going on and whether it's best to play along with the charade or to confront me. But he's not sure what I know.

'I - I - but they all deserved it, one way or another.'

'That's not the point, Callum. You were playing god. With our money.'

'I don't see what the big deal is,' he says. 'I was righting a few wrongs, that's all. It's not like I was picking people out randomly.' There's a hint of irritation in his tone.

'You took a contract out on your old PE teacher just because he bullied you at school and made you feel worthless,' I say, exasperated.

Callum glances at the floor and rubs his toe across the carpet. 'Well, he was a perv and he had it coming.'

'You know if they trace any of those deaths back to you, they'll lock you up and throw away the key? It only takes three murders for you to be considered a serial killer.'

He snorts. 'They can't pin any of them on me.'

'But it's not the number that upsets me the most. It's that you went behind my back,' I say with a disappointed sigh. I thought I could trust you. We're supposed to be married, for better or for worse.' I watch his face closely.

His mouth twitches. 'I'm sorry,' he says, although it doesn't sound like he means it.

'You're sorry for what? Sorry for going behind my back or sorry you got caught?'

'Sorry for going behind your back,' he mumbles sulkily.

'Right,' I say. He's not sorry in the slightest.

It's clear watching his reaction that the power to control life and death is a seductive siren, and he's been blinded by her allure.

'No more deaths. No more killings, okay?' I say, reaching for his hand. His skin is surprisingly cold and clammy. 'If you want to do some good with the money, give it to charity. Use it to help save lives, not take them. You're not a monster, Callum.'

He nods as he chews his lip, his eyes glassy. I think I might actually be getting through to him.

'You promise me? No more hits?'

He lowers his gaze, chastened. 'I promise.'

'Good. Now give me the phone.' I hold out my hand. 'You won't be needing it anymore.'

His head jerks up. 'What?'

'The burner phone Henry gave you. Give it to me.'

He stares at me open-mouthed as if he's trying to gauge whether or not I mean it. But I mean every word. I need that phone.

'But —'

I raise an eyebrow.

Callum's resistance deflates. 'Fine.' He slips the phone from his back pocket and slaps it into my palm.

'Not so hard, was it?' I check the screen. There's plenty of charge on it and a decent signal. 'What's the passcode?'

'Why do you need the passcode?' His eyes narrow suspiciously.

'Don't argue with me, Callum.'

He throws his arms up in submission. 'Fine. It's 2-5-1-2.'

I hesitate before I punch in the numbers. 'Christmas Day?'

He smirks. 'That's what having a hotline to Henry felt like. It was better than winning all that money. Better than sex,' he says.

'Are there any more hits scheduled?' I ask.

He shakes his head.

'Are you sure?' Again, I watch his face for any unusual ticks or giveaways, but it's a blank.

'I'm sure.'

'Good.' I slip the phone into my own pocket and sit back on the sofa with my feet curled under my legs. 'Sit,' I instruct, patting the cushion next to me.

Callum sighs but does as I ask, perching on the edge of his seat, wringing his hands. I don't think he's enjoying my resurrection in the slightest.

'I wish we'd never won that money. It's the worst thing that's ever happened to us,' I tell him, folding my arms across my chest. 'I thought it would make all our problems go away, but it's just made them worse. Don't you think?'

Callum shrugs. 'Not really.'

'I thought money would make me happy. We dreamt about what winning big would mean, but I had no idea. If nothing else, it's driven us apart in ways I could never have imagined. It's put a terrible strain on our marriage.'

Callum's hands still. 'That's not true.'

'Isn't it?' A part of my brain wants to blurt out that I know all about his sordid little affair and make him justify himself. I want to know when it started. Who made the first move. Whether he thinks he loves her. Why he didn't think I was enough for him anymore. But I can't show my hand. Not yet. It would ruin everything. He needs to believe I still don't know about him and that slut, Vicky Etheridge.

'Of course not,' he says.

'Do you still love me?'

He bristles. 'What kind of question is that?'

'Do you still love me?' I repeat.

'Yes. What a stupid thing to ask.'

It's not stupid. I can't remember the last time he told me he loved me.

'The money's destroying us, Callum. Can't you see that? I'm not any happier. And I don't think you are either.'

'I'm happy,' he says.

'Really? Deep down, are you?'

He looks at me like I've lost my mind. 'We can have anything we want. We don't have to work. We don't have to worry about anything.'

I sigh. It's a shame he can't see it.

'I want you to get rid of the Ferrari,' I say quietly. 'And cancel the order for that other car.'

'The Aston?'

'Yes.'

'But why?' He scowls at me.

'They're too fast. Too dangerous. I'm worried you're going to end up killing yourself,' I tell him.

'They're only dangerous if you don't know what you're doing.'

'Please, would you do this for me? For the sake of our marriage?'

'You're being ridiculous. You're worrying about nothing,' he says.

'I thought you said you loved me.'

'I do.'

'Then do this for me. Get rid of the fast cars. Buy something sensible. Something that's not going to get you killed.' I stare imploringly at him. 'You want me to be happy, don't you?'

Our gaze meets and we sit in silence for a moment. He's probably hoping I'll back down, but I'm not going to.

'And what if I refuse?' he asks.

'Then I'd have to go to the police and tell them everything. It's the only way I can guarantee you'll be safe. Better to lose your freedom than to lose your life, don't you think? I have a copy of the list of names you pulled together and now I have Henry's burner phone too, which I guess has a log of all the calls you've made to him?'

His mouth gapes open. 'You wouldn't,' he says.

'Of course I don't want to. I'd have some awkward questions to answer myself, but I'll do it if that's what it takes to protect you.'

'You're crazy,' he says.

'Is that a yes?'

He shakes his head and rubs his eyes. 'Alright. Fine. I'll get rid of the cars if it makes you happy.'

'Thank you. It does.'

He sinks back into the sofa with a thunderous face, but I don't care. He's brought this on himself.

'I'm sorry, babe,' I say, taking his hand and looking lovingly into his eyes. 'It's only because I'm afraid of losing you. You understand that, right?'

'I suppose,' he says grumpily.

'Will you do it first thing tomorrow? Will you return the Ferrari and cancel the order for the other one?'

'Tomorrow?'

'You might as well strike while the iron's hot.'

'But I —'

'I know it's hard. You love that car, don't you?'

'It's what I've wanted ever since I was a little boy,' he says. 'I never thought I'd be able to afford one.'

268

'Look, I'm not a total killjoy. Why don't you take it out for one last spin? A sort of goodbye drive.'

'When?'

'Now?'

'Right this minute?' he says.

'Go on, I don't mind. As long as you're careful. Get it out of your system and then tomorrow I want it gone.'

He sits up straight, playing with a tag of skin around his thumbnail. 'Alright,' he says. 'I will. If you're sure?'

'Go on,' I smile. 'Have fun. I'll see you in a couple of hours then, shall I?'

'Why don't you come with me?'

'What? No, I don't think —'

'Come on, Jade. You've not been in the Ferrari once. Come with me for a spin.'

'I can't,' I snap, panic building. 'I have things to do here. You go. You'll have more fun without me.'

'Are you sure?'

'Absolutely. Go and enjoy yourself. Just don't drive too fast.'

He jumps up with a wide grin on his face. 'Well, if you're absolutely certain.' He races out of the room and pokes his head back around the door, clutching his jacket.

'I'll be back by ten. Eleven at the latest,' he says.

'Okay, go. Drive safely. Don't kill yourself.'

'I won't,' he says as he's already halfway out of the house.

'Goodbye, Callum,' I shout after him. 'Goodbye.'

Chapter 30

I wake with a jolt, sitting bolt upright in bed, when the banging starts. For a moment, I forget where I am. The banging stops. And starts up again. Someone hammering on the door. I blink away the sleep, pawing at my eyes, and clasp a hand to my chest to quiet my thumping heart. I turn to Callum, but his side of the bed is empty. And then I remember.

My phone tells me it's two-thirty in the morning. What the hell's the emergency?

I slip out of bed, pull on a dressing gown and step to the window. When I ease back the curtain, I'm shocked to see a police patrol car has pulled up outside. It can't be good news.

At the door are two young officers. A man and a woman. Sombre-faced. Fully tooled up in bulky vests and hi-vis jackets.

'Hello?' I say meekly. 'Can I help?'

'Jade Champion?' the woman asks.

'Yes.'

'It's about your husband, Callum. May we come in?'

I shake my head in disbelief. 'What's all this about?'

'It's better if we do this inside,' the woman says with a grim smile.

I show them into the lounge, flicking on the overhead spotlights. It's too bright. Too clinical. Especially at this time of the morning, but they're not here on a social call.

'What's happened? Is he okay?'

'Please, sit down.' The male officer nods to the armchair by the lamp.

I take a seat and perch on the edge, playing with the cuffs of my dressing gown. 'Has something happened to Callum?' My voice trembles.

'I'm afraid we have some bad news,' the female officer says. She's obviously practised her sad face. A slight frown of concern. A dip of the head. Tight lips. 'I'm afraid your husband has been involved in a serious road traffic collision.'

'Oh, my god.' My hand flyies to my mouth. 'Is he alright? Is he hurt?'

The female officer lowers her gaze as if it's all too much for her.

'I'm afraid Mr Champion is dead,' the male officer announces.

Nothing like sugarcoating it.

'What? No, he can't be,' I wail.

'I'm very sorry for your loss.'

'Wh - what happened?'

'Obviously a full investigation into the circumstances is underway, but it appears he may have lost control of his vehicle,' the male officer continues.

'Where?'

'The coast road in East Sussex. It seems to have been a bit of a freak accident. It looks as though he lost control of his car along a clifftop road. Wreckage was discovered on a beach at the foot of the cliff.'

I stare at the officer, blinking, his words whirling around my head.

'Is there anyone we can call who can be with you?' the woman asks.

'What? No,' I say breathlessly.

'No one at all?'

I could call my mother, but what use would she be? She's probably in an alcoholic stupor. You'd have to bash her door down to wake her.

'No, I'm fine. Thank you.'

An odd look passes between the two officers. The female officer clears her throat. 'Efforts are still ongoing to recover Mr Champion's body, but I should warn you there was an explosion and a fire. When our teams reached the wreckage, there wasn't much left.'

'So he might still be alive?' I say, hopefully.

'Highly unlikely, Mrs Champion.'

'Please, call me Jade.'

'It's virtually impossible that anyone could have survived the drop from the cliff where your husband went off the road.'

'Oh,' I say. 'I see. Sorry, I'm forgetting my manners. Would you like a cup of tea?'

'No, but I can make one for you, if you'd like?' the female officer offers.

'No, no. Thank you. I think I might need something a little stronger.'

Chapter 31

An old lady with unkempt ash-grey hair poking out from under a woolly bobble hat, dragging a shopping trolley behind her, grumpily pushes past as I attempt to navigate through the door of a charity shop on the high street.

'Don't mind me,' I mutter under my breath as she shuffles away, grumbling to herself.

My arms are aching painfully. I probably should have made two journeys from the car with all these boxes, but I just want to get this job over with and move on.

A shop assistant, seeing me struggle, rushes from behind the counter and holds the door open for me. She has a kindly smile. The sort of woman I expect bakes her own bread and makes her own jam, and every Sunday has all the family, including the grandchildren, over for lunch.

'Can you manage?' she asks.

'It's fine. Thanks.' She must be twice my age. I can hardly ask her to take the boxes for me. 'I'm hoping you'd like to take some of this stuff.'

'Pop them down on the floor over there by the counter and let's take a look.'

I drop the boxes and rub my lower back as the woman deftly slices through the tape I used to seal them closed. She peels the first one open and peers inside.

She's probably expecting to find a load of tatty secondhand clothes, unfashionable shirts, skirts that no longer fit and jumpers that have seen better days. Or a library of dogeared paperback books and DVDs nobody watches anymore. What she actually finds wipes the smile off her face.

The first thing she pulls out is one of Callum's games consoles, still in its original packaging. I'm not sure he even played it. I think I've put all the correct games in with it, but I'm not certain.

The woman glances up at me with an uncertain frown.

'This looks brand new,' she says, as if she thinks I might have made a mistake.

'It is,' I confirm. 'I'm not sure it's ever been used. But it's all there if you want to check.'

'Are you certain? That's very generous of you.' She checks over her shoulder and lowers her voice. 'You'd probably fetch a couple of hundred quid for it if you put it on eBay.'

I hold up a hand. It's the same reaction I've had in the last three charity shops where I've delivered similar donations of Callum's crap. None of them can believe I'm giving away his things so readily. But what use do I have for them? I don't need the money, so why waste my time trying to sell them? I'd rather they went to a good cause.

'You'll be able to sell it, won't you?'

'Oh, yes, I'm sure we can,' she says, the smile returning to her face.

She dives back into the box and discovers two unused electronic tablets, a pair of expensive trainers, a laptop computer, a couple of watches in presentation cases, the expensive wetsuit Callum insisted on buying, and a drone I don't think he ever found time to fly. There's more of his unused crap in the second box.

With each item she pulls out, her eyes grow wider and wider.

'I don't know what to say. This must be worth thousands of pounds.'

I point to the watches she's placed on the counter. 'Don't underprice those. I think my husband paid a lot of money for them. It might be worth checking their value first.'

Just as in the previous three shops, her initial shock quickly turns to suspicion.

'May I ask why you're giving all these things away?' she says, standing.

She must think they're stolen. But if I'd stolen them, why would I be giving them to charity?

'They belonged to my husband. He died recently,' I say matter-of-factly.

'Oh, I'm so sorry,' she says, looking mortified.

'It's fine. I just can't cope with seeing all his things in the house.' I dab a finger under my eye, wiping away an imaginary tear.

'You poor dear,' she says, patting my arm.

'You can take all these things, can't you? He'd be pleased it's all going to a good cause.'

'Yes, yes, of course. This is wonderful.'

Another woman sweeps into the shop from a back room. Grey cardigan. Thick black tights. Tartan skirt.

'Maggie, take a look at this,' the woman at the counter says. 'This lady is donating all these amazing things. Some of them haven't even been opened.'

Maggie regards me sceptically over the top of her glasses and then glances at Callum's stuff. All the stupid impulse purchases that have cluttered up the house in the last few weeks. There's still the massive TV that dominates the lounge. That was far too big to carry, let alone get in the back of the BMW. I'll have to decide what to do with that later.

'That's incredibly generous of you,' she says.

'That's what I said. They belonged to this poor lady's late husband.'

I shoot Maggie a thin-lipped smile. 'It's what he would have wanted.' The lie falls from my mouth far too easily.

Maggie's eyes narrow as she looks me up and down.

'I know you, don't I?' she says. 'I saw you on the TV. You're that woman who won all the money on the lottery.'

A warm flush heats my cheeks and I nervously glance around the shop, hoping no one's listening.

'Guilty as charged,' I say sheepishly.

'And I read about your husband's accident. So sad. I'm so sorry.'

I shrug. I still haven't worked out what I'm supposed to say when people offer their condolences.

Maggie grimaces. 'Have the police established what happened yet?'

I stare at her blankly. Callum's only been gone a matter of days and she thinks it's acceptable to quiz me about his death. Talk about insensitive.

What the hell. She might as well know.

'He was driving too fast. Lost control of his car,' I say with a brittle tone to my voice. 'Unfortunately, they never found his body, so I'm not going to be able to hold a proper funeral. They think it would be more appropriate to have a memorial service with no coffin.'

Well, she did ask.

Callum's parents have been beside themselves with grief, of course. They want to be around me all the time, so we can 'grieve together'. But I don't want to grieve with them. I need to deal with this in my own way.

I ended up telling them exactly that after a long and emotional day yesterday, and now I'm not sure they're speaking to me at all. Still, that's their loss. At least I didn't shatter the illusion that their only son could do no wrong. I bit my tongue and didn't tell them he was screwing Victoria Etheridge behind my back. Or that he'd been responsible for the murder of at least six people. Maybe more.

Maggie tuts and rolls her eyes. I'm in half a mind to pick up my boxes and take them elsewhere.

'I'm hoping eventually they'll find his body and then maybe we can arrange a proper funeral,' I say sourly.

'I didn't realise,' she mutters. 'How awful.'

'You have no idea. Anyway, I hope you can sell his things and at least make some money for... ' I look up at the banner on the wall behind the counter, '...the hospice.'

I turn away and head for the door. I've done what I set out to achieve. I just want to go home and finish packing. I've given notice to the landlord that I'm moving out. And the sooner I've gone, the better. The house holds too many bad memories. I'm still looking for somewhere I can start over, but in the meantime, I've booked into a nice hotel by the sea.

'Thank you again,' the first woman calls to me as I head out of the door. 'We really do appreciate it.'

I have one more errand to run before I return to the house.

The landlord of the lock-up garage Callum was renting wants me to drop by. He says Callum's left some things he wants cleared out. I can't imagine what Callum kept there, other than a stack of useless begging letters, but I dutifully swing by at the prearranged time.

The landlord shakes my hand professionally, his brows knotted with sincerity as he tells me how sorry he is for my loss.

'I'm sorry I had to call,' he says, 'but I was clearing out and noticed Mr Champion had left a few belongings.'

279

He must mean the old desk and chair. I don't want those.

'Would you be able to dispose of them for me?' I ask, smiling sweetly.

He frowns, his head tilting fractionally to one side. 'You don't want to take them?'

'I'm trying to get rid of his things and I don't have space for a desk.'

'I don't mean the desk,' he says. 'I'm talking about the two big holdalls.'

Holdalls?

'I didn't open them or anything, so I don't know what's in them,' he adds. He flounders through a bunch of keys and finds the one that fits the lock on the garage door. Flips it open and steps aside. 'I left them at the back, under the desk,' he says.

'Thank you.' I smile at him but instead of leaving, he stands, watching me.

'Would you mind? I'll only be a minute.'

'Right, yes, of course. I'll wait in the car,' he says, snapping to attention and hurrying away.

I wait until he climbs into his car and I'm safe from prying eyes before I venture into the garage. Just like he said, there are two canvas holdalls partially poking out from under the desk on the back wall. Not dissimilar to the bags of cash we picked up for the drop-off with Bianca.

I pull the nearest one out. It's heavy and scuffs along the dusty, concrete floor. I double check nobody's watching, then yank open the zip.

There are bundles and bundles of notes inside. Hundreds of thousands of pounds. Millions maybe.

It's the same in the other bag. Cash Callum must have accrued to pay Henry for the series of contract killings he'd planned? Or something else? An escape fund maybe? It never even occurred to me to check our bank balance. I trusted Callum and never imagined I needed to keep tabs on the money.

What if he'd been withdrawing money in preparation for my death, in case the police became suspicious and froze our bank account? Could this be the fund he planned to use to take off with his mistress?

Bastard. I never realised how conniving he could be.

A flush of anger burns through my veins. I take a deep breath. Slowly in. And slowly out again. Centring myself. Bringing my blood pressure back under control. There's no point getting angry now. Everything's worked out for the best.

And it might be Callum's just done me an enormous favour.

Chapter 32

Julia Laverstock collapses in a sweaty mess at her desk and throws her bag on the floor. She's practically jogged from the station to make it to the office on time for her nine forty-five meeting. And now she looks a complete state. All hot and bothered, her hair coming loose from her ponytail and her blouse coming untucked. Why are there always problems on the Tube on the days she has to be in town? An unexplained holdup at Parsons Green station this morning to blame for the start of her bad day.

Actually, that wasn't true. The start of her bad day was when Jemima had a complete meltdown as Julia tried to drag her out of the door so they wouldn't be late for nursery. There was no reason for it. Jemima just chose this morning, of all mornings, to have one of her moments. A full-on tantrum with stamping feet, blood-curdling screams and real tears. Of course, Mark was long gone by then. God forbid the childcare of their daughter should impact on him making it to his office on time.

'Hi, Julia. Coffee? I was just going to pop across the road.' Petra, her faithful personal assistant, jams her head around the door with a sunny smile, tight corkscrew curls cascading over her cheeks and down the back of her neck.

'Please. You're a lifesaver.'

'And don't forget your nine forty-five with Timothy in the boardroom.' She frowns as she notices Julia looking unusually dishevelled. 'Bad morning?'

Julia rolls her eyes. 'Small children and public transport. Guaranteed to wipe the smile off your face every time.'

'Do you want me to see if I can push Timothy back till ten?'

Julia checks her phone. She still has ten minutes before the meeting's due to start. It gives her time to catch her breath and sink a skinny latte. 'No, it's fine. Thanks.'

Petra withdraws but leaves the door open. The hubbub from the central open-plan office, where all the real work happens, drifts through like sea mist floating across a flat ocean. Early morning chit-chat. People on their phones. The buzz of a busy charity going about its business.

Julia smooths down her hair, tucks in her blouse and fires up her computer. The monitor blinks into life but as she logs into the system, a message pops up in the centre of her screen reminding her she only has three days left to update her password before she gets locked out. She sighs with frustration. There's always something. She doesn't have the time right now. She'll change it later.

She calls up the spreadsheet she was working on yesterday. It lists the details of all the private and corporate donations the charity's received in the last six months. There's no hiding the worrying decline. It's clear for anyone to see in the downward trend of the jagged line on the graph she's added on a second tab. They're down five per cent year on year, and, as head of fundraising, Julia needs to explain not only why to Timothy, their director of marketing, fundraising and engagement, but more importantly what she plans to do about it.

It's hardly a surprise people aren't giving as much, even if it is for a great cause. The headlines are awash with stories of rising fuel and food prices, and how people are having to make difficult decisions, in some cases facing the impossible choice of heating or eating. It's a tough financial climate, and donations to charity are always one of the first things that get cut from household budgets when people are struggling. They're already seeing that in the worrying rise in the number of monthly direct debit donations being stopped.

Top of Julia's list to get them back on track is an idea she's had for a new advertising campaign using real people and their stories. People who've had cancer and survived thanks to the groundbreaking research funded by the charity. A handful of characters with smiling faces surrounded by their families and loved ones that will be plastered across magazines and newspapers, Tube stations and bus stops with one-line tales of victory over adversity. Hopeful, inspiring stories everyone can relate to.

But it'll cost. A campaign like that needs a big budget. Go big or go home, though. That's her mantra.

But with income dropping, it's going to be a hard sell to Timothy and the other directors.

Julia clicks open her email and groans as she's confronted by a dozen new messages all demanding her attention. It's a modern-day form of slavery with everyone chained to their inbox these days, at its beck and call twenty-four hours a day.

She quickly scans the subject lines. Most of them are internal messages from colleagues. A few from partners she's working with. But there's one that stands out from the rest. The name of the sender looks vaguely familiar, but it's the subject line that catches her eye. It's been forwarded from the team's public-facing email account.

Re: A small donation for your amazing work

They receive emails like this all the time from people who want to help. Schoolkids who've raised money from a sponsored walk. Little old ladies who want to give away a few pounds of their pension. Families whose loved ones have been saved thanks to a pioneering cancer treatment and who want to give something back. But there's something about this email that stands out. For a start, the team rarely forwards on these types of email to her.

'Here you go,' Petra says, flying breathlessly into Julia's office with a takeaway cup of coffee which she plants on the desk.

'Amazing. Thank you.'

Julia clicks open the email and reads.

It's no ordinary email. No wonder the team forwarded it to her.

'Have you seen this?' she asks, as Petra's on her way out, stopping only to inspect a browning leaf on the kentia palm by the door.

'What is it?' She returns to Julia's side and rests a hand on the back of her chair as she peers over her shoulder to read the email. Although she has full access to Julia's inbox and calendar, she rarely checks her messages unless Julia's on holiday or away at a conference.

My husband and I recently won a large amount of money on the lottery. Too much money for one couple. It brought us nothing but misery and unhappiness. We'd rather the money was used towards a good cause and to help people who are less fortunate than ourselves. And so, by the time you read this email, your charity should have received a donation of £1 million from us. We are making similar donations to other charities who support great causes. We do not wish for any publicity and hope you will respect our wishes for privacy.

Yours sincerely
Jade Champion

'I know that name,' Petra says.

'It's that woman who took her own life, who was all over the news, isn't it?' Julia says. 'The lottery winner.' She'd read about it on her phone a few days ago, completely absorbed by the story. It was heart-breaking. Such a waste of two young lives. A couple who'd won a fortune on the lottery and become overnight multi-millionaires, but who'd died weeks apart in shockingly unfortunate separate incidents.

He'd crashed his car over a cliff, if Julia remembered rightly, and days later she'd jumped from the exact same spot and her body washed out to sea. Although there was no suicide note, the police assumed she'd taken her own life because she'd been wracked with grief at the loss of her husband and unable to go on without him. It was truly awful and just went to prove that all the money in the world couldn't necessarily buy you happiness.

'When was the email sent?' Petra asks.

Julia scans the email for the date. 'A few days ago. The team have obviously only just spotted it.'

'It's a shame she's so specific about not wanting any publicity.'

'I know. It would have made a great story for the press at a time we could really do with some good publicity,' Julia muses, rocking back in her chair. The woman might be dead, but she still has the right to her privacy and Julia's determined they're not going to jeopardise that.

'That donation's come at a handy time though.'

'You're telling me. It's an absolute godsend.'

Petra glances at her watch. 'You're going to be late for Timothy,' she says.

'I know, I know. I'm just going.' Julia pulls her keyboard nearer and begins tapping furiously on the keys. 'I just need to update this spreadsheet first.'

Chapter 33

THREE MONTHS LATER

The rain is coming down sideways, soaking every-thing. It's not the heavy rainfall of a sudden cloud burst but a fine mist under leaden skies that seems to be a regular occurrence in this far corner of Scotland. Water drips from my hood, splashing over my waterproof trousers, but I keep my eyes fixed on the pontoon ahead, one hand on the tiller, tickling the throttle.

As I draw closer, I cut the engine and let the boat drift. For someone with so little experience of boats, I've become something of an expert in the last few months. I've had no choice. There is no other way of getting to the island. There's no bridge and no ferry. It's a completely different way of life here.

The boat silently cuts through the water and slows almost to a stop as I leap ashore and tie it securely to a cleat.

I push the hood up and out of my eyes, scanning the horizon for a break in the weather, but it looks set in for the day. It's no wonder everything around here is so green and lush. There haven't been many days it hasn't rained.

I miss the convenience of being able to pop to the shops whenever I need something, but it's not the greatest hardship. It just means I need to plan ahead while keeping a stock of essentials in the house in case the crossing's too rough. At least here, I can live anonymously. Nobody knows who I am or what I've done. I've cut my hair short and dyed it jet black, along with my eyebrows, and I wear a thick pair of glasses with plain lenses when I'm out, although they're not practical when the drizzle is swirling around like it is today.

I kneel on the slippery, wet pontoon and reach into the boat for six carrier bags of shopping I've shoved under a tarpaulin to keep dry. I haul them out with a grunt and stagger slowly back to the cottage which nestles beneath the rocky, gorse-covered hills I now call home. It's a world apart from everything I've known before. It's bleak, barren and remote. And I absolutely love it.

The house is far from being the mansion I'd once imagined us living in, when we had all that money from the lottery. It only has three bedrooms, a cosy lounge with a log-burning stove, and an adequate kitchen. But the views are spectacular from all the rooms, with stunning vistas across the water and beyond to a smattering of emerald islands prevalent in this secluded part of the Western Isles. Often, you can hear golden eagles screeching high above and if you're lucky, spot one gliding on a thermal overhead, their enormous wings outstretched, the gods of everything they survey.

My hands and arms are burning by the time I reach the house, the plastic bags cutting off the circulation to my fingers. I dump the bags on the doorstep and fish for my keys in my pocket. Locking the door when I'm out is the one habit I can't seem to get over, even though there's no one around for miles. It just feels like I'd be asking for trouble if I didn't leave the house secure.

The lock clicks back in its housing and I spill inside, the warmth from the stove hitting me with a welcoming hug.

I stagger into the kitchen, place the bags on the table and peel off my wet coat and trousers. I put my glasses by the toaster, fill the kettle, and start to unpack while I wait for it to boil.

It's not only my appearance that's changed. I've had to take on a whole new identity. Jade Champion no longer exists. I'm Pippa now. Pippa Charlton. Jade Champion's somewhere at the bottom of the English Channel, her body never to be found and her name existing only on a plaque in a churchyard close to where we used to live. I found that out when I did a bit of discreet digging on the internet to see how my untimely death had been received at home.

There was a fair bit of news coverage about it. I suppose it was because we'd had our five minutes of fame after we won the lottery. We weren't famous exactly, but our names and faces were reasonably well-known thanks to that press conference we should never have agreed to. And I suppose it was a tragic story. A young couple with the world at their feet after winning an obscene amount of money, who had it all snatched away by a cruel quirk of fate. But, of course, they didn't know the half of it. They didn't know anything about our association with Bianca or Gabriel Salt. That we'd become involved with a professional hitman. All they saw was the picture we presented to the world. Callum killed in a tragic accident while driving a sports car that was too fast for his abilities, and his distraught wife who couldn't go on without him.

I couldn't have done any of this without Henry, if that's even his real name. I suspect it's not, but it's probably best I don't know. It sounds strange, but he threw me a lifeline when he revealed Callum was having an affair and had paid to have me killed. It cost me a lot of money to buy my way out of that contract, but the chance to live was a price worth paying.

Henry offered me not only the opportunity to save my life, but to engineer an unfortunate accident for Callum. But I wanted more than that. I wasn't going to be made a fool of by Callum and that vacuous, money-grabbing bimbo he'd hooked up with at the garage. And so, with Henry's help, I came up with a plan to restart my life without all the money and the problems it had caused us. We talked through my options, what Henry could and couldn't do for me, and my mind was made up pretty quickly.

I needed to disappear. To vanish without a trace, with no questions left unanswered. I couldn't afford to arouse the curiosity of an over-enthusiastic detective or a keen young journalist with a nose for a scoop.

After Henry suggested he could arrange for Callum's Ferrari to come off the road and crash over a cliff, the way I could successfully fake my own death became instantly apparent. All I needed to do was leave a suicide note, along with my shoes and my bag for authenticity, and who wouldn't believe I was so distraught at my husband's tragic death that I jumped?

It took some careful planning. We had to wait until high tide and then ensure I was spotted by a few people in the area, looking inconsolable with grief. Having some eyewitnesses was Henry's idea and I admit it was a good one. It lent my story some credibility and hopefully stopped those awkward questions in their tracks when they failed to find my body.

I left Callum's BMW in a car park near the cliffs, abandoned a pair of shoes and a bag at the edge, along with a handwritten note, and fled with Henry in his car, hidden under a blanket on the back seat. Unfortunately, they never found the note, which was an inconvenience. I guess it must have blown away. In retrospect, I should have left it in the car where I could have been certain it would have been found.

I'd already sorted out the finances, preparing a series of large donations to a variety of worthwhile charities, and kept hold of the cash I'd found in the two holdalls Callum had stashed at his lock-up.

It was a fraction of what we'd won, but it paid for an entire island, which came with a small property, here in the northern fringes of Scotland. Plus, it covered Henry's not inconsiderable fee, and there was enough left to ensure I'd never have to work again.

I'm no longer financially rich, but I have plenty for my simple needs. As long as I have enough to put food on the table and to keep the house running, I'm happy.

Henry helped me with the purchase of the island, acting as my agent and paying for it in cash under my new name. He told them I was a famous recluse and anonymity and discretion were essential if we were to go ahead with the purchase.

Henry helped me set up things here, but then I told him I wanted nothing more to do with him. Financially, he's done well out of us both. He's earned more than enough to retire, although he was non-committal when I urged him to think about a change of career. I can't bear the thought that he might continue to carry out contracts and that more people, innocent or not, might die.

I've vowed never to contact him again. I gave him back the burner phone I'd taken from Callum and he threw it into the sea. It felt symbolic, like it was the end of something dark, but significant, in my life.

Things are better now. I'm happier. More at peace with the world. My only regret is that we won that money in the first place and became sucked into Gabriel's obsession for revenge.

The money's caused so much pain and heartache, and been at the root of so much death and misery. And to think I used to dream about how fabulous my life would be if only we could match those six numbers.

I finally worked out how Gabriel knew about our win when it was still under wraps and we'd hardly told anyone. As far as I was aware, the only people who knew were Callum's parents, his sister, and her husband. But it seems Callum hadn't been able to keep his mouth shut and confessed to me that he'd "let it slip" to someone he used to work with. Vicky, on reception. Did I remember her? He thought we'd met once at a party. She'd told a friend, who knew Gabriel, and he seized the opportunity. I can't say I blame him, although it was his letter that set us out on this sorry path.

I didn't tell Callum that I knew about his affair. I didn't want him getting suspicious, but I was fuming. I hadn't even told my mother that we'd won the lottery at that point. Still, I always said revenge, like good champagne, is best tasted chilled.

I've no idea what happened to my mother or whether she even mourned my death. I'm sure she would have been furious when she discovered I hadn't left her a penny. I can just imagine how her eyes must have lit up when she heard about my apparent suicide and the thought wheedled into her vodka-addled brain that she'd be laying her grubby hands on my millions. But I couldn't do it. I'd rather it went to good causes than to my ungrateful mother.

I didn't do it because I hated her. I did it out of love. We might never have been close, but she almost certainly would have spent any money I left her at the off-licence and I didn't want her death on my conscience. That money has already caused enough misery.

I stretch up on my tiptoes to put a tin of baked beans onto the top shelf of the cupboard above the microwave.

'Do you need a hand with anything?'

I whirl around and glance down at Callum, his withered legs bound at the knees, his unshaven face hollow and grey.

'I think I've got it,' I say. 'But thanks.'

As if he could do anything to help me. He can't even stand on his own, let alone walk.

It's frustrating for him, but things have worked out pretty well, even if Callum's disability wasn't initially part of the plan.

I thought long and hard about Henry's offer. For a million pounds of the money I no longer wanted, Henry would kill Callum and make it look like an accident. He even offered to "take care" of Victoria Etheridge, at no extra cost. I think he felt sorry for me.

It would have been easy to go along with it and add to the death toll. I was angry and hurt and ready to lash out. But it would have gone against every fundamental principle of my being. After Lee Greenwood, I vowed I'd never do anything as stupid again. Instead, I suggested to Henry an alternative plan in which we could both die, and yet both live. After all, for all his faults, I still love Callum. We're meant to be together.

And by faking our deaths and disappearing somewhere we'd never be found, we could escape from our past without the money tempting Callum into more trouble. He'd let the power it gave him go to his head once. I had to be sure it wouldn't happen again.

'How are your legs today?'

Callum grimaces. 'Sore.'

'Do you need some more pain killers?'

'Sure,' he says, sounding resigned.

There's not much for him to look forward to when he's restricted to a wheelchair on this island. He's effectively housebound. But I find it hard to have much sympathy after he went sniffing around that gold-digger at the garage and falling for her fake charms when she thought she could get her hands on my money. At least this way, I get to keep him out of trouble and there's no danger his head's going to be turned by another woman. He's not seen another woman since we moved here.

I run a glass of water and hand it to him with two more pills, which he swallows gratefully, throwing back his head, wincing.

'I might have a lie down for a bit, if that's okay,' he says, rolling himself backwards. He's adapted to life in a wheelchair remarkably quickly, although the house isn't really suitable. In time, I might look at getting the doors widened and replace the carpet with some free-rolling lino, but for now he'll have to make do. We're not made of money anymore.

'Sure,' I say, brushing a few stray strands of damp hair off my forehead. 'Do you need some help getting into bed?'

'Please.' He lowers his gaze and fiddles with his fingers in his lap. I know how degrading it is for him to have to ask for help to do almost everything.

Smashing his kneecaps wasn't my idea. Henry came up with that sadistic twist all by himself. He was only supposed to abduct Callum, stage the car crash, and keep him safe until I was ready to join them and we could sneak off to Scotland to start our new life.

Henry insisted it had been necessary and that it was his only way of subduing Callum when he tried to escape. He never said as much, but I think the truth is that it was Henry's way of punishing Callum for how he'd treated me and making sure he'd never cheat on me again. I would never have sanctioned it, although admittedly Callum's disability has worked in my favour. He'll never walk again, of course, but what's done is done.

I push him into our room and roll him up to the bed.

'You want to get under the covers?' I ask.

He shakes his head. 'I'll lie on top. It's fine.'

We go through the awkward routine we've developed over time to lift him out of his chair. I hook my arms under his legs and he throws his arms around my neck to support his body. I've become stronger over the weeks we've been here and it's not so difficult to lift him now, although I do wonder if we should spend some of our cash on a winch. It would make things a lot easier for both of us. And save my back.

Callum rolls onto the bed with a grunt, his eyes squeezed shut in discomfort. I help him wedge a pillow under his neck and wheel his chair to the corner. Then I sit on the edge of the mattress and massage his calves. He says it helps with the pain. Really, he should have seen a surgeon, to establish if there was anything that could have beeen done to save his legs, but I couldn't take the risk that we'd be recognised. It's been months now since our faces were all over the news, but it was such a big story, I'm terrified someone will expose us, and neither of us wants to make headlines again, let alone end up behind bars.

'I miss Jefferson and Delilah,' Callum says, folding an arm over his eyes.

'Me too, but I'm sure your parents are looking after them well.' They always had a soft spot for those dogs and we could hardly bring them with us. It would have been too difficult and not much fun for them. And, anyway, how would we have explained their disappearance?

'I've been thinking about reaching out to them,' Callum says quietly.

'Who? Jefferson and Delilah?'

'My parents. I can't stand the anguish we put them through.'

I jump up, horrified. 'No, Callum. You can't.' After all my carefully laid plans, I can't have him ruining everything by trying to contact his mother and father.

He sighs. A long, low whisper of air that rattles through his lips. 'I know,' he says. 'But don't you ever think it would be nice to turn back the clock and return to our old lives? You know, when we had money and everything we ever wanted at our fingertips. When I could walk. When I wasn't constantly in pain. When we were planning the amazing house we were going to buy.'

I swallow a dry lump in my throat.

Callum lifts his head and peers out from under the crook of his elbow.

'Jade?'

'It's Pippa now,' I croak.

'Don't you ever wish things had turned out differently?'

I glance out of the window, streaked with a pebbledash of rain, and beyond to the murky, cold waters that surround our tiny island like a velvet glove around a slender hand. I picture us in our old house. An ordinary couple struggling for money. Too poor to buy our own home. Kids and a family on hold because we couldn't afford it. And I remember the euphoria that swelled and fizzed in my stomach when we found out we'd won more money than we knew what to do with. For a brief moment, it was truly amazing.

It meant freedom and opportunity. I didn't have to work in the restaurant anymore. I didn't need to worry about looking for yellow sticker items in the supermarket. Or how we were going to pay the gas bill. I didn't think we had to worry about anything.

Now, we're alone and isolated. I have a disabled husband to care for and if we run out of food, it's a two-and-a-half-hour round trip by boat to the mainland. It's always raining, and apparently it only gets worse in the winter. We have no friends. No family. Nothing to look forward to but old age.

But we'll grow old together. We have everything we need right here in this house, on this island. Life may not be perfect, but I've long since come to the conclusion that the perfect life doesn't exist. It's a fallacy we're all chasing. Happiness is a state of mind. It doesn't matter whether you're rich or poor. It's life that's precious, not the trinkets and material things we surround ourselves with.

'No,' I say, stretching my back. I put a hand on my swollen belly and delight in the flutter kick inside. 'I don't wish anything was any different. Even if I could, I wouldn't turn back time.'

A WORD FROM THE AUTHOR

The Lottery Winners was one of most enjoyable books I've written, putting myself in Jade and Callum's shoes as they realised they'd won more than £50m on the lottery.

It's a book about money and power and how too much wealth has the power to corrupt. It's also about the difference between vengeance and justice.

What do you think – did Callum and Jade get their just desserts in the end?

Hopefully, you enjoyed reading it as much as I enjoyed writing it.

Ratings and reviews help authors (particularly independently published authors with no marketing team behind them, like me) to reach a wider audience, more than you probably realise.

You don't even have to leave a review these days – although any supportive words always go down well!

A rating will do.

I always read all my reviews, so thank you so much for taking the time. I really do appreciate it.

If you'd like to keep up to date with all my writing news, please consider joining my weekly newsletter. I'll even send you a free e-book! You can find more details at bit.ly/hislostwife or scan the QR code below.

You can also follow me on Facebook - @AuthorAJWills, find me on my website ajwillsauthor.com join me on Instagram at @ajwills_author or find me on Goodreads @ A.J.Wills

I look forward to seeing you there.

Adrian

ALSO BY AJ WILLS

The Warning
When Megan discovers a text message on a phone hidden in the loft of her new house with a chilling warning about her husband, she's forced to confront some dark truths about their relationship...

The Secrets We Keep
When a young girl vanishes on her way home from school, a suspicious media suspects her parents know more than they're letting on.

Nothing Left To Lose
A letter arrives in a plain white envelope. Inside is a single sheet of paper with a chilling message. Someone knows the secret Abi, and her husband, Henry, are hiding. And now they want them dead.

His Wife's Sister
Mara was only eleven when she went missing from a tent in her parents' garden nineteen years ago. Now

she's been found wandering alone and confused in woodland.

She Knows
After Sky finds a lost diary on the beach, she becomes caught up in something far bigger than she could ever have imagined - and accused of a murder she has no memory of committing...

The Intruder
Jez thought he'd finally found happiness when he met Alice. But when Alice goes missing with her young daughter and the police accuse him of their murders, his life is shattered.